Sile

Sophie let the wonderful sensation take hold of her. She felt safe and content in the warm hayloft. Outside the rain rattled against the wooden walls; inside Sophie watched Callum's long hair trail across her thighs and felt a growing and powerful desire creep through her. Before he had a chance to object, Sophie pushed the young gardener down on the hay and straddled him. Her new job was proving to be quite enjoyable after all.

Silent Seduction

TANYA BISHOP

BLACK
lace

Black Lace novels are sexual fantasies.
In real life, make sure you practise safe sex.

First published in 1997 by
Black Lace
332 Ladbroke Grove
London W10 5AH

Typeset by SetSystems Ltd, Saffron Walden, Essex
Printed and bound by Mackays of Chatham PLC

ISBN 0 352 33193 3

Chapter One

'Perhaps they will make you wear a uniform, Sophie!' Toby's eyes gleamed. 'You know, really tight jodhpurs and black boots.'

'Stop it, Toby,' she laughed.

'Thigh-length boots. Shiny ones, with high heels.' He leant over to push her skirt up her thigh, caressing the soft skin.

'Toby, watch the road,' she said between giggles, 'or the only uniform you will see is one belonging to a nurse!'

'Now, Miss Ward,' he said, frowning sternly, 'you know what your duties include. Quickly now, I haven't got all day.'

'Toby, I'm going to be a groom, not a French maid. I don't have to wear a uniform and servicing the master is not on my job description.' She pushed his hand off her leg. 'And you are creasing my best skirt.'

'Take it off then,' he leered, steering the car expertly through the cool, green countryside.

'Oh, good idea!' Sophie laughed, sarcastically. 'And would you like to explain to my new employers how I came to get arrested for exposing myself on my way to my new job? No, I thought not. Now watch the road.'

1

'You'd probably be snowed under with job offers if they knew you had convictions for flashing,' Toby told her. 'It could turn out to be a sound career move. You know what these upper-class families are like.'

'No I don't, now you come to mention it, and neither do you.'

'You would be surprised what I know. They're all respectability on the surface, but a seething hotbed of immorality underneath.'

'A seething what? Good Heavens, Toby! You do talk some drivel.'

'It's true. This time next week you'll be phoning me to complain that the master is trying to compromise your virtue – maybe.'

'Compromise my virtue? What have you been reading? It's that book list the University sent for you to read over the summer. By Christmas you won't be able to hold a sensible conversation.'

They were both laughing now, although Sophie thought, ruefully, that many a true word was spoken in jest. What would things be like between her and Toby once he had made new friends at university? She couldn't really see how she would hold her own in conversation with graduates and lecturers, not with just her British Horse Society certificate.

She pushed the thought out of her mind. Whatever happened she knew what she didn't want. She didn't want Toby to stay with her out of a sense of duty. She shivered.

'Are you cold?' Toby was instantly concerned. 'Here, I'll close the window.'

'I'm fine.' She smiled to show that she meant it, and he glanced across at her, uneasily.

'I didn't mean it, Sophie, honestly. I'm sure you will be fine. You're not worried, are you? If you hate it phone me straight away; I'll come and get you, I promise.'

'I'm not worried, really. It's always sad, isn't it, when

2

something has to change. It's all for the best, for both of us.'

'It doesn't have to change,' Toby said softly, taking her hand with his free one. 'I never wanted it to change.'

For a split second Sophie was tempted to tell Toby she had made a terrible mistake, that she didn't really want this job and that she would really rather get married and produce an annual chubby baby. She thought of her sisters doing just that. She thought how happy it would make Toby, and her best friend, Sara.

'Get a job round here,' Sara had urged. 'Toby would marry you tomorrow if you wanted. We could have a double wedding; you and Toby, me and Paul. Time it so we had our first kids together . . .'

Sara had been delighted at this mapping out of the next few years; Sophie had recoiled in horror. Yes, Toby would marry her, maybe wanted to marry her, but that was only because it was expected of them. Sophie had encouraged him to apply for university courses, posted the forms herself, and eagerly waited for the outcome. And it had worked. Toby had been sufficiently caught up in her enthusiasm, so that when the letter of acceptance came, they had celebrated and planned together.

Sophie patted Toby's hand and placed it firmly back on the steering wheel.

'We've discussed all this, Toby. It's all for the best, we agreed. You were too good for that crummy job, and as for me, I do not want to work in that Post Office for another day. I want to have done something before I get as old and crotchety as Mrs Cromarty. If I go back to that village, I want it to be through choice.'

'I know, I know. You're right, Sophie.' He blew her a kiss.

Toby's university place had taken a weight off Sophie's shoulders. Now she felt free to pursue her own life, to go somewhere unknown, meet people about whom she knew nothing – to re-invent herself. She

3

wouldn't be the Sophie who lived next door to the Post Office. She wouldn't be the Sophie who had three brothers and sisters, the one who worked in the village store during the holidays; she would be mysterious Sophie. Cool, capable Sophie. Sensuous Sophie. The daydream sent shivers down her spine. Toby looked across at her and smiled.

'Hungry?' he asked.

'Ravenous. I could eat a horse.'

'Well, keep your eyes open for one then, because that's about the only thing I can't remember packing.'

They stopped by a tiny pond. With its velvety bull-rushes and waxy, green lily-pads, it hardly looked real.

'It's beautiful here, Toby. Have you been here before?'

'There's a lane there' – Toby pointed – 'that leads up the hill. I came here once on a scout trip. We went badger-watching.'

'Dib dib dib!' Sophie teased him. 'I'll bet you looked sweet in shorts.'

'I'd have looked stupid – I was fifteen at the time and one of the helpers! Here, you take this blanket, I'll bring the basket. There's plenty in here, but in case you're set on eating a horse, look over there.' A small grey pony was watching them over the fence. It snorted and shook its heavy mane.

At the end of the lane they climbed a gate and found themselves on a hillside looking down on a picture postcard village, where ant-sized people went about their business. The midday sun was hot on their backs as Sophie spread the blanket and Toby unpacked the food. He had brought a bottle of wine, chilled in its own box, and the heat and drink combined to make them feel drowsy and contented.

'Thank you, Toby.'

'What for?'

'The picnic. The place. It's all just right.'

'Trouble is that now we've drunk the wine I can't

drive for a while. What are we going to do?' He was looking at her sideways, resting back on his elbows, his long, black hair sweeping the edge of the blanket.

'Hold on,' Sophie said, 'I think I've got a pack of cards in my luggage. Give me the car keys.'

She made as if to go back to the car then squealed as Toby grabbed her legs to pull her down. She rolled over, laughing, and he was on top of her, blocking out the fierce sun, sealing her mouth with his own, hands reaching under her to undo her skirt.

'Toby! Not here! Anyone looking up at the hill from the village can see us.'

It was true. Toby checked momentarily, looking over his shoulder at the distant village far down in the valley, then tugged her skirt from underneath them both.

'No one can see,' he murmured, hand sliding back up her leg. His eyes widened in surprise.

'No underwear!' He looked shocked, making Sophie giggle.

'It's no laughing matter, young lady.' Toby sat up and slowly undid the buttons on her blouse. As the last button gave, he opened the soft material, exposing her breasts and belly to the warming sunshine. Her nipples, small and pink, rose up hard to meet the gentle breeze as it caressed them playfully.

'You'll have to do penance.' Toby pulled off his T-shirt and unzipped his trousers.

'Come on,' he said, pulling her up to meet him. 'On your knees.'

She knelt between Toby's powerful thighs. Even kneeling opposite him she barely reached his shoulder and as she bent to kiss his smooth, hard penis she heard him groan in anticipation.

She let her tongue flick skittishly over him, never lingering in one place, until he was breathing hard, holding her shoulders tightly. She slipped her hand under him, weighing his heavy balls and squeezing

5

gently, then, as he caught his breath, she leant forward and let his eager penis slide firmly into her mouth. She caressed him with her tongue, feeling him hard and strong as she sucked, enjoying his gasps of pleasure. He tried to pull her up gently, then more firmly, but Sophie was delighting in her lover's prick; she wanted him to come like this, under her control.

Toby was getting frantic now and she was enjoying his panic; he never would let her suck him until he came. When she did finally give way he was panting hoarsely.

'You are a naughty girl,' he growled, and turning her round, still on her hands and knees, he delivered a stinging smack across her bare bottom. Before she had time to respond, Toby was easing himself deep inside her, filling her completely, reaching far into her womanhood. His hands, which had held her hips steady as he thrust his quivering penis into her, now slid round her hips, over her pubis, and the fingers began to rub her clitoris expertly.

'Can you feel me, sweetie? This is all for you ... you are gorgeous ...'

Sophie began to come, Toby's powerful thrusts sending his penis full-shaft into her, making every inch of her body tingle. A cry burst out of her as her orgasm peaked, roaring through her body like fire and tightening her muscles so suddenly that Toby also began to come. When he had ridden out the waves of his orgasm, they lay down, Toby still heavy on top of her, both trying to regain their breath and their composure.

'Are you all right?' Toby asked, lifting the thick curtain of blonde hair, and kissing her neck and ears.

'I'm fine, thank you, Toby.'

'Think you'll remember me then?'

'Oh Toby! Of course. But we will still see each other, won't we?'

'I'm relying on it.'

Suddenly, Sophie felt sad about losing Toby. Still, this

was the way they had planned it, and she still felt in her heart that it was right. He had so much to offer that would never have been appreciated in the dead end job he had just left. Toby rolled himself off her and retrieved her blouse and his trousers. So engrossed were they in dressing that a snort from the hedge made them jump to their feet in surprise. The grey pony, curious as to all the activity at the end of his field, was regarding them from under his long, black eyelashes. They both burst into guilty laughter and quickly hunted through the picnic remnants for a treat for him.

'Here, there's an apple left, but only if you keep quiet about what you've just seen,' Toby told the pony, who pawed the dusty earth eagerly, and then trotted back off up the field. 'I think we should be making a move, too,' Toby said as they gathered up the blanket and the basket.

Sophie shivered as the sun disappeared momentarily behind a cloud, and they set off down the lane, anxious to continue on their way. The rest of the journey seemed strained to Sophie. They laughed and chatted as usual, but when they stopped for a break at a small country pub, they were both feeling a little apprehensive about what lay ahead. Sophie told Toby about her telephone interview with the McKinnerneys, her new employers.

'The children have their own ponies and their mother does cross-country, so I should be kept pretty busy.'

Toby, in turn, told her all about the different courses he was looking forward to, and those he was dreading. 'I've been out of "school" for so long, I just hope I can still remember it all!'

'You will do brilliantly, Toby. Your only problem is that you think other people are better than you at everything. I've got great faith in you – if you don't get a first, I'll want to know why!'

'Seriously, Sophie, I would never have had the courage to go for it without you pushing me. You know what I'm like. I'm going to miss you.'

7

'Right, that's it. If you're going to come over all melancholy on me, I'm off!'

They left the pub laughing, but Sophie thought to herself that Toby was right: she did know exactly what he was like. She knew he would have stayed in that job forever if she hadn't interfered. She also had a sneaking suspicion that she hadn't urged him to try something different entirely for his own benefit.

Perhaps, she thought, it's all for the best. Perhaps Toby will thank me for this one day. She hoped this turned out to be true. Sophie wanted happiness for herself and Toby more than anything; she just wasn't sure that they could find it with each other.

When they eventually pulled into the driveway of Prospect House, Sophie had her first glimpse of her new home and a shiver ran down her spine.

'Oh Toby! It looks just like that house in *The Omen*! The one where – '

' – the nanny hung herself!' Toby cried and clutched her leg dramatically.

They both burst into laughter again, maybe a little too heartily, and Toby slowed the car as they approached the house.

An elderly woman appeared at the door, a baby on her hip, closely followed by two other children. Waving and shouting, they all tumbled down the stone steps to meet the couple as they stepped from the car.

'Sophie?' smiled the woman. 'Hello, dear, lovely to meet you. We've been looking forward to this, haven't we?'

The children continued to push and shove, looking dubiously at Sophie.

'Let's bring your suitcases, shall we? Oh well, yes, I'm sure you can help, too,' she said to the middle child, a girl of about three. 'By the way, I'm Mr McKinnerney's mother – I'm afraid he's not here at the moment. Would your friend like to stay for some tea with us? You would be most welcome,' she told Toby.

Toby, a little bewildered by all the activity, looked at Sophie, panic-stricken. 'Oh, I don't think – what I mean is – well, it's like this . . .'

Sophie put him out of his misery. 'Toby still has quite a long way to travel,' she explained. 'I think he would really rather get on, wouldn't you?'

'I think I should,' he agreed, gratefully.

'Well, come on then, children. Let's leave Sophie to say her goodbyes, and we'll go and pop the kettle on, shall we?'

They rushed indoors as quickly as they had exited and Toby pretended to wipe his brow. 'Good luck, Sophie. Get yourself a whip and chair the first chance you get.'

'Oh I shall be fine here, don't worry. Thank you, Toby, for everything. I hope your course goes well. Write as soon as you can, won't you?'

'Of course. And you to me. And remember, come and visit my exotic new residence whenever you get a free weekend.'

She smiled. 'I will. Now, drive carefully.'

She waved him off, sad to see him go , but eager to see her new residence and get settled in. She didn't see, nor was she meant to, the young man watching her from the side of the house. Sophie would have considered him very handsome in a rough-and-ready sort of way. She would have been surprised at the interest her arrival had sparked. She may have been amused at the excitement she caused swaying across the gravel in her unsuitably high heels. She would certainly have felt flattered at the way the man strained to catch a very last glimpse of her before taking a firmer grip on the rake he was holding, the corners of his generous mouth twitching upwards in an appreciative smile. As it was, she watched Toby drive out of sight then turned to the house with a sigh, oblivious to him.

* * *

Bags deposited in the hall, children chivvied off to have tea with the nanny, Mrs McKinnerney turned her attention to Sophie.

'Well, dear,' she sighed, 'your rooms or the stables first? Actually, they are all in the same block so I can show you it all together.'

They spent the next hour or so with the horses, where Sophie was inspected by her equine charges. A small black pony eyed her in a calculating way and bit her fingers crossly when he realised that she had no treat for him.

'That's Buzz,' Mrs McKinnerney told her. 'Don't trust him an inch, he's a ghastly creature. Bit of an escape artist.'

'Which of the children rides Buzz?'

'He was Catherine's second pony. He's retired now. That's his problem, really, boredom. And our problem, too!' They both laughed. 'I know there is rather a mixed bunch here,' the older woman said, indicating the odd assortment of horses and ponies, 'but do you think you can cope?'

'Don't worry, Mrs McKinnerney, I'll be fine and I'll have the children competent in the saddle in no time,' Sophie said. 'I'm sure we will have a good time together. But do I take it that you don't live here?'

'Oh no, dear. James and Catherine took this place over when we retired. It was too big for us. We live about twenty minutes drive away.' Her eyes sparkled. 'Near enough to do a mercy dash if you need us, far enough not to interfere too much, I hope! Now, let me show you to your rooms; I think we deserve a nice cup of tea!'

Sophie's rooms turned out to be a tiny, self-contained cottage to one side of the stable block. Mrs McKinnerney had thoughtfully placed a box of groceries on the table in the kitchen and once they had organised tea and toast, they settled in the armchairs in the cosy lounge.

'You may not have come to us at the easiest time,

dear.' Mrs McKinnerney said, cautiously, when they had been chatting for a few minutes. 'I feel I should make things clear to you, but this is quite difficult for me. You see, my son and his wife are having rather a tricky time of it at the moment. Catherine is a lovely girl, but, well, it seems it isn't the way of youngsters to stay at home with the children. She wants something more – a career, I suppose. Oh dear, that sounds awfully derogatory to you when you have come to teach her children. What I mean is, I think that rearing children is the most difficult and the most rewarding job in the world but Catherine doesn't. Not that she needs to work: James is more than capable of supporting his family. But she misses her social life, her work, her freedom.' Mrs McKinnerney sighed heavily. 'Things have been a little fraught between the two of them, which is why I have been here: to give the children some stability until it's all worked out.'

Sophie nodded sympathetically. That explained why her interview with the children's parents had taken place so rapidly over the phone and, possibly, why they hadn't been there to greet her when she arrived.

Mrs McKinnerney's smile was sad. 'We all have our fingers crossed that James and Catherine can overcome these problems. Meanwhile, it is our job to carry on as best we can. Your only responsibility is to the horses. James has always had other staff, so you won't have to clean or play nursemaid, and you will only have yourself to cook for. But, please,' and here she lay a hand on Sophie's arm, 'forgive us if we seem a little neglectful of you at the moment. James has taken all this rather badly and it may be a little while before we reach any semblance of normality. I do hope all this isn't putting you off too much.'

'I'm made of stern stuff,' Sophie assured the older woman, 'I'll do all I can to help, don't worry.'

'Good. Now, I hope you don't mind,' Mrs

McKinnerney said, 'but I have arranged a little drinks party later so that you can get to know some of our friends and neighbours. We are not a very formal bunch, some of them are not much older than you, and it has been so long since I have seen some of my old friends – I know you will find someone with whom you can rub along nicely.'

Sophie, pleased at the prospect of seeing some new faces, announced that she would get her unpacking done quickly in order to shower and change.

'I'll see you in about an hour and a half,' Mrs McKinnerney said, 'these rooms are for your exclusive use so feel free to do as you wish.'

The evening was starting to darken as Sophie went to draw the curtains in her room. Down on the lawn, a stone's throw from her window, a young man was carefully propping garden tools up beside a spacious shed. Sophie lingered, watching his well-muscled shoulders as they strained against the grass-stained shirt.

There's someone I wouldn't mind exploring, she thought to herself. Yes, I think we two could rub along quite nicely together.

As if reading her thoughts, the young man straightened and looked directly up at Sophie's window. He flicked his long, blonde hair out of his face and gave her a lopsided grin, making Sophie realise how clearly he could see her, lit up indoors, while he stood in the mysterious twilight. She blushed, feeling the heat spread from her cheeks to her neck, then through her whole body, weakening her knees. She was about to pull the curtains when the young man stepped forward into the light below her window, put both hands to his mouth, and blew her a kiss.

Sophie laughed despite herself. The man grinned again – a curious, knowing grin – and the moment was gone. He turned back to the shed. Sophie pulled the curtains and went to take her shower. It was only as she discarded her skirt and blouse that she thought of Toby arriving at university, and she hoped he was feeling as settled as she was.

The water from the shower hit her naked body, stimulating and invigorating her. The hot, cleansing streams were good after all the travelling and Sophie felt she could see the debris of the day disappearing down the plughole, washing away the old, ready for the new, sophisticated Sophie to emerge.

She soaped her body carefully, relishing the slipperiness of her full, heavy breasts and feeling the hardness of her nipples. Squeezing firmly, she let the other hand slide into the abundant blonde curls that covered her womanhood, and then underneath herself, letting the soap leave a slippery trail down her long legs. Eyes closed, lips parted, she stroked and massaged herself, then grasped the shower-head, removed it from its niche on the wall and let the hot pin-pricks of water cascade over her pubis, washing the soap through her glistening blonde bush. Lifting one leg to rest against the low cubicle shelf, she parted her pussy-lips gently and let the jet of water play on her inner labia, feeling the hot pressure, letting the sensation excite her until the water was incidental and she dropped the shower-head to the floor.

The water squirted upwards, unheeded, as Sophie, oblivious and obsessed, inserted her thumb into her vagina, letting her fingers creep backwards to stroke her anus. Head thrown back, the knuckle of her thumb rubbing deliciously on her clitoris, Sophie felt the heat of desire spread through her womb to her belly and then go coursing around her body until her orgasm shook her, making her gasp. When the waves of pleasure had finally abated, and she was able to breathe normally again, she bent to retrieve the forgotten soap.

What on earth is happening to me, she wondered, as she resumed her shower. For the prick she had imagined

13

riding as she had masturbated herself had not been Toby's but that of the young gardener whose eyes had seemed to undress her earlier. Surprised by her own desire, Sophie vowed to be strict with herself: what she did in the privacy of her rooms was her own affair, but in public she was determined to be very much in control of herself.

She chose a deep blue velvet dress to make her début at the McKinnerney's drinks party. She had been nervous at first: ready too early and wondering what to expect. Mrs McKinnerney made her jump, knocking on the door and calling her.

'Sophie? Sophie? Are you ready, dear? Shall I show you where to go? Come on, we'll go together. And by the way, call me Helen. Mrs McKinnerney is such a mouthful, don't you think?' And off they went, chatting and laughing, to the elaborately furnished house.

While Sophie was still admiring the beautiful furnishings, Helen pushed open the door of a room and sang out cheerfully, 'Don't be nervous, dear, none of them bite, as far as I know!'

The room was high-ceilinged and elegant. It could have looked cold, but was saved by comfortable sofas and large cushions, tasselled rugs in spicy colours and soft, red-gold lighting. About a dozen people were gathered, chatting, drinking, laughing.

'Helen!' cried a middle-aged woman, glancing across from the fireplace. 'What a treat to see you! We have all missed you so much.' The two women kissed, and then Helen turned to Sophie.

'Janie, I'd like you to meet Sophie. She is the brave young woman who has come to impose some discipline on those hooligan horses. Sophie, this is Janie Marshall, our nearest neighbour and a very dear friend.'

Sophie shook her hand. 'Pleased to meet you, Mrs. Marshall.'

'Oh, just call me Janie, dear. I must compliment you, Helen,' she continued, patting Sophie's hand, 'on your excellent taste in grooms. I had no idea they were so glamorous these days!'

They all laughed, Helen shaking her head and saying,'I'm afraid I can't take the credit. James and Catherine are the ones for that. Where are they, by the way?'

'Haven't seen them. I can take care of Sophie if you want to go and hurry them up a bit.'

'Do you mind, Sophie? Is that all right with you? Oh well then, I think maybe I should.' Helen was off again, a stern look clouding her face.

Janie linked her arm through Sophie's. 'Good, now I have you all to myself. Still, I suppose I should share you, shouldn't I? Oh come and meet my husband – he's a bit of a dry old stick, but we like to bring him out and dust him off occasionally, don't we, darling?'

The latter part of the remark was said deliberately in the hearing of a tall, handsome man whom Sophie guessed to be a good ten to fifteen years older than his wife, but still with an eye-catching physique. From the way they smiled at each other Sophie could tell that Janie and her husband were very much in love, despite her playful jibe, and she was touched.

'Nick, this is Sophie, James's new groom.'

'Lucky old James, I say!'

'No, no! Nincompoop! Not James's groom! A groom for his horses. Sophie, this is my husband, Nick. Anyone who knows us will tell you that I deserve a medal for putting up with him.'

Sophie shook hands with Nick, who leant over to whisper theatrically to her. 'If I had known grooms were like you, I'd have insisted we needed one. I thought they all wore flat caps and smoked pipes.'

Sophie laughed. 'I'm sure some do. How many horses do you keep, Mr. Marshall?'

15

'Call me Nick, please. Mr. Marshall makes me feel, well, as old as I am, really. We've only got our two old nags – they suit us, don't they, darling? Sadly, my son has never taken to horse-riding: perhaps you could persuade him of its merits? Do you have any experience of teaching wayward twenty-year-olds?'

'I don't think so.' Sophie feigned dismay. 'That sounds like too much of a challenge, even for me!'

'Quite right, too. Here he is, now. Paul, come and meet this delightful young lady. This is Sophie. She is going to be mistress of the stable here for James and Catherine. Sophie, this is Paul.'

Sophie shook his hand. 'The wayward son,' she mused.

Paul brown eyes narrowed in his father's direction. 'What has the old fool been saying about me, now?' he hissed, while Sophie smiled at the antics. 'Come over here and tell me, Sophie.' He pulled her to one side.

'Just say the word,' he urged her, 'and I will take you away from all this.' They laughed, and Paul replenished her glass from the bottle he was holding.

'There isn't an awful lot to do round here for a young man-about-town, or for a young groom-about-town,' he added quickly, 'but I will be happy to show you the sights in your free time – it should take all of twenty minutes.'

Sophie was enjoying all the attention. 'Tell me who all these other people are,' she whispered, 'I don't know any of their names.'

'Oh all right,' Paul sighed, 'but I'm the most interesting one here.' He pointed out various friends and acquaintances: the local doctor and his wife, he looking rather devious, her supercilious; the Newton-Smiths, both jovial and loud; Rosie, the fearsome child-minder, Paul confided; and a disdainful young man lounging by

16

the window who, Paul informed Sophie, was Catherine McKinnerney's brother, Dominic.

Sophie was soon giggling helplessly at the snippets of gossip Paul inserted wickedly into the monologue, and hoped that no one could overhear the things he was saying.

'I don't know how much of this you're making up.' She laughed, aware that Paul's conversation and the wine were combining to make her feel warm and relaxed.

'Ah, but that's the fun of it,' Paul teased. 'No, no,' he cried, dramatically, as a young woman tried to introduce herself, 'I'm not sharing her; she's mine, now!' The young woman, whom Sophie recognised as Rosie, the fearsome child-minder, gave Paul a withering look.

'You get worse,' she told him, then turned to Sophie. 'You are Sophie, aren't you? The new groom? Hi, pleased to meet you. Is Paul monopolising you? He's a cross we all have to bear, I'm afraid. No,' – as Paul tried to interrupt – 'she isn't all yours now. You don't need a groom; you need therapy. I'm Rosie, by the way. I look after the Flemming's children in the village. I'm a child-minder, not a nanny, I hasten to add.'

The wine sparkled, conversation flowed, and Sophie began to think that this life would suit her very well indeed. It's only a one-off, she told herself, I'm sure this has all been orchestrated to tempt me into staying, even if things get really unpleasant between the McKinnerneys. Tomorrow will be more realistic – down to earth with a bump, probably. But she knew that the elegant surroundings and amiable company were working their spell on her; she was hooked. How could anyone want to go back to work in a boring office when they had three lovely children, a beautiful house, and certainly didn't need the money, Sophie wondered, thinking of Catherine McKinnerney.

Helen had reappeared by this time, looking rather

flustered. She checked that Sophie was mixing happily, then made another departure, prompting Janie to whisper cryptically to Sophie, 'Poor Helen. She shouldn't have to be rushing around. People can be so selfish.' Sophie nodded wisely, before Paul whisked her off to meet another small group of people standing by the open French windows. She was rapidly getting giddy and couldn't for the life of her remember all their names.

The group consisted of three people. The woman, not much older than Sophie, but with stunning self-confidence, looked her idly from top to toe, wrinkling her nose as though she didn't quite approve of her.

'I didn't know James was taking on staff,' she mused when Paul introduced them. 'No offence, of course,' she added, to Sophie.

'Hello, Sophie. Pleased to meet you.' One man (whom Sophie recognised as the family doctor) held his hand out. 'You must excuse my wife. Marcie can be rude even without trying. My name is Alex Carver, by the way. Now, let us escape her wicked tongue and find you another drink.'

He led Sophie away, refilling her glass even though she protested, and sat down on one of the small sofas in a corner. Sophie, pulled down next to him and spilling her drink in the process, was just reminding herself that it wouldn't do to have a hangover on the first day in her new job, when she spied Helen entering the room once more with a beautiful, if sulky looking, woman.

'Ah ha!' Alex cried. 'Our hostess arrives, at last.'

Sophie found herself on her feet and noticed that Helen was propelling the young woman forward, despite the scowling reluctance on the latter's face.

'Sophie! Sorry to leave you to it. I hope Alex has been behaving himself. This is my daughter-in-law, Catherine. Catherine, this is Sophie.'

Catherine was pale and drawn. Her eyes looked red, as if she had recently been crying. All this aside, she was a gorgeous creature. Her hair hung sleek and chestnut-coloured, almost to her waist, and although she appeared as fragile as bone china, there was a flash of something harder in her hazel eyes.

'Sophie, I'm so sorry you have been left to fend for yourself. As you can tell things are a little unsettled around here at the moment. I hope you are having a nice time. I won't bore you with talk about the job right at this moment – plenty of time to sort that out.'

Sophie hardly had time to smile and nod before Catherine swept past her, caught up Alex's hand and pulled him off to one side, saying brightly that she had something to say which could only be discussed with a doctor.

Helen frowned. 'I'm sorry, Sophie. Problems, problems, as you may have noticed. Nothing can persuade James to join the party. I despair of the pair of them, I really do.'

The party seemed to be in full swing; various new arrivals had been introduced to Sophie, and their names instantly forgotten. Alex and Catherine were flirting rather obviously in a corner, while Helen whirled around, chatting, making introductions, and brandishing fresh bottles. It was all getting rather out of hand, Sophie couldn't help feeling, for a quiet drinks party.

She found herself in conversation with Rosie and Joanne, who was a nanny for a family in the village, finding out where to go and what to do in the locality.

'I hope they're going to make a move soon,' Joanne said, grumpily, pointing to a couple holding court in the middle of the room. The man was plump and red-faced from too much alcohol; the woman, hee-hawing in laughter, was only slightly less portly than her husband. The Newton-Smiths, Sophie remembered.

'I know they're going to ask me to drive,' Joanne moaned, 'but you see what happens if I need the car to take the kids swimming; it'll be a different story, then.

You're right to do child-minding rather than nannying,' she said to Rosie. 'When you live in you end up doing everything.'

'Jo's lot are really horrible to her,' Rosie confided.

'I'm not paid for weekends,' Jo sighed, 'but because I'm there they expect me to muck in anyway. No privacy, either. If it's not the kids barging in on me, it's that fat slob.'

Sophie looked alarmed and Rosie laughed. 'They're not all that bad but, take it from me, Sophie, when you have a day off, get as far away from the place as possible, otherwise there's always "one more little job" for you to do.'

Sophie told them about Toby and their plans to meet up at the weekends if they could make it. Talking about him made Sophie miss him, and she sat quietly, letting the conversation wash over her pleasantly, wondering what Toby was doing at that moment.

'Hey, Dopey,' Jo nudged her, 'I asked if you'd met the other help they have here. Particularly' – she and Rosie feigned swooning – 'the gardener!'

Sophie blushed causing the girls to laugh and hoot.

'Yes, he has that effect on everyone,' Rosie said. 'The mystery gardener. He can get his hands on my begonias any day!' And they all three burst into lascivious laughter again.

'Oh-oh, mine are off,' cried Jo, jumping up. 'Nice to meet you, Sophie. We'll meet up for a night out sometime soon. Hope you get on all right.' And she was off.

Sophie couldn't help noticing her employer's fat hand slap her bottom as he handed her the car keys.

'Actually, I could cadge a lift with them if I'm quick,' Rosie said, 'as long as I don't have to sit next to Mr Wandering Hands.' She winked at Sophie, then dashed off to catch Jo.

Other people were starting to call their goodbyes and Helen continued to play the dutiful hostess, her daughter-in-law being conspicuous by her absence – along with Alex Carver, Sophie couldn't help noticing. Janie and Nick Marshall left hand-in-hand, urging Sophie to pop round whenever she wished.

Sophie, feeling rather flushed, crept off to find the bathroom; easier said than done, it seemed. After ten minutes of wandering through the dark corridors with no luck, she had just decided to wait until she returned to her own rooms when she saw a door slightly ajar and hurried towards it. As she pushed it open and leant inside to check that it really was the room she was seeking, strong hands grasped her shoulders, pulled her inside and shut the door with a soft click.

'What are you – ?' A large hand clamped over Sophie's mouth and a hard masculine body pushed her up against the wall.

Furious, Sophie whipped her head round, trying to rid herself of the hand, but the grip was determined.

'Keep still,' a vaguely familiar voice warned, 'and you never know, you might enjoy yourself more than you expect.'

Sophie suppressed the urge to giggle at such melo-drama – she felt too tipsy to be afraid – as she racked her brain for the owner of the voice. Reaching sideways carefully she tried to find a light switch, but she had no way of knowing where it was.

'Don't scream, Sophie.' The tone of the voice had changed now. 'I'll take my hand away if you promise not to scream,' it wheedled.

Sophie nodded, and the hand was removed, cau-tiously; but her fingers still crept along the wall.

'What do you think you're doing?' she hissed. 'Who are you?' It sounded quite comical and Sophie had to remind herself that this could be a very serious situation she was facing, although somehow it didn't feel that way.

'Sophie, you looked so good down there.' The man's

mouth was against her neck, and his hand had slid between their bodies and was caressing her breast. He was not much taller than Sophie, but was obviously stronger, and as he and Sophie performed a clumsy tug-of-war with her dress she realised it was only a matter of time before she lost. As she got the giggles again he took advantage, reached down and feverishly hitched Sophie's dress up to her waist. Sophie knew if she really wanted to stop him she could, but she couldn't seem to think straight. Meanwhile he fumbled his trousers open and pulled Sophie's G-string aside, sliding his whole hand between her legs and groaning as he felt her sweet wetness.

Suddenly, feeling the rising of her own desire, Sophie didn't want to giggle anymore; her only concern was her own satisfaction. She felt the man's erection urgently nudging her belly, and was suddenly lifted firmly, so that she was only supported by her own shoulders hard against the wall and the man's strong hands under her buttocks. Slowly, he lowered her on to his waiting prick, and Sophie gasped as the slipperiness of her eager vagina and her own weight carried her down hard over his quivering penis. She pulled her arms free from the straps of her dress, letting her breasts fall forward like ripe, heavy fruits, demanding attention from this shadowy man. He seemed only too happy to oblige, burying his face into her glorious cleavage, then raising his greedy mouth to find her nipples. She caught her breath as he licked, then sucked, and then began to bite gently at them, Sophie wriggling and squirming in painful pleasure, pinned to the wall like a butterfly.

'Oh, but we shouldn't . . .' she gasped.

'Shhh . . .' he whispered, holding her easily as his hardness played its full length in and out of her willing vagina.

'Someone might find us. We shouldn't be doing this, not here.' And at that moment Sophie's hand found the light switch. After a moment's hesitation she tripped the switch and in the ensuing confusion, her mystery lover stepped back, letting her slide to the floor. He covered his face with one hand, the other trying to push his suddenly wilting penis back inside his trousers.

'Alex!' Sophie gasped, horrified.

At that moment the bathroom door opened and a man whom Sophie had never seen before stood, confusion and anger on his face. The man looked from Alex to Sophie, then opened the door wider.

'Go downstairs, Alex. Your wife is looking for you.'

Without a word Alex Carver slid out of the door hardly glancing at Sophie, who got shakily to her feet, tears of embarrassment in her eyes.

'He pulled me in,' she warbled, 'it was dark and I . . .'

The man looked away as she rearranged her dress.

'Don't worry. I'm afraid I know Alex Carver of old. I should also add, he is my wife's friend rather than mine. I hope he hasn't hurt you?'

'No, no! I don't think so. Oh dear, my dress; it's torn.'

'I'm James McKinnerney. Come with me, please. We'll sort this out.'

'I'm Sophie, the new groom. I was just – then he . . .'

James took her arm and led her down the corridor to a large, dark room, full of bookshelves and soft reading lamps.

'My study,' he explained. 'Sit down.' He produced a shawl which he placed gently over her shoulders, then poured two measures of brandy. Sophie shook as she took one. 'I'm sorry your first evening here had to end like this,' he told her earnestly. 'Would you like to take this incident further?'

'Oh no! Please, can't we just forget it? Mr. Carver was rather drunk, I don't want any trouble for him. And no damage was done,' she added quickly, wondering what this staid and dignified man would think if he had known how much she had been enjoying herself. Her employer gazed at her with solemn blue eyes for a long time then, just when Sophie thought he had guessed her guilty secret, he smiled, slapped his hands to his knees and got to his feet.

'OK, Sophie, as you wish. But if you have any more problems with Alex, or anyone else for that matter, you can always come to me. I know that technically you are quite capable of looking after yourself, but you are under my roof, and I feel responsible for you.'

'Thank you, Mr McKinnerney.'

'James, please. Remember what I said. I'll see you tomorrow, Sophie. I hope you sleep well.'

She made her way through the big house and back to her rooms. The night air seemed to clear her head finally, lending a dream-like quality to the incident with Alex. As she lay in the strange bed, Sophie found herself snorting with laughter at the wounded look on Alex's face when he had been sent out of the room.

She speculated that if that little confrontation hadn't cooled his ardour, nothing would. Sophie resolved to tolerate no more horseplay from Alex Carver and turned her thoughts to her new employer. He could only be in his thirties, yet he appeared to have all the worries of a much older man resting on his shoulders; no wonder, thought Sophie, with the predatory Mr Carver around. She smiled into the darkness, and let herself enjoy the memory of how he had banished Alex and his wilting penis from the bathroom. Perhaps Toby was right, maybe her virtue was going to have to be protected! And Sophie got the giggles all over again as she thought of the delicious irony in that.

Chapter Two

S ophie felt groggy and disorientated the following morning. She had just finished dressing after her shower when a knock came at the front door and Helen McKinnerney told her that if she was going straight out to the horses, Catherine would call in to see her there before she left for work.

'I'll be off to my poor, long-suffering husband shortly,' Helen told her, 'to make sure he hasn't forgotten what I look like. I'll say goodbye now, dear, and I've left my telephone number for you. I'm sure you won't need it, but please feel free to use it if you have any problems. Good luck, dear, I'll see you soon.'

And she was gone, leaving Sophie to pick at her breakfast and wonder whether she had done the right thing, coming to work for the McKinnerneys. The humour that had been so prevalent last night was long gone; Sophie felt miserable and a little homesick. She tidied her bed and opened the windows, fruitlessly scouring the visible gardens for a glimpse of the groundsman, telling herself she was merely checking the state of the weather.

She made her way to the yard and unlocked the tack

room, noticing a list of instructions, presumably for her, stuck on the wall. All the saddles and bridles seemed to be on named pegs and she noticed, without enthusiasm, that many needed cleaning.

First things first, she thought, pulling back the doors of the stable block and feeling her spirits lift slightly at the familiar sounds and smells of the horses. You knew where you were with horses, Sophie told herself: none of the complicated emotions of humans. You fed them, watered them, and exercised them and they were happy. Simple. She patted the neck of a large bay, whose nameplate announced him as Firefly – James McKinnerney's horse if she remembered correctly. Across the block Buzz bared his teeth over his stable door as if to remind this useless woman that if she didn't let him out soon she would be very sorry. Sophie laughed at him; he was barely big enough to rest his chin on the stable door but his attitude made it easy to forget his size.

She collected Buzz first, then two other small ponies and led them down to the paddock, filling hay nets and checking water troughs on the way. She was just wondering which of the larger horses to turn out and which to exercise first, when Catherine McKinnerney appeared, high heels crunching unsteadily on the gravel.

'Sophie? There you are! I'm off now, though I'll probably be back fairly early today. I've written down an exercise schedule for the horses, so please stick to it. Also, as Peter has a sleep after lunch you could make yourself useful by giving Ellie a riding lesson – nothing taxing, just half an hour or so. And perhaps an hour for Gina when she comes in from school, although I should be back by then. No problems? Good. I'm off!'

Sophie was aware that she was gaping stupidly after her employer, unable to digest all this information which had been delivered in a quick-fire manner, not designed to encourage questions. Not once had Catherine smiled, or even caught Sophie's eye; her eagerness to be away from the house and all its responsibilities was palpable. No hangover for her this morning, Sophie noticed; there was a woman who knew what she wanted.

Oh well, thought Sophie, back to work. She watched as Catherine, hair in a business-like plait, leapt into the red sports car she had left nearby and revved the engine. Then, suddenly remembering something, Catherine let the engine die, leant out of the window and beckoned to Sophie.

'I do not want to be disturbed at work for any reason,' she told the girl. 'I've said as much to the nanny, and now I'm telling you. If you have any problems go to my husband.' She flipped her sunglasses down over her eyes, wound up the car window, and screeched off down the drive, leaving dark gashes in the pale surface of the gravel.

Sophie watched her go. Yes, she thought to herself, you have made yourself more than clear. Nobody in their right mind would cross you. Perhaps I should have curtsied!

The rest of the morning was busy. Sophie exercised two of the larger horses and then braced herself for a boring couple of hours cleaning tack. At midday Ellie appeared with the nanny, who turned out to be older than Sophie expected.

'Hello, there. I'm Jean. Sorry to have missed the introductions last night,' she called across. 'I hope we aren't too early but we want to be ready to pick Gina up from school at three. Unless, of course,' she added brightly to the child, 'Mummy gets home in time to collect her.' The two adults exchanged looks, and Sophie sent Ellie into the tack room to see if she could pick out her own pony's saddle and bridle.

'Is Mrs McKinnerney terse with you, too, Jean, or is it just me? You could have cut the atmosphere with a knife

27

when she came down here this morning. I didn't know what to say.'

'Oh, I know, dear. I've been nannying for thirty years, but this is the first time I've come close to regretting my choice of career. That's between you and I, by the way. But, you know, the children are sweet and perhaps things will sort themselves out in time; we can only hope.'

'Fingers crossed,' Sophie agreed and went to saddle up Jigsaw, Ellie's tiny skewbald pony.

The lesson went well. Ellie was a confident rider despite her tender years, and Sophie was just showing her how to groom her pony at the end of a ride when Jigsaw accidentally stepped on Ellie's foot. The wail that ensued was more from shock than pain but, loath to return Ellie to the nanny in such a state of hysteria, Sophie took her into her own little kitchen – which was, anyway, much nearer – to examine the injured foot. She pulled the boot off, then left a calmer Ellie to wrestle with the sock as she went to answer her ringing phone.

'Hello? Sophie? It's me, Toby! How are things?'

'Look, Toby, could you just hold on a minute . . .'

Suddenly a screech of brakes announced Catherine's erratic return, closely followed by the terrified whinny of a horse. A shout of, 'What the blazes? Who is responsible for this?' rang out. Sophie looked out of the window to see Buzz had escaped from the paddock and come looking for Jigsaw, obviously having just had a near miss with the front of Catherine's car.

Ellie, hearing her mother's voice, renewed her shrieking, and Catherine McKinnerney appeared in the doorway of the cottage, her face as black as thunder. Ellie flung her arms around her mother's neck, pleased to have all her attention and Sophie quickly grabbed the telephone receiver.

'Sophie?' asked Toby. 'What's going on?'

'I can't talk now. I'll ring you later. Sorry.' As she put

the receiver down, Sophie realised that she didn't have his number, but there wasn't time to worry about that.

'Would you like to explain why I nearly knocked down a pony, and why my daughter is crying, while you talk on the telephone to your friends? Can you explain it?'

'I'm sorry,' stammered Sophie. 'It all happened so quickly. Jigsaw trod on Ellie's toe but I don't think she's really hurt. And I'm sorry about Buzz, I must have forgotten to padlock the gate.'

'I'm taking Ellie back to the house now. You had better go and catch that pony. Unless the conversation with your friend is more urgent.' Catherine stalked off, Ellie limping behind her.

'Pick me up, Mummy, my foot hurts.'

'Certainly not. Your jodhpurs are filthy. Let's go and find Jean. She can get you cleaned up.'

Sophie deposited Jigsaw and Buzz, none the worse for his ordeal, in the paddock, careful to secure the chain this time. She was officially off duty now for an hour or so, but she found she couldn't face her kitchen again and wandered up the drive instead. She headed round the back of the house where, from her window, she had spotted a little wooden garden seat, nestling between well-clipped hedges.

Sophie sat herself down on the seat as far from the house as possible, hoping that no one could see her. Reaching into her pocket she found a hanky and blew her nose, well aware that at any moment the floodgates were going to open and there would be no stopping them. She thought about Toby, busy at university and with no responsibilities; she thought of her family and friends at home, and wondered why she had ever come to Prospect House. She could have settled down to a comfortable, boring life as Toby's wife in her old village: instead she had travelled all this way to some place akin to a war zone to be mauled by a lecherous doctor and work for a woman who she knew she could never please, no matter how hard she tried.

Before Sophie could stop herself she was sobbing wildly, covering her mouth in the hope that nobody could hear her. As she suspected, once she started crying, she couldn't stop. Much as she tried to pull herself together and take control, it was impossible and her sobs shook her whole body like enormous hiccups. She tried to wipe her eyes but her handkerchief was sodden, which made her cry even more.

Sophie knew she was being pathetic but she didn't care, and she was in the process of searching the rest of her pockets for more tissues when a huge, rough hand appeared before her holding out a snow-white hanky. Sophie, who had been convinced that she was alone and unobserved, nearly fell off her seat with a yell of fright.

The young gardener, kindly offering his handkerchief, stepped back in alarm. 'Am I that scary?' he asked, obviously hurt.

Sophie hiccupped and tried to laugh through her tears. 'No,' she sniffed, 'I'm sorry, but . . .' and she was off again, prompting the young man to try offering the hanky once more.

'Thanks.' Sophie took it. 'I'll give it back. Clean,' she added, hastily.

'I should hope so,' the gardener said, as she blew her nose copiously into it.

Sophie laughed in reply.

'So,' he said, sitting down next to her on the bench, 'do you want to tell me what it's about? Have they sounded the four-minute warning? Earthquake? Fire? Flood?'

'Jigsaw trod on Ellie's foot and Buzz escaped on to the drive.'

'More serious than I expected, then.'

Sophie laughed again. Out loud it sounded silly, and

anyway, the problem wasn't really the horses – it was their owner.

'It's just that Mrs McKinnerney isn't very pleased with me,' she said. 'I can't seem to do anything right.'

'Oh, nobody can do anything right for that one. Take no notice. If you live to be a hundred you won't get it right for her. Now listen, I'm on my lunch break for half an hour if you want to join me. Nothing exciting; just a sandwich and some coffee round at my place – that's the shed,' he added quickly, as she looked dubious. 'Got a better offer? Fancy facing Her Ladyship? No, I thought not. Come on, then.'

He led the way, pushing his squeaky wheelbarrow. Sophie brought up the rear, taking the opportunity to observe his rather pleasing body in motion. He chatted all the way, oblivious to her eyes on him, but delighted to have the chance to talk to this gorgeous young woman. Pushing his hanky into her pocket, Sophie noticed a blue letter C embroidered on the corner.

'By the way, I'm Sophie,' she told him.

'I'm just the gardener, ma'am,' he said, comically tugging his forelock.

'I'll bet your name begins with C.'

'How did you . . .? Oh, yes, the hanky. Very clever. Go on, then, cleverclogs, guess what it is.'

'You look like – I know! Charlie!'

'Oh, thank you very much. No.' He was opening the door of a large shed and dusting off a solid table that stood in the middle.

'Colin.'

He grimaced. 'Thankfully, no.'

'Cameron.'

'Ugh!' He switched on an electric fire and the shed suddenly seemed warm and cosy. Sophie perched on one of the stools, racking her brain.

'Cuthbert!'

'Cuthbert?'

31

'Is it?'

'Of course not!' He handed her a cup of coffee which he had just poured from a thermos flask, and then unwrapped a pack of sandwiches, offering them to Sophie.

'I know! It's Craig!' she cried between mouthfuls of sandwich, her earlier misery entirely forgotten in this cheerful place.

'Nope.'

'Christopher?'

'Nope.'

'I give up, then. What is it?'

'It's quite unusual.'

Sophie bit into an apple he had given her and combed her memory for names beginning with C. 'Clarissa!'

They both fell about laughing until the young man sat up soberly and said, 'Callum. My name's Callum.'

'That's a nice name,' Sophie said, shyly.

'So is Sophie.' He had his head down, staring into his coffee cup.

'It's a boring name,' Sophie replied, aware that the atmosphere of camaraderie had given way to something much more charged. 'I always wanted to be called something more imposing.'

'Oh no,' he said, quickly, 'Sophie's a lovely name. Not boring at all. Exciting. It's an exciting name.' He blushed slightly. 'You're exciting,' he told her. And before Sophie had time to think he had knelt beside her and was kissing her.

'Do you mind?' he murmured.

'Oh no,' she breathed, 'it's the best thing to happen to me all day.'

His arms enveloped her and Sophie felt breathless with excitement. His kisses were deep and urgent, with an insistence she had never felt in Toby's. Against her leg, she felt his penis straining within his work trousers, and she desperately wanted to free it, to hold it in her hands, to see what it felt like naked against her.

Callum hesitated slightly as she unbuttoned his shirt and slid her hand into the warmth inside. She could feel his heart beating fast, his muscles, smooth and well-defined, and she longed to experience the barely-concealed power that lay within.

Almost shyly, eyes constantly flicking to hers to gauge her reaction, Callum unbuttoned her blouse and slid it over her shoulders. Breathing her scent deeply, he bent to lift one heavy breast towards his mouth and clasped his lips firmly over her erect nipple. Sophie gasped as he sucked hard, his other hand travelling down to unzip her jodhpurs and ease them over her thighs. He let his large, work-roughened hands make their way gently over her soft belly, then, getting to his feet, he pulled her up so that her jodhpurs slid to her ankles and he feasted his eyes appreciatively on her body.

He seemed speechless, unable to think what to do next, so Sophie discarded her skimpy panties, and stepped towards him. She kissed him, standing on tip-toe to reach his lips, then slid her mouth down his bronzed chest to a taut, rippled belly. Callum was frozen to the spot, his eyes closed, as she unzipped his trousers and felt for his aching rigid penis. Kneeling before him she took him into her mouth, not caring that she was with a man she hardly knew in a shed in her employers' gardens, but just wanting to experience the wonderful hardness of his manhood. His prick was larger than Sophie had expected. Gently, she let her tongue run tantalizingly over the purple head, then eased the thick, smooth shaft into her mouth, feeling it tense and tighten in expectation.

Callum's hands were wound into her long, blonde hair, holding her face between his legs so that her senses were filled with his earthy smell and salty taste. A guilty warmth started to spread through Sophie. What a good

33

job the staid Mr McKinnerney or his irritable wife couldn't see her now, pleasuring the gardener in their shed!

And what pleasure it was! Sophie was relishing being in control; she knew from Callum's straining prick that she could make him come any time she wished, but she was enjoying the feel of him filling her mouth, letting him play his full length in and out of her and hearing his heavy breathing.

Suddenly Callum pulled himself out of her and hoisted her to her feet. Without ceremony, he lifted her like a rag doll so that her buttocks were on the solid wooden table. Standing between her legs, his perfectly-formed penis rearing upwards, he looked her over hungrily, then he parted her thighs wider and ran his finger down the deep furrow.

'Beautiful,' he said. 'Now, show me how you like it, Sophie. Let me see.'

Delighted with this new game, Sophie felt eagerly through the wet curls for her clitoris. She was cold, spread-eagled on the large table, but felt the growing heat between her legs as she started to finger herself. Her thighs tightening and her buttocks lifted off the table, she became aware of Callum towering over her, watching her intently, and the thought of someone she barely knew watching while she gave herself an orgasm added to the excitement of the situation.

She felt for Callum's penis, and found it, eager to home in on the sweet wetness her pleasure had produced. She guided it, slippery with her own juice, deep into the blonde bush and gasped as she felt it pushing against her inner walls.

'Make love to me, Callum, please, just do it.'

Callum needed no further telling. Lying back on the hard surface, arms above her head, he took her harder and deeper than she had ever experienced it before. He seemed to be able to reach to the very heart of her, and

Sophie found herself getting the most out of him as he rhythmically thrust himself into her.

Despite his earlier coyness, Callum was an expert, and when she came, raising herself up to meet him, he pushed her back down on the table, so that her feeling of being in control was suddenly challenged and she joyfully abandoned herself totally to this unexpected pleasure.

Before the tautness in her vagina relaxed, Callum gave one last shuddering heave, and ejaculated spectacularly. Sophie felt the gush of his hot semen before collapsing, happy and sated, on the table.

Callum, suddenly business-like, was searching for his hastily discarded clothing.

'Do you think she is looking for you?' he asked, casually. Sophie glanced sideways and nearly died of fright as she noticed a small window in the wall of the shed. Looking through, she had a perfect view of the back of the house, where Catherine McKinnerney had just stepped out of a door.

Sophie leapt to her feet, and fumbled for her clothes. She could hear Catherine's footsteps crunching closer and closer on the gravel path. She hid herself, still only half-dressed, behind the shed door.

'Don't tell her you've seen me,' she hissed. Callum laughed and then the shed door was flung wide open.

'Callum, have you seen Sophie on your travels? She's the new groom. If you do see her tell her I'm off to pick up Gina in ten minutes – I'd like her to come.' The footsteps crunched off back down the path, and Callum shut the door.

'Do you think she knew I was here?'

'Who cares? What you do in your own free time is entirely up to you. I'd hurry up if I were you though, she's obviously on the warpath.'

'I can't go to pick up Gina now – I smell of sex!'

'You smell great, and anyway she's hardly the one to

be making judgments. If she hadn't been so ratty you wouldn't have needed comforting.' Callum pulled a lewd face in Sophie's direction. 'Do feel free to visit my shed again soon.'

Sophie rushed back to the house, only briefly wondering what Callum had meant about Catherine not being in a position to judge others. She quickly doused herself in perfume and then caught Catherine up in the driveway.

'There you are. I was thinking you'd run away already! Come on, I want to talk to you and, as I have to collect Gina, you may as well keep me company.' The other two children were already in the car as it screeched down the drive.

'I think I owe you an apology,' Catherine said eventually. 'I shouldn't be so hard on you. Heaven knows, I, of all people, can't lecture others about coping! Forgiven?'

'Forgiven.' Sophie said, smiling, and wondering if she herself would be forgiven if Catherine McKinnerney knew what she had been up to that morning. Guiltily she turned her head so that her employer wouldn't see the blush spreading over her face as she imagined herself back in Callum's shed. Who would have thought a place of such pleasure could look so ordinary from the outside? And Sophie wondered how long she would have to wait before she went back and sampled its delights again.

Catherine was her usual haughty self by the time they reached the school, Sophie noticed, making no attempt to socialise with the other mothers there. She felt sorry for Gina as she trudged out of the playground – a lonely little island in a sea of friends visiting each other for tea.

Sophie waved to Joanne who appeared to be trying to organise several small children at once at the opposite end of the playground, and then they were back in the car, Gina telling them all excitedly about her new reading book.

'Shall I read it to you, Mummy? When we get home?'

'Read it to your Daddy,' Catherine told her. 'He's the one interested in books.' She laughed and looked at Sophie as if she had just made a good joke. Sophie was appalled.

'You can read it to me,' she told Gina quietly, 'I love books. I read so many when I was little that my Mummy used to call me "Bookworm".'

The children hooted with laughter and Catherine slammed the car into gear, her mouth a tight line, furious that the intended slight of her husband had been ignored.

When they got home Catherine locked the car doors then stalked wordlessly to the house, leaving Sophie to hand over the baby, several coats and Gina's bag to a frowning Jean.

'What now?' the nanny whispered to Sophie. 'I can't keep up with her moods.'

'My fault, I think, sorry Jean. Oh, by the way, Gina has a new reading book, she needs to read to someone. Could you . . .?'

'Of course, dear. Don't worry, it can only get better – that's what I keep telling myself, anyway!'

Sophie set about organising the horses for the night; doing her last trek round the stables, filling hayracks and water buckets. It certainly didn't look as though she would be giving Gina a riding lesson today. Probably proved myself unfit to teach her children after the fiasco with Buzz, Sophie thought, and found she didn't much care.

She was just trying to decide whether to watch the little television in her room, or to have an early night when her telephone rang in the hall. She pulled it through into her bedroom and closed the door. It was Toby.

'Hi, Soph. How are things? Sorry I phoned at a bad time earlier. Is everything sorted out now?'

'Oh yes, the horses are all sorted now – it's just been a strange day, all in all.'

They chatted: he about his course, and she about the events leading up to Catherine's outburst. Sophie mentioned that she had been having second thoughts about coming to the McKinnerney household, and that she had since decided to stay.

'So, what changed your mind?' Toby asked, and Sophie had a fleeting vision of Callum, his long blonde hair hanging rakishly over one eye, as he slowly unzipped his jeans.

'Well, you know, things always seem ... strange at first, don't they?' She tried not to sound flustered. 'But something always comes up, I mean, crops up, oh, you know ... things change,' she finished lamely.

'Are you all right, Sophie?' Toby's voice was concerned. 'I was going to see if you wanted to come up at the weekend, but if you want to make it sooner – '

'Oh no! I'm fine, Toby, really. And I can't come up before the weekend as I won't have a free day.'

'It's probably just as well, I've got a really full timetable. But there's a student party at one of the houses on Saturday night; it'll give you a chance to meet the lads, if you like.'

'I do like, yes, thanks Toby. That will be good.'

'And the girls,' Toby added. 'There are some. Girls, I mean.'

'Are there? Girls?' she joked. 'Hmm, how unusual. I hope you haven't been noticing too many girls.'

'I only have eyes for you.' Toby laughed, but Sophie wasn't convinced. Not that she could object if Toby was 'noticing girls.' It would be hypocritical to mind, considering how much of Callum she had noticed!

'Do you miss me?' Toby asked suddenly.

'Tons,' Sophie lied.

'Where are you?'

'In my own room. Why?'

'Is there a bed?'

'Of course.'

'Lie down on it.'

'What?'

'Lie down on the bed, Sophie. Go on, just humour me. Are you on it? What are you wearing?'

'Just a robe-thingy. Look, Toby, what are you . . .?'

'Take it off.'

Sophie slipped the robe off and lay back naked on the bed. She was glad she had thought to drop the catch on the kitchen door.

'Are you naked?'

'Yes.' She whispered. 'But, Toby, where . . .?'

'I'm in a phone box.'

'Toby!'

'It's very secluded here.' His voice was deep, husky. 'It's very dark. No one can see me. And guess what, Sophie? I've got something for you.'

'What? What is it?' But she already knew, and a delicious shiver ran through her body.

'It's my prick, Sophie. I'm holding it and thinking of you.'

Sophie caught her breath.

'Close your eyes, Sophie. Close them properly. Now imagine I'm there with you. I've got my prick ready for you, Sophie, big and hard; just how you like it. What would you want me to do if I was there, Sophie? Tell me.'

'Stroke me,' she murmured. 'I'd like you to stroke me.'

'Do it, Sophie. You stroke yourself from me, wherever you want. Where would you like me to stroke you?'

'My neck. My arms. My breasts,' she whispered, barely touching the hard, pink buds, her whole body tingling in anticipation.

'Your breasts, Sophie? Oh yes, I'd like to stroke them now. I'd like to squeeze them and lick them. I'd like to

39

run my tongue in a path down from your nipples. Are your nipples hard, Sophie?'

'Very hard.' She pinched one experimentally, and arched her back as a sensation, half-pleasure, half-pain, shot down her body.

'Down from your nipples,' Toby's voice continued, heavy with lust, 'to where, Sophie? Where would you like me to go next with my tongue?'

'You know.' Sophie's voice was barely audible.

'Where, Sophie, tell me?'

'My clitoris. I'd like your tongue on my clitoris.' Her fingers moved down her body, anxious to feel the pleasure, and not just speak it.

'Mmm. Yes, I'd like that too. That lovely taste – your taste, Sophie. Like honey, sticky and sweet. Then what, Sophie? Are you touching yourself? Touch yourself for me until I can do it myself. Nice and firm.'

Her breath was coming in short, panting gasps by now, and her only answer was a groan as she buried her fingers deep inside herself, imagining it was Toby's smooth prick riding high up into her. Toby's breath was also more laboured.

'Do you know what I'm doing, Sophie? I'm imagining I'm sliding deep inside you. I'm feeling myself go all the way inside you, every inch of me filling you up. Are you coming, Sophie?'

Sophie was coming but she wanted more. The sensation was good, but it wasn't enough. Desperate to satisfy the urgent yearning at her very core, she was reaching blindly towards the bedside cabinet. Her fingers, slippery from herself, closed around a plastic bottle. It was a deodorant bottle with a tantalisingly rounded top. Without thinking, without stopping to question her desire, Sophie grasped the plastic bottle and ran it over her clitoris, shuddering at the smooth insistence of it.

Oblivious to Toby's voice in the phone by her ear, she inserted the rounded end into her vagina, eyes opening

40

wide at the sudden coldness and width. By levering the end of the bottle, she could move the pressure of the rounded top; forwards, backwards – that was exciting – and upwards. Never once relenting, she let the bottle work for her, pushing it in as far as she dare, and relishing its unyielding motion.

On the end of the phone, Toby was gasping to his climax, only his final exclamation making Sophie sit up, guiltily, having forgotten the phone. As she rolled herself over, the bottle wedged itself perfectly against her clitoris, and she came, too, gushing waves of heat centered around her throbbing sex.

'Sophie? Sophie, are you all right?'

Slowly she reached out a hand and placed the receiver back on her shoulder. 'I'm all right. Yes, I'm fine. What about you?'

'Great! Telephone sex, eh?' He sounded exhausted. 'Bit naughty.'

Sophie was glad he didn't know just how naughty, and wondered if he would be shocked if he knew. Whatever was happening to her these days?

'Think it'll catch on?' she asked him, and her voice sounded languid and sexy, even to herself. Should she tell Toby what she had just done? But she decided not to; he might think it odd. Weird, even.

She continued to chat to Toby for a while but her mind was on other things. She had always been such a good girl, she thought; her act with the bottle seemed rather out of character, even perverse. But the very perversity had been part of the pleasure, she couldn't deny that.

They parted affectionately, Sophie arranging to drive up and visit Toby that weekend and maybe to take Rosie, too. She put down the phone feeling restless, strangely jumpy, and went to have a quick shower. Her feeling of agitation did not abate all evening and she paced her room like a caged lion. She switched the television on, couldn't get interested in any of the channels, and switched it off again, irritably. Her concentration that night didn't stretch to reading, and after trying unsuccessfully to ring home, she gave up and pulled on her outdoor clothes. The house was quiet, although she could see a light coming from the window of James McKinnerney's study. She didn't want to disturb James and, she reasoned, as she was off-duty where the horses were concerned, she deserved a bit of freedom.

She crossed the stable yard swiftly, enjoying the chilly autumn night. The drive was well lit, curving away towards the road, but the gardens were less so; only the occasional outdoor lamp glowed, surrounded by disorientated, fluttering moths.

She breathed in the smell of damp earth mingled with the faint smokiness that seemed to hang in the air. Sophie wrapped her coat tightly round her and strode towards the shed, site of her adventurous tryst earlier in the day. As she had expected the door was padlocked, so she made her way back to the wooden bench where she had been fortuitously found by Callum.

She sat quietly, surrounded by night noises, listening to an owl in the woods behind the house, and wondering what was happening to her.

I know I wanted something different to happen in my life, Sophie thought to herself, but this isn't quite what I expected.

She thought about Callum, about Alex Carver, and about Toby's phone call. If this was what discovering your sexuality was about, it was fine by Sophie. Toby's phone call had been fun, naughty, daring – but whatever had made her want to use that bottle? She felt she had acted quite out of character. Sophie had always been ready and willing with Toby, but she had never felt the need for any kind of sex toys, or to do anything particularly out of the ordinary. Or perhaps that was 'ordinary'. She had no way of knowing.

She remembered Callum's initial shyness, and how it had excited her, how she had wanted to impose her will on him, bully him a little, and she thought of her mild feeling of disappointment when he had taken back control of the situation.

That's it, she told herself, one night away from home and you've turned into a pervert. She sat a little while longer, turning over recent events in her brain, then, her mind alive with the possibilities afforded by her new-found sexual freedom, she meandered slowly back across the lawns, looking forward to being back in the warmth.

She checked on the horses, let herself into the cottage, made herself a cup of tea, then went to bed. Her head was still buzzing with the idea of herself as a temptress; a seductress who took what she wanted without fear. Sophie lay awake a long time, and when sleep did finally claim her, her dreams were sensual, lurid and fairly exhausting.

She awoke sometime in the early hours, befuddled and agitated. Something had surely woken her; her sleep had been too deep to have been disturbed by anything insubstantial.

Loath to disturb her sleep still further by turning on her bedside lamp, Sophie lay motionless, listening, her senses tuned to anything out of the ordinary. Was it one of the horses, stamping or snorting? But no, she could barely hear them even when they whinnied; the stable buildings were old with good, thick walls. In the yard, maybe? But Sophie felt that the noise had been closer than that.

There was just enough light for Sophie to make out the shapes of the furniture in her room: the wardrobe, dressing table, and the small couch where she had thrown her robe. The door that led into her own small bathroom was recessed, set back enough so that it was in complete darkness, the bathroom beyond a mystery. Sophie thought carefully. Could she just have had a bad dream? But much as she wanted to accept this explanation, she was still sure that something external had awoken her.

And then, with a horrible jolt, Sophie remembered what her last action had been before she got into bed. She had hung tomorrow's – today's? – clothes on a hook on the door adjoining her bathroom and bedroom; then she had shut the door. Her heart somersaulted wildly, and the sound of its beating seemed to double, as Sophie, eyes wide, gazed at the door, which now stood open.

Reaching for her bedside lamp, eyes never leaving the door, Sophie felt herself beginning to shake. It couldn't be her imagination, she had definitely shut that door, she knew. Then came her second shock – her bedside lamp was missing. Immediate relief flooded through her. Burglars, she thought foolishly, before she realised that with the house full of valuable paintings, silver and antiques, burglars were hardly likely to bother with bedside lamps in the out-buildings!

While she sat frozen in bed, every atom of her was tuned to catch the slightest smell, sound or sight of anything untoward. She wondered if she should just run for the hall door. But, she told herself, going towards that door means going towards the bathroom door. In any case her legs felt as though they were encased in plaster, so heavy had fear rendered them.

She had almost convinced herself that she had imagined the noise, and that she had been mistaken in her belief that she had left the bathroom door open, when a minute sound came from the bathroom, sending her brain into overdrive. It could have been the sound of a shoe on a tile, the brushing of a hand against clothing, or someone shifting from one foot to the other. Sophie could not tell but, before she could stop herself, she had cried out.

'Who's there? Is that you, Callum? Catherine? Who is it?' And in the split second after she spoke out loud she was sure it was one of the house cats, and was relieved.

But the shadow that appeared in the doorway was no animal shadow; it was tall, purposeful and anonymous. The figure hesitated just long enough for Sophie to draw breath then it was across the room, a gloved hand was over her mouth and a thick, soft gag cut short her intended scream.

Despite her racing heart and shaking limbs, Sophie tried hard to think straight. If this turned out to be another of Alex Carver's little routines, he was in for a shock this time. No way, she thought to herself, is that slimy little creep getting any more thrills at my expense. Even just thinking like this made Sophie blaze with fury, and she was aware of holding herself in readiness like a coiled spring waiting for the right moment to release its energy.

The quilt, still over Sophie, held her down. But you wait, she found herself thinking. The minute you get off me, you just wait . . .

The man (the size and strength of the figure gave this much away) leant over her to carefully check that the gag was not covering her nose, and she felt a little of the tension ebb from her muscles. His slow, unhurried movements were completely unlike the frantic gestures she associated with Alex; perhaps her first guess had been right, the man was a burglar. Trying to think straight, she made herself look for any feature, any give-away clues, that might later identify this man to the police. It made little difference: from the shape of his head, blunt and round, she was sure he was wearing some sort of mask and she had to fight down the rising hysteria – her life could depend on how she reacted now and she knew she mustn't blow it.

Once she was gagged the intruder seemed to hesitate, then, reaching into what seemed to be a lightweight

45

jacket, he produced a handful of scarves and pushed Sophie's head back onto her pillow.

Okay, she thought, calmer than she had a right to be, so let him tie me up. The sooner he gets on with looting the place, the sooner he will be gone.

She allowed the dark figure to tie the soft scarf around her wrist, let him test it for tightness, then gasped in surprise as he eased her wrist backwards, securing it skillfully to the post of her wooden bed. Suddenly having an insight into what was going on, Sophie tensed and began to fight against having her other hand similarly tied, but to no avail. A burglar would not have wasted time tying both her hands separately, she realised. No, this intruder had something else on his mind, and a burst of anger made her flail a fist, good and hard, at the man's face. It was too late. The second scarf was already wound round the bedpost and Sophie's spirited effort just succeeded in tightening the knot at her wrist.

The darkly-clad figure, pulling backwards to avoid Sophie's punch, was off the bed now, and stood looking down at her before he strode to the window and pulled back the curtains. A pale shaft of moonlight fell through the window and, startled, Sophie blinked and tried to pull herself into a sitting position.

The figure, seeming now to be keeping to the shadowy edges of the room, moved in order to stand beside her. Sophie, heart beating wildly again as the man leant towards her, was convinced that her earlier fears were about to be justified when the gloved hand reached out and tentatively stroked her hair. Sophie was confused. The mischief she had assumed was in the mind of this mysterious intruder was not consistent with the gentleness of his actions.

His movements were hesitant enough to make Sophie wonder what the purpose of tying her hands could be; although her assailant was obviously nervous, he gave no signs of being aggressive. Sophie, her imagination working overtime, reflected on the possibility that the man might not be the stranger she had originally supposed. But who would do this? She was as certain as she could be that Alex Carver did not have the imagination nor the self-control to carry this through. But who else did that leave?

Sophie racked her brain. Callum? Surely not. She knew he didn't live in the grounds of Prospect House, so he would have had to return, surreptitiously, to do the deed. But why? Even discounting the fact that there was no real reason for him to do it, Sophie could not imagine Callum acting this way. He had an open and honest way about him; he did not seem the sort of man to lurk in shadows.

But then, thought Sophie, what do I really know about him? He could be a mass murderer for all I know! She just had time to reflect that even the worst despots probably had someone, somewhere, who thought they were quite harmless, when the figure stepped forward, took hold of one edge of the quilt, and pulled.

Sophie gasped as her only covering was instantly whipped away, exposing to the moonlight her ivory-white breasts, sculpted waist and long, tapering legs. The stranger seemed to stand, transfixed with awe, and even Sophie, agitated as she was, had to admit it was an alluring sight. The shifting light threw her body into relief, emphasising the curves even more. Her treacherous nipples stood out against the soft pillows of her breasts, a mute confession of the mounting excitement she was beginning to feel, despite her best intentions.

The figure seemed to stand, captivated, for several seconds. Sophie was beyond feeling threatened by the situation; she was wondering now what those smooth, warm, leather gloves would feel like running over her skin.

Before she could fantasise further, the figure at last

47

dropped the corner of the quilt, and half-turned his back on Sophie. With a jolt of anticipation she realised that he was unzipping his trousers, and as he turned back to her she saw that he had managed to free a massive erect penis from his straining crotch. Sophie's heart leapt with lust, her earlier worries forgotten, but the stranger stayed where he was, his manhood pushing insistently towards her. She was beginning to feel hot with desire now. It was a beautiful penis, and Sophie wanted very much to throw herself on to it, to feel it moving inside her. It seemed to stand out very pale in the moonlight, as if created especially for her, and she could feel the thick sweetness spreading between her thighs.

With a barely audible sigh the man took hold of himself and planted his feet just a little farther apart. Then, with a few deft strokes, he began to thrust his hardness in and out of his closed fist, making Sophie moan crossly through the gag that she wasn't going to be the recipient of that magnificent prick. Her mind raced; was it Callum's penis? It was difficult to tell. She wished she hadn't got quite so carried away in the shed earlier. What about Alex's? But it had been dark in that bathroom; and anyway when she had eventually caught a glimpse of it, it had been somewhat deflated!

For Heaven's sake, Sophie chided herself, here she was playing Spot The Penis, and all the time that wonderful erection was going to waste! She wanted to feel it against her very badly, it seemed so unfair . . .

She spread her legs wide, raising her hips, inviting the stranger in, but he just gasped and moved to the foot of the bed, all the better to view her. He was working hard now. Sophie could only imagine what she must look like from his angle, but his breath was hard and rasping, making her even more furious at what she saw as her exclusion.

When he came, with a soft groan, the semen drops scattering like glimmering opals onto the bed, Sophie couldn't help feeling desperately disappointed. She lay, angry and let down, her clitoris a hot hard bud, aching for fulfillment. The mysterious visitor tucked himself back into the dark trousers, then came to stand beside the bed. Sophie turned away, frustrated, trying to convey her disgust at his selfishness; when a movement beside her told her that he was sitting down beside her. Suddenly, without warning, he was parting her thighs, and stroking her hard with a still-gloved hand. The result was electric. Sophie's body bucked in unexpected pleasure, while the stranger held her firmly and put first one, then two, and finally, very carefully, three gloved fingers into her eagerly pulsating vagina. He moved them firmly, expertly, and Sophie forgot any misgivings she may have had, opening her legs wide to give herself the full benefit of him.

His very presence, looming darkly over her, was exciting in itself; the element of mystery, embodied by a masked lover, and all the danger that implied, was driving Sophie ecstatically towards her climax. With one last, luxurious spasm, she came, eyes closed, body gradually losing its rigidity, and felt from somewhere far away that one of her hands had been gently released.

When she opened her eyes she was alone in the room, a single smooth-stemmed rose lying, soft and perfect, beside her; but no sign of the dark, mysterious stranger.

Chapter Three

'You just don't want me to work! You don't want me to have a life of my own! I've always done every-thing – everything – you wanted! Now it's my turn to do what I want!'

'Catherine, please! The children will hear.'

'Don't give me, "Catherine, the children will hear!" They are my children, too. I gave birth to them – with very little help from you, I might add.'

'Well, I did . . .'

'I haven't finished yet! I gave birth to the kids; I've done everything for them. I've done kid-things until my brain turned mushy! Now I've had enough.'

'All I asked was . . .'

The row raged on. Sophie, Jean and an unperturbed Gina huddled behind the kitchen door, out of sight but well within hearing. Sophie's sense of the unreal was deepening by the day – was anything normal in this place?

'I only asked who was bringing Gina home.'

'Well I can't do it. You do it. Or sort something else out. I've got a job to go to, remember?'

'I wanted to know if you had made any other arrangements, that's all; so that I didn't go down there and find . . .'

'You assume I will because I always have before; not any more. I've had years of caring for kids – '

'You've always had nannies!'

'I hope you're not implying that having nannies around has made running this house any easier, because it hasn't. Half the time they are more trouble than the kids. And anyway, I'm a hands-on mother – always have been.'

Here Gina snorted sarcastically, and Jean rolled her eyes at Sophie. Sophie's main worry was that they were in danger of getting caught eavesdropping; but, as Jean pointed out, they would have to be in the stables not to hear this furore.

'This could go on forever,' Jean sighed.

'Meanwhile, I'm going to be late for school,' hissed Gina, 'again.'

'Okay, hold on. I have a plan. Stay here.' Sophie dashed through the kitchen, out of the back door and round the side of the house. Trying to compose herself – this had to look natural – she slipped through the utility room and ran straight into Catherine's brother, Dominic, who was obviously doing a spot of eavesdropping of his own.

'Sophie!' At least he had the good grace to look embarrassed, but only momentarily.

'I was just coming to see Mr McKinnerney,' she stammered, 'I wanted to have a quick word.'

'Oh really?' Dominic was instantly his aloof self again. 'There are quite a few words flying about at the moment. Perhaps I can help?'

'No, thank you,' Sophie said firmly.

She and Dominic hovered hesitantly by the hall door, neither of them wishing to interrupt the heated debate. Dominic's eyes – as strikingly hazel as Catherine's – took blatant and appreciative stock of Sophie.

'Nice jodhpurs,' he murmured, moving towards her.

Sophie dived through the door into the entrance hall, to arrive looking as flustered as if she had run the whole way. The phrase, 'out of the frying pan and into the fire' seemed ridiculously appropriate as both James and Catherine turned to stare at her.

'Good morning, Sophie,' James said, as polite as ever.

'Welcome to the Happy House!' snarled Catherine to Sophie; then – making the most of the intrusion – 'I'm off. You sort out picking Gina up. I'll drop her off. See? I've done my bit. Gina!'

James watched her go, then turned back to Sophie.

'I could arrange for Rosie to pick Gina up and bring her home,' Sophie gabbled, anxious to be away from the front line in case Catherine returned. 'I wanted to see her, anyway. Rosie, that is.'

'Yes. Good idea, thank you, Sophie.'

Catherine came stomping back dragging a surly Gina. 'Move yourself, Gina, or we'll both be late.'

'Sophie suggested asking Rosie to pick Gina up from school, Catherine.'

'How lovely!' spat Catherine. 'Aren't you a little treasure, Sophie?' Then they were out of the door and gone, leaving an uncomfortable silence.

'My deepest apologies, Sophie,' James sighed. 'There are no excuses for dragging you into this. I shall have a word with my wife tonight.' James set off in the direction of his study; his walk was slow and measured like that of an old man. Sophie felt sorry for him.

'So?' Dominic's sudden closeness startled her and she turned quickly, determined not to be thrown off guard by him again.

'So what?' she snapped.

'So, what did you want to talk to James about?'

Sophie had come up to the house to see whether or not there had been an intruder, although she had no intention of admitting that. What had her excuse been for visiting the house, though? She couldn't remember.

'I don't . . . I'm not . . . I wanted . . .'

'Come on, you can tell me.'

'I can't remember. Oh yes, I know. I wanted to find out if they needed me at the weekend.'

'Is that all?' He looked disappointed.

'Well, I need to know. I might go away on Saturday.'

'Going somewhere nice?'

Sophie glared at him. What with Dominic's arrogance and Catherine's rudeness, Sophie couldn't help feeling that brother and sister weren't over-blessed with charm.

'I think that's my business.'

'Okay, keep your jodhpurs on! Just asking. I'll have a word with James, shall I? Unless you want to do it yourself.'

Sophie, who just wanted to be away from the Madhouse – as she was beginning to think of it – shook her head. 'You do it. Thanks.'

'Right then. And I'll pop down to the stables later to let you know the outcome.' He sidled up to her, sliding his hand round her hip to fondle her buttocks.

'Don't bother!' She slapped his hand away and gave him a dirty look. 'Leave a message with Jean; it'll get to me.'

She marched into the kitchen and slammed the door, leaning against it heavily. Jean, still giving the two little ones their breakfast, flashed her a sympathetic look.

'Are they really all mad here, Jean, or is it just me?'

Jean gestured towards Ellie, who seized this pronouncement gleefully.

'All mad here!' she crowed happily. 'Mad! Mad! Mad!'

'Eat that toast now, Ellie.' Jean told the child sternly. 'Look at Peter – see how good he's being.'

The two women turned their backs on the curious child while Sophie related in a whisper what had just happened with Dominic.

'What I really came to find out,' Sophie said, keeping her voice low and choosing her words carefully, 'was whether you had had an intruder up here last night.'

Jean looked alarmed. 'Oh no, dear. Not as far as I know; and I'm sure someone would tell me. Have you had a problem with one at the cottage?'

'Well, more of a prowler, really.' Sophie couldn't see herself telling Jean about her strange experience. Not in a million years.

'Foxes!' Jean said in relief. 'We get a lot of foxes coming up to the house at night; especially once the weather turns colder.'

'Foxes, eh? Well thanks, Jean. That's put my mind at ease.' Sophie smiled, reassuringly. 'Anyway, I'll pop up later to find out what the answer is from James about the weekend. I think I'll wait for Dominic to go, though.'

'Oh, he's an odd kettle of fish, he is,' Jean confided. 'I'd keep out of his way, if I were you.'

'Kettle of fish?' Ellie hooted. 'Fish in a kettle?'

Sophie laughed with Jean, and then set off back to the stables, relieved to be out of the house.

Well, she thought, that wasn't exactly a success. No signs of anything untoward at the Madhouse – furious rows were the norm, it seemed – and Jean fobbing off her prowler as 'foxes'. Something odd was going on and it wasn't confined to Prospect House. Perhaps there had been burglars but, in all the excitement of this morning, nobody had realised yet.

Sophie decided to keep her story to herself, for now. Who could she tell, anyway? Jean would be shocked, Catherine unsympathetic, and Callum would think she was as mad as the rest of them. Sophie thought hard. Rosie! She could talk to Rosie.

Suddenly she felt desperately in need of the weekend. To get away for the night. To return to the world outside Prospect House. To talk to someone. Rosie would know what to do; she would be sympathetic.

Sophie worked her way through the morning, her thoughts swimming wildly in all directions. By the time she phoned Rosie at lunchtime to arrange Gina's transport home, she had decided that she would not tell her friend the story of the intruder. At the very least Rosie would want to know why Sophie hadn't reported it; and Sophie had no easy answers to this herself. At worst, Rosie would think she was making it up; Sophie couldn't bear to be thought a liar.

Sophie managed to keep her composure well on the phone, until they had planned Gina's lift and were finalising details for the weekend.

'It will be great, Sophie. Thanks for asking me. Are you sure you won't just want time alone with Toby?'

'No!' Sophie said, too quickly. 'We have some talking to do, it's true; but what I really need is moral support.'

'No problem. I'm looking forward to it. Are you worried about seeing him?'

'I suppose a little. Why?'

'You just don't sound yourself, that's all. Is anything else wrong?'

'Well, yes, there is. But I can't talk about it now. I wasn't going to say anything, but . . .'

'Look, don't worry. We'll have a good talk on the way to Toby's. I'll take my car; we can share the driving. I'm sure it's nothing that can't be sorted out.'

'Thanks Rosie, I'm sure you're right. See you later.'

She was silly not to have wanted to tell Rosie, she decided; it would be good to talk it through with someone. Rosie would be able to shed some light on it. She wouldn't blame Sophie, who had been powerless to resist, after all. Sophie gave a little shudder of excitement as she thought about it.

Stop it, she told herself, angry at her body's refusal to see it as a problem. Still thinking hard about how to tell Rosie the truth without presenting herself as too willing an accomplice, she set off back to the horses.

Throwing herself into her work didn't help Sophie to think any more clearly about the previous night; she was preoccupied and unorganised. In her agitation she nearly fed Buzz twice, to his great delight, but caught herself just in time. When Jean tracked her down to pass on the message that she was free to go on Saturday, Sophie was relieved and exhausted in equal measure.

'You look wrecked,' Rosie told her, bluntly, when she dropped Gina off from school. 'For Heaven's sake, get an early night and stop worrying – it can't be that bad, whatever it is. We'll talk in a couple of days.'

Sophie did her usual round of checking stable doors and filling haynets, her mind whirling incessantly over the same thoughts. She noticed how dusk was falling noticeably earlier each evening now. Making her way wearily back to the cottage, she felt a fleeting sadness for the spent summer.

Lost in melancholic thoughts, the shock was even greater for her when a dark figure stepped from the shadows at the side of the house. Sophie let out a terrified scream.

'It's me – Callum!'

'For crying out loud, Callum! What are you trying to do to me? For a big man you really can creep around.'

'I'm sorry. I wanted to see you.'

'Let's make it daylight next time, shall we?' Now he was closer and she had calmed down, it was obvious it could only be Callum. It was only half-light now, but even in the dark she would recognise the curve of his muscular shoulders and his earthy, musky smell.

Or would I, she wondered, trying hard not to compare the masked figure with Callum. She mustn't think like that; it was verging on paranoia.

There was a brief embarrassed silence, as they both recalled their last meeting, and Sophie was glad he couldn't see the blush spreading across her cheeks.

'I just wanted – '

'I thought – '

They both spoke at once, then laughed.

'You first.'

'I just hoped you hadn't got in trouble.'

'In trouble?' She wasn't sure what he meant.

'For yesterday. In the shed.'

'Oh. No, no! Mrs McKinnerney didn't know I was there. She didn't say anything, anyway.'

'Oh right. Good.'

Trawling her addled mind for something to say, Sophie's thoughts turned once again to the previous night's prowler. 'Have there been any break-ins, Callum? At the house? Or prowlers; anything like that?'

'Break-ins? I don't think so. No one mentioned any. I would have had windows to mend this morning, if there had been. Why do you ask?'

'Oh, no reason. Just wondered.'

'I told them to get a proper lock put on that door of yours. Have you been bothered?'

'No, no. Probably just foxes.'

'Foxes don't usually break in.' They both laughed, then Callum said suddenly, 'I don't want you to think that I do that all the time.'

Sophie's mind was alert. What did he mean? Do what all the time? Surely he wasn't the prowler? Not Callum! He couldn't be, could he?

'Do what all the time, Callum?'

'You know . . .'

She was tense and scared, but she kept her voice calm. 'I'm not sure what you mean.'

'Yesterday.'

'That was you?' She wanted to scream and shout, to plead with him to tell her a lie rather than the awful truth.

'Course it was me.' He sounded proud; she wanted to hit him.

57

'Are you sure?' She was buying time, readying herself to get through the door and slam it in his face.

'Of course I'm sure! I think I'd remember, don't you? Do you feel OK, Sophie?'

'Fine, yes! You. Yesterday. Of course.' Her hand tightened on the handle. She had one chance to escape; she mustn't blow it.

'In the shed,' he said, happily.

'In the shed?' She stood, rooted to the spot. 'What do you mean, "in the shed"?'

'Don't you remember? Me and you? In the shed, yesterday?'

Light was beginning to dawn. Relief flooded through her; they had been talking about two different things! 'Oh! Yes! I'm sorry, Callum. It's been an horrendous day. The shed. What about it?'

'I don't want you to think I do that all the time.' He sounded unsure of himself. 'Look, are you really all right, Sophie? Would you like me to come inside and make you a cup of tea?'

'No, it's OK, thanks. I'm sorry Callum. I'm just so tired. Another time, maybe. Thanks.'

'I'll go, then. Take care, Sophie.'

'Goodnight. Oh, and Callum,' she called after his receding figure, 'I don't do it all the time either. In sheds. With strange men.'

'What a shame,' he called, his voice drifting back to her.

'Sophie!' The car swerved dangerously, making Sophie think that she had made a bad error of judgment in deciding to tell Rosie the truth. The car in the next lane sounded its horn and Rosie – adept at driving, looking for 'talent', and gesturing simultaneously – pulled a face at the driver.

'Be careful, Rosie! I should never have told you while you were driving.'

'Don't you worry about me; I can drive, read a map and sort out kids fighting on the back seat. But you! Well! What a dark horse you are!'

'It wasn't something I planned to add spice to your life, Rosie.'

'Why didn't you tell me earlier? Why didn't you tell anyone earlier?'

'I don't know, really. I didn't know what to say, or who to tell.'

'Me, for a start. James. Catherine. The police.'

'No, I couldn't. James had already helped me out of one tricky situation: I wouldn't have wanted to face him with another. It would just seem like I went looking for trouble. Catherine hates me; she would have assumed that I had made it up. And by the time I thought about the police, it seemed too late.'

'It's not too late,' Rosie said carefully, 'if that's what you want.'

'Well, no,' Sophie's cheeks were burning, 'it isn't really. I couldn't stand all the questions. And anyway ...' She had a sudden vision of herself raising her hips off the bed to lure the mystery man to her. How could she tell the police, or anyone else, knowing the part she had played?

'Anyway, what?'

'Anyway, it wasn't like that.'

'Wasn't like what?'

'Well he didn't hurt me or anything like that.'

Rosie's eyes were searching her face, dancing mischievously. 'Oh well, that's all right, then. What a relief! I thought for a minute he had done something you didn't want him to do.'

In for a penny, thought Sophie. 'No,' she said, quietly, 'he didn't do anything I didn't want him to do.'

The car swerved again, to more furious honking from the car behind.

'Sophie!'

'Stop saying "Sophie!" like that. I'm confused enough as it is, without you piling on the guilt.'

They drove in silence for a while. Rosie glanced surreptitiously at Sophie, whose head hung forward, blonde hair hiding her face.

'Did you enjoy it?' she asked eventually. She couldn't hear Sophie's murmured reply, so she leant over and brushed the curtain of hair back. 'Well?'

'Yes!' Sophie's eyes were shining, her face flushed. 'It was the most exciting thing that ever happened, Rosie! Do you think I'm terrible, saying that? Am I turning into a pervert? What would you have done? Help me, Rosie, I don't know what's happening to me.'

Rosie hooted with delighted laughter, and deliberately swerved the car several times.

'Stop it, Rosie! It's not funny! You're going to get us killed.'

'So, come on,' Rosie prompted, 'details!'

Sophie told the whole story, not worrying now that her friend should know of her complicity in the affair, just relieved to have someone to talk to.

'And that's it,' she finished. 'I suppose in itself it's not a problem; I'm not worried or frightened or anything. It wasn't like that. I wasn't meant to feel frightened, if you see what I mean. I just don't know what to think. I mean, was it really just a case of me being in the wrong place at the wrong time?'

'Or the right place at the right time,' Rosie leered. 'Of course it was. Why, what's the alternative?'

'Someone who knew me. Someone who had a key.'

'Why do you think that?'

'There was no sign of a break-in. I'm no expert, but I would have expected there to be broken glass, or something. Whoever got into my rooms must have had a key. I definitely dropped the catch.' But, she thought suddenly, had the door been locked? After all, she had gone

60

out for a walk once she had spoken to Toby. Maybe she was wrong.

'Well?'

'Maybe I didn't drop the catch. I've just remembered, I went out again afterwards.'

'There you are, then. Stop worrying; the main thing is that you're OK now. It won't happen again – unless you leave your door unlocked!'

'Rosie! You're terrible!'

'Not terrible – just frustrated! I hope there's plenty of talent at this party tonight. That story of yours has got me quite hot under the collar!'

'Stop here. I'll do some driving.'

'Only if you promise to tell me the whole story again from beginning to end.'

They drove and chatted, laughing at Rosie's various exploits. Sophie felt she had known Rosie for years, and was glad she had someone like her to turn to. The conversation took Sophie's mind off the dread she was feeling at what she must tell Toby. As they pulled up outside the pub where they were to meet him and his friends, the rush of anxiety overtook her again.

'You go in and get some drinks,' she told Rosie, 'I need to walk around the block to clear my head.' She could feel the beginnings of a headache and was determined not to let it spoil her night.

When she entered the dim, smoky atmosphere, Rosie was already in full swing, chatting animatedly to a man at the bar.

'Here she is!' Rosie cried. 'Sophie, come and meet my new friend, Harold. The party is at his house.'

Sophie took the empty stool beside Rosie and leant over to shake Harold's hand. He was a large, jovial-looking man with an easy smile and knowing blue eyes. He raised Sophie's hand to his lips and kissed it, making her laugh self-consciously.

'Pleased to meet you, Sophie.' His deep American drawl made Rosie beam with pleasure at her friend.

'Isn't he lovely? I've only been here ten minutes and I've found my very own lecher!'

'I think you mean lecturer. I'm a law lecturer.' He smiled at Sophie.

'I know exactly what I mean!' Rosie hooted.

Sophie laughed; Rosie was determined to have a good time. And why ever not, Sophie thought. She peered at the other people in the pub; mostly students, she surmised, but no sign of Toby yet.

'Just off to the – what would you Americans call it? – the john!' Rosie, putting away drinks as if there was no tomorrow, staggered to her feet.

Sophie's headache was back with a vengeance. As her friend tripped off to the toilets, she became aware that Harold's attention was fixed firmly on her.

'Who are you looking for, pretty lady? Who is the lucky man?'

Sophie smiled at him. 'My boyfriend, Toby.'

'I think I know Toby.' He nodded, thoughtfully. 'You don't look like it's a meeting that you're too excited about, if you don't mind me saying so.'

'No, I'm not.'

Harold had a sympathetic face, the kind of face that invited confidences. Sophie found herself telling him all about Toby and their imminent break-up. Harold nodded lazily and sipped his drink.

'And now,' Sophie heard herself saying in the tones of a petulant child, 'and now I have a headache.'

'Oh, well, hey! Don't you worry! It seems to me like you're doing the right thing by this Toby guy. And as for that headache, I can cure it like that!' He snapped his fingers, and smiled. 'I do good massage – guaranteed to cure headaches.'

Sophie felt her insides go quite liquid at the thought

of abandoning herself into Harold's easy, sensuous hands, but she shook her head.

'No, I've got to get things straight with Toby before I do anything else. Business first, pleasure later.'

Rosie returned, explaining that there was another room around the opposite side of the bar.

'Is Toby there?' Sophie asked.

'How do I know, dimwit? I've never met him, remember? You're on your own.' So saying, Rosie eased herself on to the stool next to Harold, letting one hand drop onto his tightly-jeaned leg.

Bracing herself, Sophie set off on the pretence of finding the toilets. In actuality she scanned the groups and couples for Toby. It didn't take long. Although the corner he occupied wasn't brightly lit, he and his companion were drawing many eyes. Sophie paused, then made her way to the bar and ordered herself a drink. She had no worries that Toby would spot her because he was too engrossed in the conversation with his friend.

Sophie watched them, fascinated. Why were so many people's eyes drawn to the couple? They were both attractive, but no more so than many of the other young couples laughing and chatting around her.

It came to Sophie in a rush of recognition: they were so obviously in love! Their happiness was palpable; he was leaning towards her, his face glowing as he explained something. She in turn, was enjoying his company so wholeheartedly that her face had an unusual radiance.

Sophie could remember the first time she and Toby met but she was willing to bet that they had never looked like that together. She felt a fleeting jealousy, a regret that Toby had never looked at her that way, but it was only momentary. If she were honest with herself, she would have been alarmed to have seen that intensity of emotion from Toby; her sadness was more because nobody had ever looked at her that way. After the brief, dizzying surprise, Sophie could only feel relief, not to mention happiness for Toby. Not wanting to spoil their pleasure, she finished her drink and went to find Rosie.

'Come on. Let's get off to the party now.'

'I thought you wanted to see if you could find Toby first.'

'No, I've changed my mind. Come on, I'll explain on the way.'

They braved the chilly night, walking briskly in the direction of the house where the party was to be held. Sophie explained about Toby as Harold led the way. Part way there, Sophie collapsed on to a low wall, clutching her head.

'I'm sorry, just give me a minute. My head is killing me. I don't know if it was the smoke in the pub, worrying about Toby, or Rosie's driving.'

'Charming!' Rosie snorted. 'It's probably a combination of things. Tension.'

'Probably,' Sophie agreed. 'You go on, I'll catch you up in a minute.'

But they wouldn't hear of it and ended up half-supporting, half-carrying her to Harold's large shared house. The warmth and noise assailed them at the door and Sophie groaned. The bright lights made her head whirl and pound; she only vaguely noticed concerned faces as they were turned towards her and heard Harold's voice, seemingly muffled, as she was borne up one flight of stairs after another.

Her last remembrance was of more than one pair of hands undressing her in a darkened room. Then the coolness and quiet washed over her grateful body, and Sophie let herself drift into hazy half-sleep.

When she woke up, Rosie was beside her. The room was still dark, although candles cast soft light from a marble mantelpiece. There was a clear, fresh aroma in the room, and as Sophie tried to sit up she realised her headache had gone.

'She's awake!' Rosie called over her shoulder. Sophie just had time to wonder why her friend was wearing only a man's robe, before Harold appeared, shirtless, from another part of the room.

'Hi there! Better now?'

Sophie tried to nod, but her neck and shoulders were as stiff as boards. She winced and placed her hands behind her head, becoming aware for the first time that she was completely naked. She had neither the energy nor the inclination to cover herself; it didn't seem important.

'Stiff?' Harold helped her with a cup of water. 'Come here.'

She shut her eyes and felt his large, unhurried hands close gently on her shoulders. It hurt at first but gradually his fingers smoothed away the tension and she felt her muscles begin to move freely again.

'Thanks.' She still felt a little fragile, self-conscious too, but Rosie's presence was comforting. 'That feels great.'

'How's the headache?' Rosie held Sophie's long hair off her neck, while Harold moved round to run capable hands down her spine.

'Gone,' Sophie sighed. 'It was bad, though; I've never had one like that before. But you two are missing the party because of me. Why don't you go down? I'll join you when I feel better.'

'Plenty of time for partying,' Harold replied with a smile, 'and anyway we couldn't enjoy ourselves if we thought you were feeling bad now, could we?'

Sophie saw the look that passed between them and realised they had probably done quite a lot of enjoying themselves without her. For the second time that evening she felt a twinge of jealousy. Lucky Rosie!

'He's great, Rosie,' she hissed as Harold went to find massage oil.

'You don't know how great,' Rosie said, smirking, 'but

I'm not a selfish person; I'm willing to share. How about it?'

'Well ... I don't know. I've never ...' The thought of herself, Rosie, and Harold together made Sophie shiver with excitement. 'Are you sure about this?'

Rosie nodded and Harold, returning with the scented oil, smiled to see the two women giggling together on his bed.

'There's a sight to warm an old man's heart,' he drawled, slipping out of his jeans and uncorking the bottle.

'You're not old,' Rosie murmured, kissing him. 'I'll bet you have the stamina of a man half your age.'

Harold's laugh rumbled round the room and he began to smooth the sweet oil over Sophie's shoulders. Sitting behind her, he worked his hands expertly down her back, while Rosie watched from the bedside chair.

Despite her earlier illness, Sophie couldn't help feeling how good Harold's hands felt on her body. He was a man who loved women: their shape, their scent, the very feel of them. He was in no hurry and Sophie felt warm, relaxed and, above all, desired; her body seemed to blossom in the light of his obvious enjoyment. What a turn-on it was, she thought, excitedly, to be in the capable hands of a man with so much experience and appreciation.

Sophie's body was tingling with his languid attentions; she was aware of Rosie, unable to contain herself any longer, undressing and joining them on the bed. Harold's hands slid under Sophie's arms and cupped her breasts. Her nipples, already hard, stood to attention at his firm grasp, and Sophie felt a familiar hot loosening inside.

Pulling her to him, so that she leant her back against his broad chest, Harold slid his hand down her belly and into her pubic hair. Sophie let him take the weight of her and abandoned herself to the sensation. The scented oils and his own musky smell combined to make Sophie feel irresponsible and eager; she pulled herself out of his grasp and watched as Rosie claimed him. His strong arms flexed as he lay back, propped on pillows, and lifted Rosie on to his waiting penis.

She gasped, and Sophie felt a thrill of delight at her friend's pleasure. She was unaware that her own fingers had crept down to tease her clitoris, unconsciously wanting to be part of their energetic love-making.

Harold was letting Rosie do the work now, his beaming face relaxed and his appreciative eyes fixed on her body. Sophie was not surprised that Rosie was claiming so much of his attention; her lithe body was glistening exotically with the oil. Sophie thought that she looked wonderful. She herself was just starting to feel left out when Harold pulled her gently towards him, urging her to straddle him. She gasped as he began to use his tongue as a penis, and held on tight to the bedpost, so as not to miss any of the delicious action.

With her back to Rosie, she heard rather than saw her friend reaching her climax. The ecstatic cries excited Sophie further, especially when Harold began to heave and shudder in turn. His deep moans seemed to reverberate through her belly, making her plunge her sex again and again towards his eager tongue.

When she came, arching her back and crying out loud, Sophie was sure she must have alarmed her two partners. She was relieved to see Rosie exhaustedly draped over Harold but watching her with interest; Harold himself had a satisfied glow about him.

Letting herself fall to the other side of Harold, and feeling his arm curl round her in tired embrace, Sophie smiled as she caught Rosie's eye. The two grinned conspiratorially at one another without embarrassment.

'Wow!' mouthed Rosie.

Sophie gave her a thumbs up sign.

'What are you two up to?' Harold's voice drawled

from above them and they giggled like two schoolgirls caught making mischief.

If anyone at the party knew what had been going on in the room at the top of the house, they made no mention, although Harold received a few envious glances when the three did eventually join the crowd.

In the sparse kitchen, pouring herself a drink, Sophie was unreasonably shocked to bump into Toby.

'Toby! I'd forgotten about you,' she cried, confusing him and embarrassing herself.

He had the good grace to look pleased to see her, although she noticed, with mild amusement, that he took great pains not to get too close to her.

'Sophie! So you did come after all.'

'I certainly did!' She laughed, and gave his hand a squeeze. 'Come on, let's go somewhere quiet and get this conversation over with.'

He looked puzzled, then resigned, then panic-stricken. 'I've just got to tell someone . . .'

She waited outside for him, grinning to herself at Toby's predicament, too relaxed to feel any awkwardness. Closing the front door behind him, Toby joined her, blowing clouds of warm breath into the cold night.

'Sophie,' he began immediately, 'I've met someone else.'

He poured out the story while she made understanding noises and smiled sympathetically. Poor Toby, she thought, I'll bet the deception was killing him. But he couldn't have told her on the phone – he was too much of a gentleman.

He paused for breath and glanced down at her.

'You're not angry, then?'

'No, Toby. I hope you will both be very happy together. She looks lovely; I saw you in the pub.'

He looked as though a great weight had been lifted off him. 'Oh, thanks, Sophie. It means a lot to me – us not falling out. I wanted to say, "Let's stay friends," but it sounds so trite, no matter whether you mean it or not. And it means you are free to find someone else.' He blushed slightly. 'Someone you love, rather than just like.'

He's more astute than I gave him credit for, Sophie thought. And they made their way back to the party – together but apart.

Chapter Four

'Come on, Gina! Heels down! Head up! Polly can watch her own feet; you concentrate on steering. Bring her over here, and whoa!' Sophie watched as the child brought the pony to an untidy halt beside her. 'I think we need more practice on the lunge rein.'

'Do we have to?'

'I think we should.'

'Can't I just go to your place and watch children's television? Can't we just say I did my jumping practice?'

'Not really; Mummy will be back from her ride soon, and she'll want to see how you are doing.'

'I wish I didn't have a pony; I wish I had a gerbil.'

'You'd never get a gerbil over those jumps,' Callum informed her, helpfully, from his position by the jumping ring fence. Gina laughed.

'Honestly, Callum! If you don't get that hay shifted, you'll be there all night.' Sophie was having enough problems with Gina, without Callum's surreal humour. 'And anyway,' she added, as child and pony set off round the ring again, 'Her Ladyship will be back soon; you know what she said.'

'She says too much,' Callum grumbled. 'If you ask me, women should be seen and not heard!'

Sophie squealed in fury, and hurled a clod of earth at his grinning face. With immaculate timing, Catherine McKinnerney rode into the yard and fixed them with a superior stare.

'Have you finished moving those hay bales, Callum? No, I thought not. Well, perhaps you should leave them for now; I can see you have too many distractions. The fencing on the small paddock seems to be coming down – first priority is to fix that. No, no, darling!' She had just caught sight of Gina's jumping attempts. 'You mustn't pull her mouth like that! Hold the saddle if you can't keep your hands still. I'll show you.'

She pranced past Sophie and Callum on her showy grey Arab mare, pausing only to snap briefly in Sophie's direction, 'I don't pay you to chat up the gardener, you know. Please feel free to throw yourself at him in your own time – not in mine!'

Sophie's face was a furious red as she scooped up the lunge rein and strode back across the yard. Callum followed to get his tools from the shed.

'I've had just about enough!' Sophie exploded when she got into the tack room. 'I don't have to take this! I'm off. I don't get paid enough to be insulted.'

Callum, leaning in at the tack room window, seemed unaffected by Catherine's rudeness. 'Don't leave me,' he pleaded cheerfully. 'Don't abandon me with these nutters.'

'Really, though, Callum! "Throw yourself at him in your own time!" She's so rude.'

'Perhaps she's right, though. When are you free to throw yourself at me?'

Sophie laughed at his refusal to take anything seriously. 'That depends,' she told him, 'on whether or not it will be worth my while.'

'In what way?'

71

'I don't want you thinking you can just buy me a bag of chips and take me to your shed.'

'No?' Callum feigned disappointment. 'That's a shame. I was going to ask if you wanted to give me a hand moving those hay bales before the rain starts.'

'You know how to turn a girl's head, don't you? No, I don't want to help with the hay. And anyway, I'm off out with Rosie tonight. I won't be free until the weekend.'

'The weekend, then. I'll think of something nice for us to do. Let me know if you change your mind about the shed!' He left, his cheerful but tuneless whistling barely drowning out the squeaky wheelbarrow.

Sophie had to smile. Callum refused to let Catherine get to him. It was easier for him; it was rapidly becoming obvious that Sophie was the main target for her vitriol.

Never mind, Sophie thought. If it all got too unbearable she could leave. Although not, she smiled to herself, before that weekend date.

She set to, filling hay nets in preparation for the evening. Catherine was going to blow a fuse when she saw how few of those bales Callum had moved; it looked like it would be a late finish for him tonight. At that moment Catherine and Gina trotted into the yard. Catherine dismounted and flung her reins in Sophie's direction.

'Sort out Jasmine for me, would you, Sophie. She'll need a good rub down; it was quite hard work for her today. She definitely needs more exercise. I want her up to scratch for the weekend. Did I mention that to you?'

Sophie's heart sank as she lifted the heavy saddle off Jasmine's sweating back. 'The weekend?'

Catherine helped Gina down and looped Polly's reins over the fence. 'I thought I'd told you. The Newton-Smiths are having a weekend house party. They have a rather fine cross-country course I've been dying to try so we're taking horses, children, the lot. I seem to think

72

they have a covered ring so I shall expect to see an improvement in Gina's jumping. Anyway, we'll need you to take charge of the horses, travel with them, sort out all the paraphernalia. Leave on Friday, return Sunday. Think you can manage that?'

'I expect so, it's just that . . .'

'I'm sorry if you had plans for the weekend but your job description did state that the occasional weekend would be involved.'

'Yes,' Sophie said, gritting her teeth, 'it did. No problem; I'll get the horse-box ready tomorrow.'

'I want the tack cleaned too,' Catherine added, casually. 'We want to make a good impression, don't we?'

'Of course,' was all Sophie could trust herself to say.

'Bloody woman!' Sophie exclaimed to Rosie later in the comfort of the village pub. 'Bloody, bloody woman!'

'Who can you mean, Sophie? Not your kindly employer, surely?'

'Honestly, Rosie, she's impossible! If I had a suspicious mind I'd think she did it on purpose.'

'Now you're getting paranoid,' Rosie informed her. 'This weekend has been planned for ages. I know because Jo has been roped in as nanny for about a dozen kids – no extra dosh, of course.'

'Poor Jo. What can you do with that many kids for a whole weekend?'

'I know what I'd do with them,' said Rosie darkly, 'but I doubt it would be a good career move on my part.'

'Are your lot going?'

'I don't think so. And even if they were going, I wouldn't be. I don't do weekends. I got that clear from Day One.' Rosie smiled smugly. 'No, I've got my weekend entertainment planned: scented candles, Black Cherry Massage Oil, and a bottle of wine.'

'Oh Rosie! You're going to see Harold, aren't you? I

73

hope you have a great time, I really do. Send Harold my love, won't you?'

'No I won't! He's all mine from now on.' Rosie regarded her friend's gloomy face. 'Oh do cheer up, Sophie. The weekend can't possibly be that bad! There will be time for other dates with Callum. Anyway, there's bound to be someone interesting there – enough people are going. You know what the Newton-Smiths are like: if you've got it, flaunt it.'

'So, who else is going? Cheer me up.'

'The Carvers.'

'Oh no! I said, "Cheer me up." That's more likely to drive me to drink.'

Rosie gave her a strange look. 'Why is that then?'

'No reason. Who else?'

'The Marshalls. You met them, didn't you? At the party.'

'Oh yes, I remember.'

'The Fields. Do you know them? They've got hundreds of really obnoxious kids. If you had met them, you would remember, believe me. The Edwards are going, I think.'

They chatted on, Rosie smugly content in the knowledge that she would be safely ensconced in Harold's arms; too many miles away to be bothered with the whole fiasco.

Sophie was mortified. The weekend should have been her first proper date with Callum; instead she would be cleaning tack and rubbing down sweaty horses. She tried to remind herself that there would be plenty of other dates, and that if Callum was keen he would ask her again; but it didn't help.

She sipped her drink while Rosie babbled happily about her plans. The pub was fairly empty tonight; the promised rain had started to fall in huge, pendulous drops as the two women arrived. It had continued to splatter against the low, dark windows while they chatted, keeping the village regulars at home in the dry.

Acutely aware that the weather matched her mood, Sophie only half listened to her friend. Outside, the last of the season's bedraggled hanging baskets spun disconsolately in the gathering wind.

'You haven't listened to a word I've said, have you?' Rosie was losing patience with Sophie's melancholy mood. 'Look, I'll tell you what we'll do. If you have to work at the weekend you should be due a day off during the week.'

'That's no good to me,' Sophie sulked, 'Callum works all week.'

'Oh, for pity's sake! Never mind Callum. If you can get a day off this week we can go into town, look round the shops, that sort of thing. What do you think?'

'OK. Yes, if I can get a day off.'

'Wow! Steady on, Sophie! You almost showed some enthusiasm there. I get paid on Thursday, so let's make it Thursday or Friday – that way I can have a serious spree. I've only got the baby this week, so I'll bring him along. I'll even buy lunch. Sound good?'

'Yes, it'll be great.' Sophie tried to smile at her friend. 'Thanks, Rosie.'

'My pleasure. My next tactic would have been to relieve your suffering by having you put down. Get some drinks in.'

Sophie went to the bar trying to look more cheerful than she felt.

Stop being such a misery, she told herself. Think of someone else for a change. Poor Jo, for instance: all those children to supervise for the weekend. And, she thought, a trip into town with Rosie would be good; there were a few things she needed. Perhaps she could persuade Catherine to let her buy some new jodhpurs for Gina who had been moaning that her old ones were splitting.

And I could always treat myself while I'm at it, she

thought, to some new riding boots. Her favourite pair had split when Buzz had trodden on her toes.

By the time she drove Rosie home through the dark, wet night, she was feeling more enthusiastic about their outing.

'Check it out with Catherine,' Rosie called back as she made a dash for her front door. 'Thursday or Friday – let me know. Tell her you need to go.'

Sophie drove home carefully; she didn't know these lanes very well and the little car was really more for Jean's use than hers. With swimming lessons, play groups, dance school and parties, the children needed transport.

They have a more exciting social life than I do, Sophie thought. The only thing they seemed to lack was contact with their parents: the very thing they craved.

Sophie was glad she dealt with horses rather than children; she didn't envy Jo her job. It would be nice if she could be of some help to Jo over the weekend. Pulling into the drive and round the side of the house, she was surprised to see a light on in her cottage.

I'm sure I didn't leave that on, she thought, edging up to Jean's parking spot. She squeezed the Mini between Catherine's sporty little number and Dominic's ancient Rover.

The lights from Prospect House shimmered in the puddles on the drive as Sophie ran for the cottage, raincoat flapping around her head. She fumbled with the door. It was locked. So only she could have left the light on. Unless . . .

Opening the door and stepping in out of the rain she looked nervously round the kitchen. Everything seemed to be in order. She crossed the room to flick the switch on the kettle and then she smelled a faint, but familiar, smell. It sent her stomach lurching and her heart into a beating frenzy; the smell of soft, expensive leather.

With legs like lead, she kicked off her shoes and

76

padded silently to the hall door. Clicking on the light she quickly checked the living room – empty – and then made her way clumsily to the bedroom.

The smell, though still faint, was strongest here and Sophie had to swallow hard before she could reach round the door to trip the light switch. With relief she noted that nobody was in there. A quick glance in the bathroom confirmed that she was alone in the cottage.

But someone has been here, Sophie thought, and this time I know they used a key. Shutting the bathroom door behind her, she crossed the bedroom and was suddenly struck motionless. Something was wrong, not as she had left it. Sophie scanned the room, desperate to find the source of her unease. At last her eyes came to rest on an envelope lying on the dressing table.

She picked it up reluctantly and saw her own name in block capitals on the front. Sitting shakily on the bed, she opened the envelope, her fingers feeling awkward and stiff.

The contents spilled out: soft gauzy material in irides-cent colours. It was a silk scarf, filmy and bright. Sophie caught her breath. It was very beautiful. As she turned it over in her hands the colours danced like butterflies in front of her eyes: pink, blue, silver, green. She draped it round her neck, where it seemed to whisper softly against her skin, releasing another faint whiff of the expensive leather. Despite her previous anxiety, Sophie was enchanted.

But why not just put it through the letterbox? The flimsy material was fine enough to put in an envelope, she thought, so it would surely have been small enough to post. Because, she realised with a jolt, he wanted me to know that he had been here, in my room, while I was out.

She sat and stared at the scarf for several seconds, then picked up the envelope to see if any clues to the sender could be gleaned from it. A piece of paper fell out and

Sophie bent to retrieve it, noticing that block letters had been used again on this note.

My beautiful Sophie,
Please accept this small gift as a token of my admiration for you. I want you to wear it close to your skin, and think of me. I will be watching you, waiting for a time when we can be together again. I am not in a position to tell you my name but please rest assured that I mean you no harm. I shall make arrangements very soon. For now, gorgeous creature, wear the scarf and always think of me.

There was no signature, no clue as to who had sent the note.

Who would have the keys to her cottage? Catherine and James, of course. But who else? Callum? Maybe; she would have to find out. Could anyone else have keys, or even have borrowed a set? She racked her brains. She must find out how many people had keys and where they were kept.

Sophie read the note again. It sounded quite formal, almost as if she and the writer were well-known to each other and were trying to arrange a perfectly innocent dinner date!

'I will be watching you,' sounded quite sinister, but, 'waiting for a time when we can be together again,' gave the impression of an old-fashioned courtship. And why wasn't he in a position to tell her his name? Did he think she would reject him? Would his name mean nothing to her? In other words, was he a total stranger? Was he married? Could he lose his job if the truth of his infatuation were known?

Sophie sat on the bed, her breathing heavy and her head spinning. What was this man's secret? Should she tell someone? But that would mean she had to reveal details of the first meeting, and she couldn't face that.

She could tell Rosie, but not on the phone – when they met for lunch.

She pulled herself unsteadily to her feet, her heart still pounding from the unexpected shock.

What would have happened if she had been in tonight? A persistent thought was buzzing around her head: did he know when she would be out? Sophie caught her breath. Was he watching her?

She instinctively glanced at the open curtains, noting the anonymous blackness outside.

Is he watching me now? she wondered, and was seized with a surge of anger. Sophie dashed through the cottage, pausing to pull on her boots, determined to confront her fear. Out in the yard and suddenly remembering the rain, she stopped and glanced around her, nervously.

What if he was still here? What exactly did she intend to do if she saw some stranger lurking in the shadows? Accost him? Accuse him of leaving her an expensive present?

No, she thought, I would take him back to the cottage, demand an explanation. A little voice piped up in her head; why take him back to the cottage? You could demand an explanation here, in the yard. Be honest with yourself, Sophie, it continued. You want to see him again. You are looking forward to seeing him again. The idea of being made love to by a mystery man excites you beyond belief.

Sophie felt uncoordinated and shaky. It's true, she thought, I am excited by the situation. I didn't come out here to confront him; I came out here because I felt disappointed to have been out when he visited.

She stood, in a turmoil, the rain soaking her hair and shirt. I want him, she thought. I want the danger, the desire, the excitement.

A noise from the side of the barn caused Sophie to

start. Heart surging in anticipation, she began to creep slowly along beside the wooden partition.

In the dim glow from one electric bulb, placed high in the roof of the barn, she could see tools and a wheelbarrow. Beside them, half a dozen bales of hay sat under a sheet of polythene, waiting for their turn to be stored safely on top of the towering stacks.

As she watched, the wind fretted at the polythene, making the snapping noise that Sophie had heard earlier. Callum, long hair hanging damply over his face, came into view, still whistling tunelessly despite the dull job and the late hour. His T-shirt was plastered across his chest; the muscles, pumped up from hard labour, looked as solid as carved wood.

Not quite like wood, thought Sophie; wood is too unyielding. Too cold and dead. If I touched him now he would feel warm, firm, and very much alive. I want to touch him.

She watched the determined ripple of his arms as he hefted another bale into the barn, and thought of how easily he had lifted her on to the table in his shed. Then, just before he disappeared from view – and almost as if to inflame further Sophie's desire – he clumsily pulled the wet T-shirt over his head.

His blonde hair, made darker by the rain, clung to his shoulders, and he used the T-shirt to wipe the trickles of sweat from his chest. The wet rag was then discarded into the wheelbarrow, and Callum stepped out of sight to continue his job in the barn.

Sophie glanced furtively round the yard; it was deserted.

That's typical, she thought. On a night like this they leave him to store all the winter feed for their animals while they stay indoors in the warm.

Still in her lustful frame of mind, but telling herself that she just had Callum's best interests at heart, she crept silently up to the barn door. Slipping inside she could hear Callum, high up on top of the stacks of hay.

He deserves a treat, she thought, giggling to herself. A sudden urge to be wicked made her quickly pull off boots, socks, jeans and shirt. After a second's hesitation, she added her underwear to the pile and stood shivering in the chill night.

Sophie could still hear Callum's whistling from somewhere up above, so – aware that the longer she stood there the more likelihood there was that someone would see her – she flung Callum's coat around her and went to find him.

A ladder led upwards into the topmost reaches of the barn. Glad to step on to the smooth rungs after the prickly sharpness of the barn floor, Sophie scaled it quickly and peeped over the top.

Callum, his back turned, was trying to make room for the last few bales. Sophie pulled herself up, flung off the coat, and said softly, 'Surprise!'

Callum leapt a good way into the air, cracking his head mightily on the barn roof. On seeing Sophie's nakedness his mouth dropped open and he staggered backwards. She only just managed to save him from falling the twenty feet to the barn floor by grabbing one of his flailing arms.

Collapsing back on to the relatively safe platform of hay bales, Sophie cradled his head against her breast.

'I'm sorry, I'm sorry,' she told him, absently picking bits of hay off his back. At least she felt warm now, protected from the wind by the hay bales, and covered by Callum's body. 'Now you know how it feels,' she couldn't help telling him, casually.

'What, to have your whole life flash before you?' he mumbled happily from between her breasts.

'No, when people creep up on you, I mean.'

'Creep up on me anytime. Where are your clothes, by the way?'

'Down there, on the floor; I thought I would surprise you.'

'Surprise me? You nearly killed me!'

'Well at least you would have died happy.'

'Not very happy, knowing I had left behind an opportunity to satisfy a beautiful woman.'

'Well then,' – Sophie shook him off and arranged herself provocatively on his coat – 'satisfy me now. In case you have heart failure in the next few minutes!'

Callum came towards her on his hands and knees. His hair hung in damp coils around his face, and Sophie realised he wore a gold hoop in his ear, making him look for all the world like a pirate. He straddled her, his head low and hands on her wrists, looking at her from under his eyebrows.

'I should get my revenge for that little trick,' he told her, while Sophie feigned indifference. And then he growled ominously, like a large and dangerous dog, and swooped down to pretend to bite her.

Sophie squealed and wriggled as he darted at her, his mouth finding her most sensitive places but only just making contact. She was breathless and aroused as his lips skimmed playfully over her, teasing her with their promising closeness. Suddenly, burying his head deep between her legs, Callum began to lick and nuzzle at her, making her gasp. She tried to push him off, but he kept his head clamped firmly in place; burrowing his face into her bush of blond hair.

It felt to Sophie as if she was being eaten, that she was a fruit, ripe for the picking, with her lover devouring her mouthful by delicious mouthful. She could only groan and squirm, holding his heavy head where she wanted it, and offering herself up to his hungry mouth.

Sophie let the wonderful sensation take a hold of her. She let herself relax, lying back and gazing at the ceiling of the barn above her. She felt safe and contented in the warm, fusty hay loft. Outside the rain rattled in vain against the wooden walls; inside Sophie watched Callum's long hair trail across her thighs, and felt a growing and powerful desire creep through her body.

This time, she thought to herself, this time I'll have him how I want him. It was my idea, after all; I call the shots.

With a supreme effort she pulled herself out from under Callum's greedy mouth. He moaned and tried to pull her back but she resisted, grabbing his belt-buckle to remove his jeans. Happy to comply, he fumbled with the buttons and eased the denim down to reveal his decidedly eager penis. Before he had a chance to object, Sophie pushed him down on the hay and clambered on top of him. He tried rather half-heartedly to sit up, but Sophie kissed his lips, still glistening from their impromptu feast, and used her weight to keep him where she wanted him.

Callum's eyes roved appreciatively over Sophie's full breasts, tiny waist and mass of honey-coloured hair; which she swept back impatiently from her face. She grinned at him cheekily, although not quite sure what his reaction would be to her taking charge of the proceedings. He smiled, encouraging her, as she steadied herself above his quivering penis. As Callum strained his hips up to her, eager to be inside that dark, mysterious place, Sophie grinned again and slowly lowered herself on to his waiting penis, closing her eyes in satisfaction.

Callum groaned and heaved, pushing himself as far into her warmth as he could reach, but Sophie pulled herself away, teasing, refusing to take all of him into her so soon and making him groan all the more.

Sophie's face was a mask of concentration as she fought not to be thrown off balance. Callum's muscles were tense and tight, his penis insistent, but still Sophie played herself over him, never letting him get as deeply into her as he desired. She smiled to herself, knowing that this time she controlled his pleasure as well as her own; it felt good to have a powerful man like Callum at her mercy!

Not that she wasn't enjoying it herself – far from it! She felt she could let herself go at any time but she wanted to enjoy her dominance just a little longer. Reaching behind herself, Sophie let her fingers find Callum's thighs. Leaning back, she trailed one hand between his legs, eager to feel the place where they fitted together so perfectly.

Callum's reaction was instant: bucking like a particularly lively horse, his eyes opened wide and he tried to pull her hand away.

'Sophie, don't! I'll come too quickly!'

She instinctively tightened the grip with her knees as she had been taught to do when a horse was trying to throw her. She smiled to herself as he relaxed beneath her once more, then, before he could raise any more objections, she braced herself against any kind of reaction and slid a cool hand firmly round his balls.

'Sophie! No, don't!'

But she was enjoying herself, enjoying her power over him, and the fact that his every movement took him deeper inside her. Sophie locked her hands underneath and forced herself down on him, ignoring his moans. They were moving together now, Callum lifting himself off the hay to plunge as deep as possible into her. Sophie felt the tightness in her thighs, the looseness in her stomach, and wanted to keep Callum there for ever, underneath her.

He was coming now in huge jerking spasms, his eyes open but unseeing. He was gasping out her name but she carried on, determined to make the most of his last few moments of hardness. She let herself enclose him, her own climax coming in waves of almost unbearable pleasure, before she allowed herself to sag forward on to his chest. A huge sigh racked them both simultaneously, making them laugh.

It felt good to have Callum's arm round her, Sophie thought; her head felt right resting on his solid chest. His other hand stroked her hair thoughtfully, prompting her to look up at him.

'Are you all right?'

'Yes, sure. I'm fine. Just a bit taken by surprise.'

'You didn't mind?'

'Did it seem like I minded? You can take me by surprise any time you like. In fact, you can take me any time you like, surprise or otherwise! There is one thing, though.'

'What?' She was instantly alert to the change of mood that his voice indicated. 'I meant what I said about you not leaving.'

'What did you say?'

'I asked you not to leave without me.'

Sophie was stunned for a few seconds; this all sounded rather more serious than she had expected. She decided to try to laugh it off.

'Oh that! I'm not leaving; if I do, you'll be the first to know.'

'I like you, Sophie.'

'I kind of suspected that!'

'Even though you're a shameless hussy who lures unsuspecting gardeners into temptation!'

She sat up and gave him a playful slap. 'You love it!'

'I had no choice.'

'You wish! Come on, I'm getting cold. Help me find my clothes.'

Giggling, they collected up her clothes only to discover that the driving rain had managed to seep in and soak them all through. Callum pulled his coat round her again, bundled up her wet clothes and, lifting her into his arms, made a dash for the cottage.

After a few seconds fumbling for the key they fell, wet

and dishevelled, through the front door. Callum struggled to shut it, then bent to retrieve something wedged between door and jamb.

'What's this?'

Frozen in the act of filling the kettle, Sophie turned to see him waving a sodden, but unmistakably expensive, leather glove. She felt her knees go weak and had to put the kettle down quickly before she dropped it.

'Sophie! What's wrong? You've gone white.'

Slowly, shakily, she sat down at the table; she felt as though the mysterious stranger was haunting her life. 'It's . . . it's something I've got to deal with.'

He was all concern. 'Let me help. What is it?'

'I can't tell you.'

'What? Why not?'

'I just can't tell you, Callum.'

His voice was gentle. 'You can tell me anything, I hope.'

'No. Not this.' She tried to smile. 'It's only a glove, anyway; it was just a shock, seeing it there.'

'Whose glove is it?' He was getting angry now. 'Is there something I need to know?'

'I don't know whose it is. Please don't make this more difficult for me.'

'For you? It's not exactly easy for me, you know. I meet a woman I could really fall for only to find she's keeping things from me!' He turned away, exasperated. When he turned back, his face had softened. He came to stand beside her. 'It can't be that bad, Sophie. Just tell me, please.'

'I can't, Callum. I just can't. It isn't that there's some-one else – well, there is, but not what you mean.'

His face glowered darkly above her for an instant. Then, without a word, he turned on his heel and left while Sophie sat, shaky and miserable, at her kitchen table.

Chapter Five

Sophie crunched across the gravel, blowing puffs of warmth into the chilly air. The bushes, trees and grass had a lacy white sheen, and she marvelled at how sudden and total autumn's arrival had been.

Beside the shed, Callum was pulling on heavy boots, hopping about so ludicrously that Sophie had to tell herself not to laugh. She stopped and held out the coat she had borrowed two nights previously.

'I brought this back.'

'Thanks.' He took it from her without meeting her eyes, threw it into the shed, and then started rooting about amongst the tools again.

'Is that it, Callum?'

When he straightened up to look her full in the face, Sophie was taken aback. His eyes, normally so full of life, were dull and expressionless. He stared at her for some thirty seconds before he spoke.

'What do you want me to say?'

'Just talk to me, Callum. I'm sorry if I've hurt your feelings, but I've got to sort things out for myself.'

A flash of pain seemed to pass across his face before he managed to rearrange it into the blank mask once again.

'Don't worry about my feelings – I'm just a gardener, I don't have them.'

Sophie made an exasperated gesture and marched off towards the house. If he wanted to act childishly, let him. She didn't have time for Callum's tantrums; she had been summoned to see Catherine.

Once inside the hall, she glanced at her watch. Sophie hoped she hadn't missed her employer; what she had to ask was important, no matter how casually she phrased it. At length Catherine appeared, immaculate as ever in a navy blue suit. She waved at Sophie to follow her as she finished the preparations for her departure.

'Jodhpurs for Gina,' she announced, dropping car keys, lipstick and purse into her bag. 'I shall phone Butlers on Queen Street to tell them to expect you. We have an account with them, so it should be all ready for you to collect. As for the riding boots, which I know you need, Mr Butler will be told to add them to our account.'

As Sophie tried to protest, Catherine held up her hand.

'I don't want to hear another word about it. I know that our plans have messed up your weekend, and I know that it was that wretched Buzz that split your other boots. This is my way of trying to make amends. That's a lovely scarf, by the way.'

'Thank you,' Sophie stuttered, as taken aback as if Catherine had given her the crown jewels. She absently fingered the soft silk draped round her neck.

'I can't let you have the car keys, I'm afraid; Jean will need the car later to collect the children. I can drop you off in town, though, if you're ready now.'

'That's all right, thanks. Rosie is coming to pick me up later.'

'Rosie? I didn't realise you were going shopping with Rosie.'

'Well, yes, it was her – '

'Can you find Butlers?'

'I expect so . . .'

'Right, then, I must be off.'

'Wait!'

Catherine's eyebrows arched towards her sleek hair. 'Is there a problem?'

'Well, no. Not really.' Sophie took her courage in both hands. 'It's just that I wanted to ask you something. Could you tell me who else has keys to the cottage?'

'Well, us; James and I. And you. Does that answer your question?'

'Sort of. Nobody else has access to them, then?'

'Not that I know of.' Catherine, impatient to leave, was on the move again, bustling Sophie into the hall.

'These keys,' Sophie persisted, bravely, 'where are they kept?'

Catherine stopped fussing with her bag and regarded Sophie keenly.

'There,' she said.

Sophie looked at the wooden plaque on the wall by the front door; it bristled with keys. Slowly the realisation dawned on her that the spare keys to her cottage were kept, hung on a hook, in plain view, beside a door that was never locked. She felt slightly queasy.

'Is there a problem?' Catherine asked again, gimlet-eyed.

'I would feel better,' Sophie said, faintly, 'if the keys for the cottage were kept somewhere safer. I mean, the front door is always open.'

Catherine waved a perfectly manicured hand at her. 'Nonsense! Who would want to steal the keys to the cottage? And anyway, if a stranger ever ventured on to the drive, Brin would cause an uproar.'

Sophie thought hopelessly of the deaf, toothless Labrador blundering round the yard, getting trodden on by horses whose approach had taken him totally by surprise.

'Brin,' she repeated, stupidly.

'Of course,' Catherine reassured her, having lost all

patience with the conversation. 'Look, if it's worrying you I'll get James to lock the keys in the study. How's that? Now I really must fly.'

It's a bit late for preventative measures, Sophie thought, watching her employer make a hasty departure. Why don't I just leave my door unlocked with a big ALL INTRUDERS WELCOME sign stuck to it?

She stumbled down the steps, fell over Brin – who hadn't heard her coming – and headed back to the cottage, still dazed at Catherine's complacency. The only thing that cheered her up slightly was the thought of what Rosie would say when faced with this latest outrage.

She got ready for her friend's arrival amidst a riot of emotions. Callum's surliness was depressing, but Sophie knew she was right not to let him dictate the terms of any relationship they might have; her privacy was important to her. It wasn't as if she had known him that long. She had no way of knowing how he would react if she told him the truth about her mysterious visitor. And anyway, she thought, telling him the truth was hardly likely to heal the rift between them.

But, thought Sophie, what about Catherine? Now there was a surprise! Why had she insisted on paying for Sophie's boots? She had no need to; the others had been old and cheap. It wasn't Catherine's responsibility to make sure that Sophie had decent boots.

Guilt, thought Sophie. She's probably regretting the way she's treated me recently, and so she should.

She applied her make-up carefully. It was not something she wore often, but today was different. It was nice to have an excuse to wear something other than jodhpurs, nice to imagine lunchtime in a restaurant, as opposed to the usual rushed bowl of soup in her tiny kitchen.

When the car horn sounded outside her window,

Sophie bounded out of the door, turned to lock it, then thought, why bother?

Rosie was fiddling with the tape deck, while the baby in the back seat appeared to be yawning protractedly, its face red and damp. As Sophie opened the passenger door, the noise from within hit her like a brick. She was appalled that such a small human could make such an ear-splitting racket.

'Heavens, Rosie! Where's its volume switch?'

'I'm just going to put some music on; that usually works.'

'Good idea, out-noise him. Is it a him?'

Rosie turned to peer absent-mindedly at the squawking child on the back seat. 'Yes, its a him. Patrick.'

Sophie looked at Patrick; Patrick paused in his protest.

'Hello, Patrick,' Sophie said, uncertainly.

Patrick launched into his loudest screams yet, and Sophie recoiled, horrified. 'Is he always like this?'

'Oh no.' Rosie seemed undaunted. 'He's teething.'

'Is he?' He looked as though he were exploding to Sophie. 'I thought babies were supposed to go to sleep in cars.'

'This one doesn't.'

'That's a shame. Can't you do something for him?'

'Like give him away, you mean?' Rosie found the tape she was looking for and put the car into gear. 'He's got stuff on his gums.'

'Stuff?'

'He had a teething ring but he launched it at the back of my head about ten minutes ago. It bounced under your seat, I think. Took me by surprise, I can tell you.'

The baby's cries subsided once the motion of the car and the music began to work their magic. Patrick grumbled fretfully to himself and then fell asleep. The two friends breathed a sigh of relief.

'I don't know how much they pay you,' Sophie told Rosie, 'but it isn't enough.'

'You're right, it isn't. But never mind that – how are things with you?'

Sophie recounted the strange tale of Catherine's generosity.

'Guilt,' Rosie agreed. She was satisfyingly outraged at the accessibility of the spare set of keys to the cottage.

Then Sophie told her of the return to the cottage with Callum, and of them finding the glove.

'A clue!' Rosie gloated. 'This is exciting, isn't it?'

'That's not all.' Sophie showed her friend the scarf and told her about the note. 'And now Callum's not talking to me. He's sulking because he thinks I should tell him all about it and, even if I wanted to, I'd be too embarrassed.'

'You do have an exciting life, don't you?'

'It's not very exciting knowing that a stranger can get into my house any time he likes; it's sinister, Rosie.'

'Oh, come on! If you truly felt threatened, you would have called the police, changed the locks, moved out, something like that. He's obviously not going to do you any harm; he's mad about you. Anyway, he doesn't sound like a nutter.'

'Oh great! And what exactly do nutters sound like? I'm anxious to know.'

'You know what I mean. Anyway, I wish I had an admirer who left me expensive silk scarves; it's lovely.'

'But why the secrecy? That's what puzzles me.'

'It could be any number of reasons. At least this time he left you a clue. What's this glove like, then?'

'What do you mean, "what's this glove like?" It's a glove, Rosie! It hasn't got a name-tag in it, if that's what you mean.'

They drove in silence for a while, Rosie scouring the streets for a parking spot. Eventually she pulled erratically into a recently vacated space and they jumped out.

'Anyway,' Rosie said slyly as they unloaded baby and

buggy, 'what was Callum doing at your place so late at night?'

'Don't ask,' sighed Sophie, determined not to let her disagreement with Callum cloud the rest of her day off.

They worked their way systematically through the new shopping precinct, the reality of a day in town bringing them down to earth with a bump. Patrick grizzled and moaned, punctuating this delightful behaviour with ear-splitting shrieks and a spot of shop-lifting. Rosie was unconcerned.

'It's the shop's own fault,' she announced. 'If they didn't put everything so low down, and the aisles so close together, this couldn't happen.'

They sat having coffee, surveying the grumbling toddler as he pawed through his newly-acquired loot. Sophie sighed. This wasn't quite how she had imagined her day off. So far, they had spent half the morning in the chemist, trying to find something to ease Patrick's teething pains and the other half had been taken up trekking from one baby-changing facility to another.

Rosie seemed unbowed by the inconvenience of it all. She had been positively ecstatic to find free nappies in one of the cubicles.

'Free nappies!' she told Sophie, as she exited, holding a wriggling Patrick.

'Hold me back,' Sophie said sarcastically, regretting it as soon as she saw her friend's face.

Even lunch was spoilt when Rosie's meal was allowed to go cold so that some evil-smelling gunk could be spooned into the surly Patrick. As they finished their coffee, Patrick began to wail once more and they were forced to pay the bill and leave quickly, to the obvious relief of the other diners.

'The trouble is, we're not really baby-orientated in this country,' Rosie explained, trying to strap Patrick into his buggy. He arched his back and trumpeted furiously, aiming wild smacks at her head.

'The question is: do we want to be?'

'He's not always like this.'

'I'm sure.' Sophie felt sorry for her friend. Rosie's patience seemed astounding to her; she was acutely aware of the fact that, placed in Rosie's position, she wouldn't have a clue how to cope.

'Listen, Sophie, if you don't mind, I think I might get Patrick back. He's not going to settle, and at least at home he might have a sleep. I'm sorry if it's messed up the day, but this way you get to look round the shops in peace.'

Sophie smiled. 'You get back. I hope he gives you a break soon. I'll get a taxi home when I've finished.'

Rosie looked relieved that her friend hadn't taken offence.

'Rosie,' Sophie called after the hurrying figure, 'if I had kids, I'd want someone like you looking after them.'

'Thanks, Sophie,' Rosie smiled, 'but I don't know if that's a job I'd want.' They both laughed.

It was a relief to be able to wander the brightly lit shops without Patrick yelling and attempting to grab at displays as he passed. Sophie stocked up on her favourite toiletries, bought herself a couple of books, and then, wandering into the old part of town, found a shop selling hand-made chocolates. Inside, she bought a small box of chocolates for Rosie, then set off again in search of Queen Street.

All the shops in this part of town seemed ancient. They were smaller and dimmer than the ones in the precinct, their contents not as uniform. Each window held something unique and, looking at the few customers on the darkening pavements, Sophie wondered how these interesting little places managed to survive.

Butlers – Equestrian Specialists Since 1855 – was larger than its neighbours. On closer inspection this seemed to be because it was three shops knocked into one, giving it the appearance of a series of dimly-lit caves. From the outside the shop looked closed but the door opened when pushed, creaking and groaning as if this were the first time today that it had done so.

They certainly seemed to be well-stocked, Sophie thought, peering into the gloom. There were saddles and bridles, grooming kits, jumbles of books, jewellry and pens, even a sign on a door at the back, marked DRESSING ROOMS.

Sophie waited for someone to attend to her. The place seemed deserted, even though they were expecting her.

'Hello!' she called, 'hello! I'm here to collect an order.'

A door behind the counter swung open and an elderly man, presumably Mr Butler, peered out. From the room behind him a very loud television could be heard.

'Ah! Good afternoon to you – you must be Mrs McKinnerney's girl. What did she say the name was? Sophie.'

Sophie nodded and smiled, although the thought of being 'Mrs McKinnerney's girl' didn't appeal to her much.

'It's here.' The elderly man patted a parcel on the counter. Sophie was amused to see that it was wrapped in brown paper and tied with string. Just like carrier bags had never happened, Sophie thought to herself.

'Mrs McKinnerney said something about boots,' he continued, racking his brain for the specific message. 'Ah yes! I remember. She said you would be choosing some new boots which were to be added to her account.'

'That's right,' Sophie nodded.

'Excuse me?'

'I said "that's right!"' Sophie bellowed.

'In there.' He pointed to the door with the DRESSING ROOMS sign. 'That's where I keep all the footwear.' He waved her towards the door, obviously not wanting to miss too much of his television programme.

The room was pitch black. Sophie found the light switch, letting the door thump closed behind her, and set about finding the right-sized boots amongst hundreds of identical white boxes.

It wasn't easy. The boxes were stacked to the high ceiling so that Sophie had to climb a rickety ladder to find a pair of boots, then struggle down to try them on. As she rejected what felt like the twentieth pair, she heard a shuffling noise behind her. Glancing down, Sophie noticed a pale envelope which appeared to have been pushed under the door.

Getting off the ladder, Sophie picked up the envelope with a shaking hand. The familiar block capitals leapt out at her, and she had to take a deep breath before she could rip it open.

Darling Sophie,
I am here to see you! I am delighted to note that you are wearing your gift; it looks even more becoming than I imagined. Please, my darling, do exactly as I ask; it is important that you act quickly if we are to be together today. Go into the changing room. Put the scarf around your eyes. You must trust me, Sophie; it is imperative that you don't see me yet. Do this now.

Sophie caught her breath. It took two readings before she comprehended the note, then she froze in shock. Desperately trying to collect her wits, she lurched forward to open the door. In her eagerness to confront her seducer, she heaved pointlessly at the door handle, before realising that it was being held firmly on the other side.

What should she do? Sophie tried to think quickly. If she complied with his demands she might just find out his identity. On the other hand, defiance on her part might antagonise him, make him angry. It seemed unlikely. What seemed more likely was that she would drive him away. Sophie wanted to solve this mystery; she couldn't stand the thought of never knowing who this man was.

She would be forever wondering, looking into the eyes of strangers and thinking: was it him? If she was honest, Sophie thought, the idea of being with this strange, silent man again excited and aroused her. She could no more resist him than she could change her nature.

She stumbled across the room, kicking discarded boxes out of the way. She let herself into the changing room, pulling the door closed behind her, and fumbled with the scarf. Sophie could still see the light under the changing room door through the flimsy material.

Doesn't he realise, she wondered frantically, that I can almost see through this thing? And in that split second she realised how far she was prepared to abet her admirer in his fantasies. The thought of maybe being allowed to see the man's face this time excited her as much as it filled her with dread.

Should I shout for someone, she wondered. But who would hear, anyway? Mr Butler was as deaf as a post, as well as a television addict, and the chances of there being any other customers in the shop were virtually zero. This place looked as though they were lucky to get a dozen customers in a week. Anyway, thought Sophie, did she really want someone to come and rescue her? Hadn't she really wanted this to happen?

Sophie lowered herself on to a small, velvet-covered stool that sat in the corner of the changing room. Her legs were shaking. She seemed to sit there for ages, and was just considering taking off the blindfold to reread the note when there came the unmistakable sound of the dressing room door opening. Almost immediately, the line of light that Sophie had seen under the changing room door was doused.

He's turned the light off, she thought, fighting an overwhelming agitation as she heard the outer door close to behind him. Then footsteps, and the sound of a hand groping for the door. Sophie, unable to contain herself, leapt off the stool and pushed open the door.

'I'm here,' she whispered.

Immediately, strong hands pulled back the door and Sophie felt the swish of air as her unseen lover entered and closed the door.

Before Sophie had time to draw breath, his arms were around her and she was crushed urgently against his chest. By the texture of the material she could feel against her face, Sophie thought he wore only a shirt. She could hear as much as feel his heart racing beneath the taut, crisp cotton.

He held her tightly, both of them trying to control their breathing, for what seemed like a long time; then strong hands pushed Sophie away gently, and she stood shakily waiting for his next move.

She didn't have to wait long. The hands found her in the darkness, and running intimately over her face, found her lips. An eager mouth found hers, firm and greedy, with an insistent, probing tongue. The kiss was deep, sensuous and hugely arousing. It was the sort of kiss that made Sophie's knees feel weak: a possessive, demanding kiss. When Sophie and her lover finally broke to draw breath, she realised she was almost panting with desire.

'Who are you?' she gasped. 'Please tell me.'

A finger was placed on her lips, as if to quieten her, and a hand slid downwards to cup her breast. Sophie jumped as the large hand squeezed and fondled, her excitement becoming immediately obvious as her aroused nipples brushed the fine material of her shirt.

The fingers dealt expertly with the delicate buttons, then the garment was slipped over her shoulders. Her skirt followed almost immediately and Sophie was gratified to hear the sharp intake of breath that accompanied the discovery that she was wearing stockings rather than tights. For several moments the playful fingertips trailed across Sophie's belly and between her thighs, pausing only to fondle her breasts through the lacy material of her bra. Then, suddenly, she felt the clip on her bra being undone, as the other hand inserted itself between her soft bush of hair and her knickers, teasing them gently down.

Sophie felt light-headed as the smooth hands toured her body, cupping the mounds of her breasts, squeezing her buttocks and stroking her pubis, before dipping downwards to investigate the valley of her womanhood. The hands moved eagerly, deftly, so that she was never sure which part of her body would be the grateful recipient of their attention. Every inch of her body was explored with relish, making Sophie feel appreciated and languid. These hands seemed to have a life all their own so that Sophie couldn't tell where they ended and her own skin began.

She groaned and held for support to the rail she had found beside her on the wall. Her lover's vocal responses were minimal: a groan when he felt her wetness, and a gasp when Sophie's hand had found the bulge of his straining penis. She tugged at the zip as her lover held his breath; then, to the relief of both, it gave and the smooth penis sprang into Sophie's hand as if it belonged there.

She tried to unbutton the man's shirt but he was impatient, refusing, by firmly removing her hands, to let her even lower his trousers.

In the dark, and with an ease that made Sophie suspect forward planning, he found the velvet stool. Turning Sophie round he leant her over it so that the prickly material caressed her stomach and she shivered in anticipation as he ran his hands greedily over her exposed buttocks, lifting her high into the position he wanted, despite the taut suspenders. She felt him edge himself into position behind her and groaned as his fingers found her secret place and entered her carefully. He played teasingly inside her, making her arch herself towards him in the hope of feeling more of him. She felt as if she were a flower, opening itself up on the first day of spring.

She felt her lover kneel behind her and braced herself, knowing that she was more than ready for what was to happen next – for what she wanted to happen next. Even though she was prepared, Sophie had not imagined it could feel this good; his penis slid into her like a hand into a glove. He seemed to fill her beautifully, not because he was a big man – he wasn't – but he knew exactly how to move himself to best advantage and Sophie was bewitched by the sensations his deeply probing penis provoked.

The man's hands now moved down to locate and tease her clitoris so that Sophie felt herself start to move with him, anxious to satisfy him as well as herself. Her small, animal moans of pleasure became noisy, guttural gasps as he held her hips firmly and moved himself rhythmically, almost mechanically, deeper and deeper inside her.

Sophie's orgasm took her suddenly by surprise, and she cried out. It was followed by another, then another, and Sophie arched and squirmed over the stool as wave after wave of pleasure swept over her body.

Her lover, who had seemed to ease off while the glorious sensations tumbled over her, now seemed determined to renew his efforts. Tucking both hands under her hips, he held her exactly where he wanted her, and set about satisfying himself.

There was a naked desire about him now. Sophie was aware of his power and strength as he hunched over her, her presence almost incidental to his enjoyment. Whoever this man was, he was used to getting what he wanted. Gentle though he seems, Sophie thought, she would not like to be the recipient of the savage selfishness that also seemed intrinsic to his character.

His fingers were digging into her sides now, and Sophie could feel his balls slapping hard against her behind as he stiffened and strained, finally holding her tightly to him as he shuddered and jerked. He collapsed, satisfied, on top of her, and Sophie, for a few brief moments, thought of him as being as vulnerable as herself, just a flesh-and-blood man like any other. It didn't last long. Before she could start to get used to his more human side, he was standing to tuck himself away, a mechanical lover once again.

Before Sophie could protest, or even remove the blindfold, the waft of air told her that he was on his way out of the changing room.

'Wait!' she cried, trying to struggle to her feet, hampered by her numb knees.

The click of the shop door came while she was still fumbling for the changing room door handle. Sophie tore off the blindfold and, praying that nobody came in, staggered across the room to the light switch. Catching sight of herself in the mirror – naked, flushed and dishevelled – she fled back to find her clothes and compose herself.

Bursting through the door into the shop several minutes later, Sophie looked wildly around, as if she really expected the man to be waiting for her. The shop was, of course, deserted.

'Mr Butler,' she called, with more ferocity than was strictly necessary. 'Mr Butler! Are you there?'

The elderly gentleman rushed through the door looking most alarmed.

'I'd forgotten you were here,' he said.

'Did a man just leave?'

'A man?'

'Was there a man came in after me?'

'Well I didn't see anyone. But, you see' – he gestured to the bellowing television – 'I don't hear very well.'

Sophie collapsed on to the wooden chair beside the counter. It was perfect, really: a shop that was routinely empty of customers, an assistant who couldn't hear the door, and a handy changing room where they wouldn't be disturbed. Sophie had walked straight into it, in every sense. The risk to her seducer had been minimal, just enough to make it all the more exciting.

What was really bothering Sophie was how he had known where to find her. Had it been planned? In which case, someone had found out about her day off and, even more sinister, about her intent to visit this particular shop. The alternative scenario was that her mystery lover was watching her every move and had just grasped the opportunity to get her alone. Sophie shivered; she wasn't sure which option appealed to her least.

'I wonder,' she asked faintly, 'if you could call me a taxi?'

'Of course, of course.' Mr Butler set off back to his little room, then half-turned. 'Do you feel quite well? You look a little peaky, if you don't mind me saying so. Did you not find any boots to fit you?'

Sophie stared at him blankly, then leapt to her feet. Back in the dressing room she grabbed the first pair of size five riding boots she could find and staggered back to the chair.

'These are fine,' she stammered.

Mr Butler started the interminable process of encasing them in brown paper, chuckling to himself – inappropriately, Sophie thought. As he tied the last knot in the string, he leant across to gaze into Sophie's glassy eyes.

'I do believe,' he whispered, 'that you have had a little surprise. Am I right?'

Sophie turned her uncomprehending face towards him and blinked stupidly. 'What do you mean?'

He pulled himself proudly up to his full, but still meagre, height. 'People are always a bit flabbergasted,' he boasted in his cracked old voice, 'at the sheer volume of merchandise I manage to store in that back room. Oh yes, it's a real Aladdin's Cave in there.'

Chapter Six

'Tell Sophie what she told you about breakfast.' Jo giggled through a mouthful of toast. 'Go on, tell her, Mrs C.'

Sophie – who never normally ate a large breakfast – tucked enthusiastically into scrambled eggs, tomatoes and mushrooms, providing an attentive audience to the double-act that was Jo and Mrs Clegg, the Newton-Smith's housekeeper.

'Oh, that woman!' Mrs Clegg was an entertainer of the highest calibre. Any conversation with her was littered with asides, gossip and much animation; her announcement of breakfast had deserved an award in itself.

'Tell her,' Jo urged, swilling coffee.

'You wouldn't credit it,' Mrs Clegg declared, throwing her hands in the air. 'All that money, and no class! And I know; I've worked for the best. She says to me – this was yesterday, before you all arrived – she says, "Mrs Clegg, try to remember; toast and cereal only for the kitchen, cooked breakfasts for the dining room." Can you believe that? So I pretend to look confused, and she says that this weekend is costing them enough, without having to provide meals for "hangers-on". Her very

103

words! So I told her that them "hangers-on" are the workers, as far as I'm concerned, and should have what they want for their breakfast. That shut her up!'

Sophie looked suitably disgusted, which was all the encouragement Mrs Clegg needed to share more of her wisdom.

'It isn't as if they haven't got the money,' she assured Sophie. 'Oh no! Loaded, they are.' She lowered her voice as if she had something a little shameful to impart. 'Football pools win,' she announced, wrinkling her nose. 'Doesn't know what to spend it on, she doesn't. But I'll tell you what she doesn't spend it on, shall I? New underwear!'

She paused for Sophie to realise the full horror of this revelation. Sophie tutted and tried not to look at Jo, who was shaking with silent laughter.

'Will she buy new underwear? She will not! I've even offered to take her shopping – but no!'

Sophie, who was not at all sure that she wanted to know any more about Mrs Newton-Smith's underwear, shook her head sadly.

'Grey, it is! Grey!' Mrs Clegg proceeded to empty the washing machine, still pouting with disapproval. 'My mother always said that some people were all show and no knickers,' she added, pointedly.

By the time Jo and Sophie escaped they were red in the face with suppressed laughter.

'She's a scream,' Sophie spluttered, 'but I hope I never get on the wrong side of her!'

'Oh, you don't need to worry about that. Her disapproval only extends to people who don't live up to their income. She actually keeps me sane in this place; she's always been very good to me. Anyway, I'm off to entertain ten horrible kids – what are you up to?'

'Apparently my first job is to take poor Gina for a jumping lesson. I thought at least this weekend she would get a break – you know, get to play with some other kids for a change. Poor little mite. It would be just what she needed.'

'Can't you get a couple of the others to join in? Tara's got her own pony and Katie Field is a good little rider. She could easily handle Jem's pony.'

'That's not a bad idea! I could organise some races and games; that would get a few off your hands, too.'

'Tell you what; I could bring the little ones down to cheer them on, if you're doing races.'

'Great! Just give me an hour to take Gina for a quick jumping lesson. Her mother will throw a fit if she thinks the whole day has been wasted having fun!'

Sophie had spent the previous evening settling horses and ponies into the Newton-Smith's stables after a nightmare journey that began and ended with a row.

Catherine had been her usual peevish self; insisting on supervising the loading of the horse-box, despite the fact that she was obviously needed at the house. When James had come to find her, there had been a furious argument which resulted in Catherine refusing to lift a finger in the rest of the preparations. The screaming and shouting had so unsettled the horses that Sophie was obliged to travel with them in the back of the horse-box with James at the wheel. Catherine had followed behind, complete with children and luggage, ensuring another angry disagreement by then overtaking the horse-box at breakneck speed en route to the Newton-Smiths.

While this had delighted the over-excited children, it had goaded James McKinnerney into an uncharacteristic shouting match with his wife when they arrived at their destination.

Needless to say, while Sophie unloaded skittish horses from the trailer, the McKinnerneys gave a performance *par excellence* for all their gathered friends and acquaintances, ending with Sophie having a headache so bad that she went to bed at nine o'clock.

She shuddered to even think back on it now. She had

been hoping that the beautiful surroundings and casual luxury of Wynholm – the Newton-Smith residence – would work their charm on Catherine and James. A weekend somewhere different, time to relax, no distractions; it had seemed perfect.

Although, Sophie thought, while trying to ignore Alex Carver who was waving at her from a bedroom window, there seemed to be more distractions here than she had imagined. What a shame that her employers couldn't seem to get on together, even for a couple of days.

She mused over how two people could appear to hate each other, when they had obviously once been very much in love; it couldn't have been that long ago. Somewhere along the way, something had gone wrong. True, James McKinnerney had the appearance of being a little cold; but that didn't seem to be where the problem lay. Sophie sighed, and set about preparing Jasmine for Catherine's arrival.

When she did appear, Catherine was pale and withdrawn. She hardly glanced at Sophie, making it obvious that she just wanted to be off. Jasmine snorted and danced, earning a stern rebuke from her rider before they both disappeared; rather more erratically than seemed safe.

Gina's jumping lesson went well, especially once Sophie had promised that her hard work would be rewarded with something much more fun later. Jo's arrival, heralded by several small children, signalled the start of the games. A good time was then had by all as they dashed to collect beanbags and swapped ponies for relay races.

After lunch – food and entertainment by the tireless Mrs Clegg in the kitchen – Jo took the smaller children for a rest and quiet games, while Sophie supervised a horseback treasure hunt for the older ones. This turned out to be much less fun than the morning's games, mainly due to the over-competitive nature of Jeremy Newton-Smith and his whining younger sister, Tara.

'You really are hopeless at absolutely everything,' the supercilious Jeremy informed his sister. 'Whatever did I do to deserve you on my team?'

Tara, two years younger and still at the snivelling stage, muttered something about 'telling Daddy', at which point Catherine McKinnerney rode into the stable yard.

She still looked small and fragile perched on top of the snorting mare, but the cold weather had put lovely blushes of colour into her cheeks, and the chestnut hair – escaping from its hair net – hung in tendrils round her face.

'Have they managed without me?' she asked Sophie, dismounting and nodding towards the house. Sophie was tempted to reply that they always had to manage without her anyway but she stopped herself in time.

There was something about Catherine, Sophie thought, that prevented one from biting back at her, even though Catherine could be so unpleasant to others. She had a vulnerability, a sadness, that discouraged unkindness, no matter how much it was deserved.

She's very insecure, thought Sophie, definitely not as confident as she pretends to be. While this uncustomary tolerance towards her employer's failings prevailed, Sophie took Jasmine's bridle and held it while Catherine climbed down.

Tara and Jem were in full flow: his voice, raised and mocking, hers a miserable screech that set one's teeth on edge.

Catherine paused, her top lip in the familiar sneer. 'There should be a law,' she drawled, 'which decrees that children as horrible as those may be taken outside and shot.'

Sophie sighed. It was hard to have sympathy for Catherine for very long.

It was only by an enormous effort that Sophie got through the afternoon with her sanity intact. Tara and Jem argued about everything on principle, and were egged on by their contemporaries at any opportunity. Sophie was overjoyed to see Jo at four o'clock, and even more delighted to see the back of the children.

'Speak to you later,' Jo called. 'I should be free by seven. I'll come and find you.'

Sophie was sharing a room with Jo in the part of the house given over to the children. There was a playroom, bedrooms, television room, and a bathroom containing a bath so large that several children could be dunked at once.

It was into this bath that Sophie poured a large quantity of Barbie bath foam, and relaxed, groaning, into the sweet-smelling bubbles. The children were downstairs being fed by Mrs Clegg and Jo; if Sophie timed it right, she wouldn't have to have any dealings with anyone under fifteen until tomorrow.

She shampooed her hair and rinsed it in the bath, aware that she was being lazy, but aching too much to care. She thought about Jo and how long her working day was; she had been up before Sophie that morning, and wouldn't finish until past seven o'clock tonight. Sophie wondered what tales Mrs Clegg was regaling the children with, and hoped it was nothing to do with underwear.

Sophie submerged herself, her ears filling with the strange booming sound only heard underwater, so that she couldn't be sure that she had correctly heard the sound of the bedroom door, closing in the next room.

'Jo?' she called. 'Is that you?'

Almost immediately the bathroom door was flung open and Sophie saw a familiar face grinning down at her.

'Get out, Mr Carver,' she snapped, 'or I shall shout so

loud the whole house will hear, not to mention your wife.'

He shut the door behind him and looked her up and down. 'Don't be unfriendly, Sophie. We were in the middle of something the last time we met, but we were disturbed, remember?'

Sophie, determined not to let him get the better of her this time, lay where she was. All the time she stayed in the bath, the bubbles covered her; if she moved, she would be exposed and that would only encourage him.

'Get out now,' she hissed, 'or I will scream blue murder!'

'Sophie, Sophie,' he murmured, coming closer.

Fury overtook her. Pulling herself up out of the water, she stood to face him. The foam slid in shimmering blobs down her body. Her nipples, bright pink from the warmth, stood to attention in the sudden cold. Her hair hung in sinuous ringlets over her shoulders, causing tiny rivulets of water to trickle between her breasts.

Alex was visibly excited as she stepped out of the bath towards him, foam still sliding down her body. The arrogant smile told her that he thought she was finally about to succumb to his charms. Sophie felt almost sorry for him. Smiling coyly, she arranged her body in an alluring pose and opened her arms.

'Come and get me, then.'

Alex beamed at her stupidly. 'Dry yourself off, then.'

'No, I don't think so. If you want me, you can have me. Now, as I am.' She started towards him, scooping up more foam to lather across herself.

'Hold on!' Alex was backing up towards the door. 'Just dry yourself off first. This suit cost a fortune. Come on, Sophie, be reasonable!'

There was a small explosion of foam as Sophie grabbed him and pulled him to her, hard. He tried to back away but found himself up against the airing cupboard door. Sophie leered at him.

'Isn't this what you wanted? No? What did you want, then?' she reached between them to find his penis through the soggy material of his trousers. 'Did you want me to touch you? Like this?'

'Get off, Sophie! Are you mad? This jacket's worth a bomb. It'll be ruined!' He shook her free and headed for the door, slipping comically on the wet floor.

Sophie helped herself to more of the scented foam and pelted him with it. For one glorious moment he seemed to run on the spot as he negotiated a particularly slippery patch of floor, then he made it to the door and fled.

It took Sophie ages to clean the bathroom floor, but she did it happily, giggling to herself as she did so. Poor Alex didn't seem to have a lot of luck in bathrooms, she thought to herself. He would have had to go back to his room to get changed, she thought. Served him right if his wife caught him and started asking tricky questions.

'Oh Sophie!' Jo laughed when her friend related the incident later, 'I wish I had that sort of courage! I would have died!'

'Knowing him, that wouldn't have put him off,' Sophie snorted, and the two girls fell about laughing.

Mrs Clegg had retired to bed leaving Sophie, Jo, and several bottles of wine in the kitchen. It was a nice room at night. The large stove kept the room warm, while small lamps on matching Welsh dressers gave a cosy feel.

'That's my problem,' Jo sighed. 'No confidence in myself. I've done this job since I left school. I like the job – don't misunderstand me – and I'll miss it when I leave, but there aren't many opportunities to meet people.'

'You should come out with Rosie and me. Anyway, why do you say that? Are you leaving?'

Jo shrugged. 'There's been a lot of talk about Jem and Tara going away to school. I don't know whether it's true or not, but I can't say that I'd be surprised. They're getting a bit old to need a nanny, now. Anyway, it might do me good, to go somewhere different; meet new people. Do you know,' Jo leant closer over the table, as if worried that someone might overhear, 'I've never had a boyfriend!'

Sophie didn't know what to say. Jo's tone didn't make it clear whether she looked on not having a boyfriend as a virtue or a curse. Sophie tried to look non-committal.

'Not one!' cried Jo, outraged. 'And I'm not that bad, am I?'

'Jo! Of course not! There's nothing wrong with you – you're just more choosy than other people, perhaps.'

'That's not it, Sophie. I just find it hard to talk to men. Anyway, the only one who seems remotely interested is Creepy Colin – that's Mr Newton-Smith, by the way – and even then only when he's drunk. I don't think I'll ever be that desperate.'

'I'm glad to hear it. Have some more wine – drown your sorrows.'

They laughed and got steadily more tipsy, safe in the knowledge that all their duties were done for the day: the children had gone to bed too exhausted to wake before morning.

They were contemplating a second bottle of wine when there was a knock on the kitchen door. Mrs Newton-Smith appeared, looking around jumpily, as if she expected all manner of debauchery to be happening without Mrs Clegg to supervise.

Perhaps, thought Sophie, she was worried in case Mrs Clegg was here, giving us the low-down on her employer's underwear situation. She regretted the thought immediately as it conjured up the image of an enormous pair of greying knickers, making her want to giggle.

Jo had been on her feet the minute her employer appeared, as if she had been doing something she shouldn't have, but Mrs Newton-Smith seemed hardly to notice.

'Hello, girls,' she trilled, nervously. 'Glad to see you're enjoying a well-earned rest.'

When she got no reply, she coughed and hopped from one foot to the other, as if even just being in a kitchen made her uncomfortable. 'I wondered,' she chirruped insincerely, 'that is, we all wondered, if you would like to join us? Mrs Fields was saying how well you have done with all the extra work, Jo. And I know that Tara and Jeremy had a wonderful time this afternoon. So, maybe, if you aren't too tired –'

'How lovely!' Jo babbled. 'We'll just have to –'

'Marvellous!' screeched the older woman and fled, relieved, from the kitchen.

'Jo! What did you say that for? It will be horrendous. They'll all be drunk and Alex will start again.'

'I'm sorry.' Jo looked so mortified that Sophie couldn't be angry. 'She makes me nervous. I said it to get rid of her!'

'Oh, never mind,' Sophie consoled her. 'Let's go and get changed. You never know, we might find a man for you!'

Their arrival at the festivities was announced by a large woman who brayed, 'Here they are; the men of the match!'

Sophie was unsure as to whether this woman – who turned out to be Mrs Fields – was completely drunk, or merely insane. The two girls then had to endure a painful few moments of polite applause when it became obvious that they had been responsible for the enjoyment of a child-free afternoon.

Sophie, resplendent once again in the reliable dark blue dress, accepted the attention gracefully. Jo could only blush and stammer, spilling her drink and cringing painfully.

Once the excitement had died down and Jo had mopped the wine from her skirt, they were free to enjoy themselves. Sophie recognised many faces from her first night at Prospect House and was particularly pleased to see Nick and Janie Marshall. Polite inquiry ascertained that their son Paul hadn't accompanied them and that they would be travelling home that night, rather than staying the whole weekend.

'We're too old for over-nighting,' Janie confided playfully to Sophie. 'We like our own beds. Poor Nick gets quite put out waking somewhere different, don't you, dear? Disorientates him, poor old soul!'

Sophie suspected that the truth was that they could only take so much of their hosts, and for that she couldn't blame them. Mr Newton-Smith – Creepy Colin – was in frighteningly high spirits; it was comical to see his guests trying to avoid him, and failing.

Sophie's own employers were pointedly ignoring one another, James favouring an uncomfortable-looking stance by the fireplace while Catherine held court on a sofa by tall bookshelves. Catherine's demeanour had undergone a dramatic change from earlier: her eyes danced, her skin glowed, and her chestnut-coloured hair shone like lovingly polished copper.

As Sophie glanced across at her, Catherine threw back her head and laughed at something Alex Carver had said. Sophie couldn't remember seeing her laugh like that before and it seemed out of character.

'She's very beautiful, isn't she?' Jo remarked, following Sophie's gaze. 'Look at the way James watches her, as if he doesn't want to, but he can't help it.'

James seemed to become more erect and uncomfortable the more Catherine relaxed. His pretence at holding a conversation with Nick Marshall was laughable; his eyes kept straying across to his wife. When Catherine leant across to touch Alex Carver's arm, James seemed to hold his breath; when she relaxed back on to the sofa, he gulped his drink down with a pained and frantic look.

'We're not going to find a man for you here, are we?'

113

Sophie joked to Jo. 'Not unless your esteemed employer gets his hands on you.'

'Ugh!' Jo shuddered. 'If he doesn't it won't be through lack of trying! Don't look now but here comes someone who fits the bill much better.'

Sophie looked up to see Catherine's brother, Dominic, slide into the room as if he were gate-crashing.

'Oh great,' muttered Sophie. 'That's all we need.'

'I think he's lovely,' Jo breathed, 'really handsome. He's an actor, you know.'

'Why is he always hanging around at Prospect House, then?'

'I've heard he's resting at the moment,' said Jo, airily.

'Honestly! You're so gullible. That's what all two-bit actors say when they can't get the work. It doesn't change the fact that he's rude, arrogant and thinks he's God's gift to women,' Sophie scoffed. 'Get a grip on yourself, Jo, he's coming over.'

'Sophie! What a lovely surprise. Hello – Jo, isn't it?' He beamed at them both.

Jo tried to stutter a reply, then gave up, much to Dominic's obvious amusement.

'I have that effect on women,' he said with a grin, 'I render them speechless.'

'She's just got an olive stuck in her throat, I expect,' Sophie told him, patting Jo on the back.

He laughed. 'Well, it's nice to see you without the jodhpurs, Sophie. Catch you later.' He winked at them and sailed off to join his sister.

'Sophie! Why did you say that? Fancy telling him I had an olive stuck in my throat. What's he going to think?' Jo had recovered from her speechlessness.

'He'll think you like olives. Do calm down, Jo. It's not that important, is it?'

'In case you hadn't noticed, he's the only eligible one here.'

'Not as far as Catherine is concerned,' Sophie nodded

across to where Catherine was now head to head with Alex Carver. Whatever they were discussing was either very serious or very private; their giggles indicated the latter. Opposite Catherine and Alex, Marcie Carver sat, keeping a watchful eye on her husband.

'It must be awful,' Jo said, sloshing more wine into her glass, 'not to be able to trust your husband.'

'Or your wife,' Sophie agreed, looking at James.

The party seemed to be breaking up. The Marshalls had left some time before, Marcie was trying to reclaim her husband and the Fields were making much of their retirement.

'Don't drink too much,' Mrs Fields brayed at the two girls. 'The brats will expect you in peak condition tomorrow.'

'Bloody cheek,' muttered Sophie. 'She's drunk enough to sink a battleship. The only reason she's still standing is because she's leaning on him.'

'She's right, though,' Jo said, putting down her glass. 'I've got to be up early again tomorrow. Are you coming or staying?'

'I'll come.'

Back in their room Sophie generously gave Jo first use of the shared bathroom and settled down on her bed with a magazine. A noise at the door made her get cautiously to her feet and, fearing Alex had returned, she rolled the magazine into a handy baton; she was determined not to let him get through the door this time.

The shuffling, whispering noises continued, so after several seconds Sophie threw caution to the wind and flung the door open. Alex and Catherine plummeted through, obviously having been indulging in a spot of foreplay right outside her bedroom door.

Sophie stared down at them. They were both drunk and dishevelled, suggesting that the courtship was well advanced. Alex was the first to his feet, leaving Catherine to struggle gamely on her own on the floor.

'Well,' leered Alex, 'we meet again, Sophie.'

She glared at him. 'What a coincidence.'

Catherine staggered to her feet. 'What does she mean by that? What do you mean?' she slurred at Sophie.

'Look' – Sophie's patience was wearing thin – 'the children are asleep in those rooms. If you wake them up, we'll never get them back to sleep and we will all be up for the rest of the night.'

'Not me,' muttered Catherine, smiling blearily at Alex. 'She's right, though. Let's find somewhere else.'

They started up the corridor, Catherine having to be held upright by Alex as they wove their way past the rooms of sleeping children. Sophie felt helpless. It was not her place to interfere, but Catherine was surely too drunk to know what she was doing.

What should she do? Sophie was about to run after them when a door opened further down the landing and Marcie Carver stood like an avenging angel, framed in the light behind her.

'Did I hear Alex?'

Sophie nodded miserably, and pointed. This was turning out to be just what she had been trying to avoid.

'Right!'

Sophie, anxious to prevent any real nastiness, set off to catch up with Catherine, while Marcie, pausing only to throw a robe over her silk slip, followed closely behind.

'There you are!' Marcie's voice, though not loud, stopped Alex in his tracks.

Which was probably as well, thought Sophie, considering where those tracks seemed to be leading.

'Come on,' she said gently to Catherine, 'let's find your room.'

'I don't want to find my room,' Catherine whined. 'James is in there.'

'Let's go and get you some coffee then,' Sophie said, taking her arm. 'That will make you feel better.'

116

'I don't want coffee. Don't take me to my room. I don't want to go. You can't make me. I won't go.'

Sophie was getting exasperated. 'All right then, come to my room; anywhere but here.'

'I'll come to your room,' Alex leered.

'Alex!' Marcie was trying, unsuccessfully, to drag him away.

'You stay out of my room,' Sophie snapped before she could stop herself. 'You go in there again and you'll be sorry.'

There was a prolonged silence, while they all took in the implications of this statement; then Sophie was aware of everybody starting to talk at once. Marcie was snarling something at her, while Alex denied all knowledge of what she was talking about. Catherine had started to snivel so it was with profound relief that Sophie saw James coming to join the fray.

He looked gravely at the four of them before taking Catherine firmly by the arm. 'Excuse my wife,' he said with his customary politeness, 'but she doesn't seem to be quite herself at the moment. Could you lend a hand, Sophie? Excellent.'

Together they propelled Catherine up the hall to her own room, leaving Marcie and Alex still arguing behind them, although this time Sophie could hear her own name being hissed instead of her employer's.

Catherine seemed to be in a daze, which made getting her back to her room relatively easy. Once there it was a different matter and she became belligerent and angry, convinced that James had dragged her away in the middle of the party.

'How dare you?' she kept shouting, despite his patient assurances that the party had ended some time ago.

'Should I get some coffee?' Sophie asked.

'Would you mind? Thank you, Sophie.'

'I don't want any coffee,' she heard Catherine snarling as she closed the door behind her.

Back along the hall a muted but angry row was proceeding unchecked in the Carver's rooms.

'You're so suspicious of me,' Sophie heard Alex say, as if Marcie was being utterly unreasonable.

'And you are a practised liar,' Marcie shouted back. 'So don't be too surprised if I don't believe you.'

Sophie's nerves were shattered. Why, she wondered, did they come to these parties, knowing full well what the likely consequences would be? There was a sort of masochism about it all; everyone knowing it would end in tears, but going ahead regardless.

Sophie crept into the kitchen to make coffee. Half the house still seemed to be awake and rebuking the other half for misbehaviour, real or imagined, that had occurred that evening. It was, Sophie thought, how one imagined a bedlam to have been.

'And another thing!' Marcie's voice exploded through the door of her room as Sophie passed by in the corridor, nearly dropping the tray of coffee things in alarm.

Somehow, Sophie made it shakily back to the McKinnerneys' rooms. Inside, Catherine was more agitated than ever, refusing to put on the nightdress which James was holding and insisting that she wouldn't drink the coffee.

'Ah, Sophie,' James sighed, with obvious relief, throwing the nightdress over a chair, 'thank you so much.'

'You can't make me drink that,' Catherine slurred. 'I don't drink coffee; it poisons the system.'

'Ten gin-and-tonics don't exactly have a cleansing effect,' James snapped, before turning away, crossly.

'Don't shout at me,' Catherine wailed. 'You shouldn't shout at me!'

'I'm sorry.' He looked worn down and old; Sophie felt sorry for him. 'You're right, I shouldn't have shouted. Sophie, would you mind giving me a hand? Bit of a cheek, I know, but I can't really ask anyone else . . .'

Between them they managed to get Catherine's shoes off, much to her renewed fury.

'Get off me! What do you think you're doing?'

'Catherine, be reasonable. You can't go to bed like that.'

'Go to bed? Who said anything about going to bed? Get off! How dare you? Who do you think you are?'

'Sophie is trying to help.'

'Trying to help, is she? Miss Goody-Two-Shoes! She's always trying to help! Helped herself to the gardener, didn't she? Probably help herself to you, too, given half a chance.'

Sophie was aware that she was blushing bright red, but she kept her head down and hoped that James wouldn't notice. How did Catherine know about Callum? she wondered. And how much more of Sophie's private life had come under her scrutiny?

'Come on, Catherine, for Heaven's sake! You're going to wake the children.'

'Oh no, we mustn't wake the children, must we? Oh no, not that. What are you doing now? Oh no you don't! Not my dress . . .'

James held her arms while Sophie slipped the black dress down. A bit of inspired teamwork meant that James had the nightdress over Catherine's head before she knew what was happening.

'I'm not wearing that! That's not mine! Take it off! I don't wear a nightdress.'

James patience was monumental. Sophie had only admiration for the way he handled his wife. It was a struggle, but they got her into bed at last. James managed to persuade her to drink a cup of coffee before she fell into a mumbling, restless sleep.

James heaved a sigh of relief and beckoned Sophie to follow him on to the balcony. It was bitingly cold outside but, ever the gentleman, Sophie's employer found a blanket to drape around her shoulders. Producing a bottle of brandy and some glasses, he proceeded to pour them a large measure each.

'Cheers,' he said, miserably. 'We earned this.'

They drank in uncomfortable silence for a few minutes, then James poured out some more.

'Thanks, Sophie,' he said quietly.

'No problem.'

'It is a problem, though, isn't it? It wasn't always like this, you know. We were very settled once. With a bit of luck we may be again – if you can bear to stay with us until then, that is.'

Sophie felt like saying that she would stay as long as she was needed – such was the loyalty she was starting to feel to this man – but her common sense stopped her in time. Who could tell how much worse things could get before they got better? Assuming things are going to get better, she thought. Somehow she doubted it.

'I can cope,' Sophie told him, noncommittally.

'I'm just sorry that you had to witness all that.'

'I've seen worse.'

'Have you?' he suddenly looked brighter, as if the fact that Sophie had seen worse behaviour was cause for optimism. 'Bit unnecessary to bring old Callum into it, though,' he muttered.

Sophie felt herself blush again. 'I didn't know ... I mean ... well ...'

'Oh please, Sophie! I beg your pardon! I didn't mean to pry. Heavens! Not my business at all.' He was blushing worse than she, and they both gave a forced laugh at their mutual embarrassment.

'As long as there's no house rule about it,' Sophie mumbled, trying to alleviate the tension. 'I wouldn't want to, you know ...'

'Lord, no!' James waved his glass in the air. 'Nice for you to have friends your own age. Can't be much fun for you; stuck in the middle of nowhere and us arguing our heads off.'

120

The brandy had warmed Sophie through; she felt secluded and comfortable wrapped in the thick blanket, talking to James. She watched, mesmerised, as he swirled the liquid round in his glass, gulped it down, then poured another.

'He's a good chap,' he said suddenly.

Sophie, her mind elsewhere, was caught off guard. 'Sorry?'

'Callum. A good chap.'

'Yes,' she said, thinking of their recent disagreement, and feeling sad, 'he is.'

James seemed lost in thought, as if he had forgotten Sophie was there and was talking to himself. 'The trouble is that we all try to be good chaps. Try to do the right thing, give someone what they want. Then, of course, when they've got it, they don't want it any more. Sometimes it's very hard being a good chap.'

Sophie felt immensely touched; this was the longest speech she had ever heard James make. It was obvious that he had been brought up to hide his feelings, so for him to make such a declaration to Sophie seemed totally out of character, and all the more moving. If James McKinnerney had asked her at that moment for an assurance that she would stay, Sophie would have given it gladly.

'Sorry, Sophie,' he said before she could voice her feelings, 'I don't mean to blather on, especially when you've been so good already.'

'We all need someone to talk to,' she said quietly.

'You are very easy to talk to,' he mumbled, struggling with the words. 'How can I put it? You are too easy to talk to; perhaps I say things I shouldn't, you see.'

'We all do that sometimes.'

'Just seems, you know, disloyal, somehow.'

'I would never repeat our conversations to anyone. I just wish I could help you more. I don't know what is at the bottom of Catherine's unhappiness – she wouldn't tell me even if she knew herself – but that doesn't automatically make it your fault.'

He had placed his glass beside his chair and held his head in both hands. Sophie edged closer. She wanted to comfort him in some way. If it had been anyone else she would have put an arm around their shoulders or held their hand, but this man seemed so untouchable.

'People change,' she told him, quietly, 'and not always for the better. Sometimes what you think you want is not the thing that will make you happy.'

He raised his head and smiled at her. 'Has anyone ever told you that you have an old head on young shoulders? I am sorry to burden you like this.'

'It's not a burden, really. I wish I had some way of helping you, that's all.'

'I don't think anyone can help us at the moment; we must try to help ourselves.' He stood and swallowed the rest of his drink. 'Now I must get some shut-eye. I am truly exhausted.'

Sophie tried to hide her disappointment. She could have happily stayed there talking to James all night. Finishing her brandy, she rose too, wearily. She was just about to enter the room where Catherine slept when she felt James take her arm and hold her back.

'Many, many thanks for your kindness, Sophie. I don't know what I would have done without you tonight. I sincerely hope you do stay and aren't put off by all our silliness. It would be terrible to lose you.'

Sophie felt frozen in time. She didn't know what to say, transfixed as she was by the earnest blue eyes and the closeness of the generous mouth.

What would it be like to kiss him, she wondered. I could; I'm close enough. What would he do? Would he pull away? Or would he respond? Her knees felt stiff and her heart seemed to be beating very loudly, as she fought to find something appropriate to say. When she did speak, her voice was unexpectedly husky.

'You won't lose me,' was all she said.

James smiled, seemingly oblivious to the turmoil of emotions he was causing in her. He slid his hand down her arm, to hold her hand lightly.

'Whoever gets you will be a lucky man,' he told her, before holding open the door back into his and his wife's bedroom.

Catherine was fast asleep, the peevish look gone from her face now she was unconscious. She looked very young in the white cotton nightdress, her long hair spread out across the pillow. James looked down at her with a tired expression and frowned.

'I seem to remember thinking how lucky I was when Catherine and I got married,' he said. 'Things are rarely what they seem, are they?' And he showed Sophie back out into the hall.

Chapter Seven

Sophie forked hay into the last corner of the loose box and stood back to admire her handiwork. It seemed strange to take pleasure from the gruesome task of mucking out, she thought, but when she glanced over the half-door to see clean straw and full hay nets, she knew it was a job well done. Better still was bringing the horses back into their respective stables and seeing their reaction. Sophie shut the door of Jasmine's box and leant over to watch the mare.

Jasmine examined everything minutely, like a particularly fussy housewife; then, with a relieved sigh, she dropped into the thick straw bed and rolled happily.

Sophie smiled and turned to place the pitchfork and shovel on top of the wheelbarrow. Now that was out of the way she felt she had earned a shower and breakfast, assuming there was any left.

Stowing the tools round the back of the stable block where she had found them, Sophie was surprised to hear an engine start up. She was even more surprised when Catherine's car went down the drive at a speed suggesting some urgency. It couldn't, surely, be Catherine driving; for Sophie was convinced that this morning her employer would have the hangover to end them all.

She herself was regretting at least two of the brandies she had drunk with James. Restlessness had kept her awake most of the night and got her up early this morning.

Sophie trudged back to the house, glancing at the ominously dark sky. It was due to pour down, she thought. Still, Gina would be pleased: no jumping lesson. Then Sophie remembered the indoor ring and her heart went out to the child.

After a quick shower, Sophie was glad to find Mrs Clegg in the kitchen, still turning out vast quantities of food.

'You were out and about early this morning, dear,' she said approvingly, handing Sophie a huge breakfast. Nodding at the loaded plate, she added, 'Must look after the workers!'

Sophie experienced a moment of queasiness before her hunger kicked in and she went to sit with Jo, who was staring gloomily at her toast.

'What's up with you? Got a hangover?'

'It's going to be wet weather,' Jo informed her, miserably. 'Can you imagine? All those brats. Indoors. All day. And yes, thanks for your concern, a hangover, too. Anyway,' she sat up suspiciously, 'where were you last night?'

'Being helpful.' Sophie had no wish to discuss the previous night's antics in front of Mrs Clegg. It was unnecessary caution; the housekeeper made it her duty to know everything that went on in the house; even if it happened when she was asleep. Especially if it happened when she was asleep, in fact.

'Mrs McKinnerney!' she thundered, banging a plate on the table so hard that a loose sausage somersaulted through the air to be deftly caught by Megan the spaniel.

The two girls froze in surprise at this unexpected

outburst while Megan, who had waited all her life for an opportunity such as this, made good her escape.

'Mrs McKinnerney,' Mrs Clegg said again, shaking her head. 'Drunk as a lord!' She bent down to whisper to Sophie. 'What is she thinking of? And Dr Carver should know better.'

She went back to the stove while the two friends exchanged glances. Jo's eyes were like saucers.

'Is it true?' she mouthed to Sophie. Sophie nodded.

'Mrs Newton-Smith says to me this morning, "Take her a tray, Mrs C. She's not very well, poor dear." Trays!' Mrs Clegg was outraged at the very idea. 'Trays, indeed! I said to her, "Now you look here! I've enough to do without your trays!" You start with trays and where does it end? One gets a tray, they all want a tray!'

Sophie tried not to look at Jo, who was waving her toast about, excitedly.

'Quite right, Mrs C. Put your foot down. Trays today, full breakfast in bed tomorrow!'

Mrs Clegg shuddered. 'Breakfast in bed? Never! Over my dead body! Crumbs in the beds! Marmalade on the sheets! And what Mr Newton-Smith does with a boiled egg is nobody's business.' Mrs Clegg had to sit down.

Jo patted her hand. 'Don't worry, Mrs Clegg, I'm sure Mrs Newton-Smith won't mention trays again. You've seen her off.'

Sophie was struck by a thought. 'If Catherine is still in bed, who took her car just now?'

'Mr McKinnerney,' Mrs Clegg said firmly. She didn't hold with calling employers by their first names. 'He said he had business. Urgent business.'

'On a Sunday?'

'If you ask me,' Mrs Clegg confided, pulling herself to her feet, 'he just couldn't face anyone after his wife's disgraceful performance.'

Sophie thought hard. Maybe Mrs Clegg was right and James McKinnerney couldn't face anyone. Or perhaps, she reasoned, he just couldn't face her; Sophie. Maybe he had said more than he intended to last night, and was feeling a little ashamed of himself.

'Did he get a phone call?' she asked. 'About the urgent business?'

'Well, no,' Mrs Clegg looked puzzled, 'now you come to mention it, I don't think he did. But, then, you see, he may have one of those mobiles that they all seem to have. It must have been very urgent, though; he didn't even pack a bag.'

Sophie kept her head down on the pretence of doing justice to her breakfast. She hoped she was wrong and James really had just been called away but she suspected otherwise. If she was right, he would have to face her sometime. And anyway, he hadn't said anything out of turn last night, just been a little more open than was usual for him.

Sophie sighed. Why did everything have to be so complicated? She thought fondly of Callum, and his down-to-earth approach to life, vowing that her first priority when they returned to Prospect House would be to sort out her differences with him. 'Thank you, Mrs Clegg,' she said, pushing her plate away. 'That was just the job.'

'I wish I could eat huge breakfasts like that,' said Jo, ruefully.

'I don't know why you don't,' Mrs Clegg told her. 'You should; a growing girl like you. You can't survive on toast.'

Jo rolled her eyes at Sophie. 'Because, Mrs C, it goes straight to my hips. And stays there.'

'Nonsense! You carry it well. Besides, men like big women.'

'They don't, Mrs C. That's a rumour put about by thin women so that they continue to get all the men.'

'Rubbish! Go and get yourself some bacon and eggs; there's plenty left upstairs. Too much, for my liking . . .'

'Not a chance.' Jo got to her feet. 'Anyway, I've got things to do.'

'And I'd better get Gina for her jumping lesson,' Sophie sighed. 'I'll make it a quick one today. It's not as if Catherine is going to check up on us.'

Mrs Clegg snorted and went to clear the dining room.

'I was thinking,' Sophie told Jo, 'why don't we organise some games indoors for the kids? Things they can all play: hide-and-seek, charades, blind man's bluff. Stuff like that?'

'I think we're going to have to,' Jo said glancing out of the window as the first heavy drops of rain began to fall. 'The little ones may have trouble with charades, but we can sort something out. Are you free to help? Brilliant! Thanks, Sophie. See you later.'

'We're going to play games later,' Gina informed Sophie as she led her pony into the covered ring. 'Are you going to come?'

'Why not? Will I enjoy these games?'

'Oh yes,' Gina predicted with all the confidence of a six-year-old. 'You'll enjoy them very much. Do you know any games?'

'Hide-and-seek.' Sophie helped Gina adjust her stirrups. 'Sardines.'

'Sardines?'

'It's a bit like hide-and-seek. I'll explain later. For now, show me a nice sitting trot over the poles while I set up some proper jumps for you.'

Gina chatted away happily, not in the least resentful, this morning, to be having a lesson while the other children played.

'I like it here,' the little girl confided. 'There's walls all round so nobody can say, "I was watching you from the house and you weren't doing it right." If I don't do it right, there's only you to see, and you don't shout.'

'So who shouts at you if you don't do it right?'

'Mummy.'

That figures, Sophie thought. 'I expect she's got a lot on her mind,' she told the child. 'Grown-ups often shout without meaning to.'

'She has got a lot on her mind,' Gina sighed. 'But really it's Daddy I feel sorry for.'

Me too, Sophie silently agreed. 'Don't worry about Daddy,' she said, gently. 'He's all right.'

'Well, he is now.' Gina reined in beside her, and Sophie was alarmed to see that the little girl's eyes were full of tears. 'But what about if Mummy leaves him? What then?'

Sophie lifted her down and cuddled her. 'Why do you think that's going to happen?'

Gina was sobbing now. 'Because I heard her say, when she was on the phone once, that she would leave him tomorrow if she only had the money. I hope she never gets any money.'

Sophie didn't know what to say. She patted Gina's heaving back until the sobs subsided, then found a hanky for her. 'You know, grown-ups often say things they don't mean, just because they're angry.'

'She meant it,' Gina said sadly. 'I'm sure.'

The atmosphere for the rest of the morning was strained. Sophie tried to make Gina laugh but failed miserably. When they parted company it was a relief for Sophie and she hoped that the presence of the other children would cheer Gina up before the games.

At lunch time Sophie found herself alone in the kitchen and able to mull over her own thoughts, something she wasn't able to do with Gina around. She wondered whether Catherine had been serious about leaving James. Whether she had or not, it was a cruel thing to say in front of Gina. Unless, of course, Gina had been eavesdropping again; it wouldn't be the first time. Sophie wondered who Catherine had been talking to on the phone when Gina overheard.

She picked at her lunch, broodily. No matter which way you looked at it; it wasn't good news. At the very least she could be out of a job soon. At worst, Sophie imagined a long drawn-out divorce, anger and accusations on both sides, and – at the end of it all – she would still be out of work.

Sophie felt selfish worrying about her job. After all, not so long ago, she was talking about leaving anyway. The real victims in all this were likely to be the children; they had no choice in the proceedings.

First things first, she thought. Get this weekend over with. Get everyone settled back at the house. Talk to Callum, see what he thinks. And Jean might have heard something. If things don't look too good, I can always get the job recruitment papers the next time I go into town. The idea of starting again with job applications didn't fill her with joy, but the very process of making a decision – no matter how tentative – made her feel better, and she finished her lunch quickly.

She went and found Jo, who had settled the younger children down for a rest before they launched into the full-blown games of the afternoon.

'You look exhausted already!'

'I'll just bet I do! You try playing I-Spy with such a variety of ages! It took me what felt like hours to persuade Ellie to stick to the usual wording of the game. She kept saying, "I-Spy with my little eye, something beginning with cushion." Still, it sped the game up!'

They laughed and went to supervise the older children who were enjoying a relatively quiet game of charades in the playroom.

'Have you seen Catherine yet?' Sophie asked Jo. 'I need to know what time she's intending to leave.'

'The last I heard, she still hadn't surfaced.'

The charades got noisier and noisier until the smaller children woke, and then the clamour for hide-and-seek began. After a few ground rules had been laid about which rooms were out of bounds, the participants set off, Ellie announcing her intention of hiding under a beanbag in the playroom.

'That's one I won't lose then,' laughed Jo, as she and Sophie stayed behind to count to fifty. 'Shall we just leave them hiding and go for a coffee?'

The little ones were easy to find. Ellie, unsurprisingly, was right where she had said she would be, although Sophie and Jo feigned amazement at such an unexpected hiding place. The older children were more imaginative; Jem, having climbed high into a linen closet, was declared the winner.

With Jem and Ellie next 'on', everyone else, Sophie included, bounded off in search of the ultimate hiding place. Racing through the house, Sophie came upon a double-doored cupboard, and paused to investigate. It appeared to be in use to house cleaning supplies, no doubt so that Mrs Clegg didn't have to trek back down to the kitchen every time she needed polish or dusters.

How thoughtful her employers were, Sophie smirked, climbing in amongst the dustpans. She pulled the door closed behind her and settled down in the fusty darkness. She didn't have long to wait; footsteps hurried up the corridor and paused at the door of the cupboard. Sophie shrank back. Anyone opening the wrong door wouldn't see her and there was always the chance that she could remain undetected even though, technically, the cupboard had been searched.

She held her breath. The pounding of her heart must surely give her away, it seemed so loud. No matter how old she got, the thrill of hide-and-seek remained the same as it had been when she was five years old; the excitement of concealment and the dread of being caught were almost more than she could bear.

It seemed ages since the footsteps had stopped outside her door. Was the seeker still there? Or had they crept off, unheard by her straining ears? Impossible, Sophie thought. They are still there, wondering where to look next.

She wanted to peep through the keyhole but fear of knocking over a clattering dustpan, and giving the game away, stopped her. At that moment the door was flung open, flooding the half of the cupboard next to Sophie with light. She shrank even further back and screwed her eyes up against the sudden brightness, hoping not to be detected. Instead of closing the door and leaving, or opening Sophie's door, the figure quickly climbed into the cupboard and pulled the door closed.

Sophie didn't know what to do. She hadn't seen clearly who entered, although it was obviously one of the bigger children. Still, she didn't want to scare them.

'Hello,' she whispered. 'It's me, Sophie. Who's that?'

'Hello, Sophie. It's me, Alex.'

'Alex! Get out, now!'

'I thought anyone could play.'

'Not you.'

'Jem said I could play.'

'Well he didn't ask me first, so you can't.' They were both talking in whispers: Sophie hissing angrily, Alex jovial.

'Oh, go on! Let me play.'

'No. Anyway, this is my hiding place – find your own.' Sophie couldn't believe what she was saying to Alex. She sounded, even to her own ears, like a petulant six-year-old. At that moment small footfalls pattered up the hall and carried on towards the stairs. The two fell silent for a few moments, then Alex spoke again.

'Do you think we've won the game?'

'Not yet. Sit tight for a while.'

'My pleasure.' His hand met hers in the darkness. 'Fancy livening this game up a little?'

Sophie snatched her hand away. 'You never learn, do you? What are you doing in here, anyway? Don't tell me it was coincidence, because I won't believe you.'

132

'All right, I won't, then. I saw you hide in the cupboard and shamelessly followed you.'

'I'm surprised that you're allowed out on your own after last night.'

'Last night? Oh, I can't be held responsible for that,' he said, airily. 'I was drunk.'

'That's no excuse.'

'It's the best excuse. Shh!'

Several pairs of feet trotted up the corridor. Ellie's voice drifted through the door. 'I expect she's under the beanbag in the playroom.' The footsteps trotted on.

Alex's hand crept across the divide again, nearly poking Sophie in the eye.

'Alex! Pack it in.'

'Come on, Sophie. You know how I feel about you. How about some encouragement?'

Sophie sighed. He was so predictable, it was almost sad. 'You don't need any encouragement. Anyway, you're married and I'm not interested.'

'I won't be married forever,' he said, sadly. 'Marcie's divorcing me; or so she says.'

'I can't say I blame her.'

'So,' he said, suddenly cheery again, 'you won't have to worry about my wife for much longer.'

'Alex, I won't have to worry about her at all, because I'm not interested in you. I can't help feeling I've made that as clear as crystal.'

There was a moment's silence while this fact filtered into Alex's brain. Then he decided to ignore it. 'Give me your hand, Sophie, go on! I've got a surprise for you. Feel this.'

Sophie recoiled. 'You must be joking! Get off me before you get a surprise of your own. I mean it, now! If you touch me again, I'm going to your wife. Then I'm going to Mr McKinnerney.'

'He's gone home,' he snapped, angry at being rejected yet again, 'so he's no good to you.'

'I'll make a point of telling him the minute we get back.'

Alex chuckled and moved closer. 'He'd love that, banning me from the house. He's been dying to do that, anyway, only he has to keep up appearances, doesn't he? Stiff upper lip, and nothing else. Can't satisfy his wife himself so he worries that someone else will. What both you and Catherine need is a real man.'

He braced his hands either side of her as she backed against the wall of the cupboard. She just had time to feel his erection digging into her belly before the cupboard door was flung open.

'She's here!'

'We found Sophie!'

'You won! You won!'

'Oh look! And Dr Carver, too! Hello, Dr Carver.'

Alex stumbled back in the sudden turmoil of light and noise, upsetting several buckets, and fumbling with his trousers.

'Good hiding place,' cried Gina, her earlier traumas forgotten. 'You're on, now. Can I be on with you?'

They played the game without incident for the rest of the afternoon, Sophie being careful not to give Alex the chance to get her alone again. She needn't have worried as, after several meaningful looks and hissed asides which she totally ignored, he sloped off to join the adults, leaving her in peace. Eventually, the children started to bicker. Jo suggested quieter games and they all returned to the playroom, happy to watch videos and draw.

One by one, various parents appeared to claim their offspring and to thank Jo and Sophie for their efforts. Everyone seemed subdued and bleary after the previous night's excesses, and Sophie was just considering going to prepare the horses for their return journey home, when Catherine walked into the playroom.

'Mummy!' Gina leapt up, closely followed by a yawning Ellie.

'Hello, girls. Have you had a nice time?' Catherine looked pale and drawn, but otherwise seemed none the worse for wear. The girls danced round her, making her smile, wanly. 'So, are we ready to go home? See how Peter's doing? And Jean.'

'And Daddy,' Gina yelled, making Catherine wince. 'I want to see Daddy! I want to tell him about hide-and-seek.'

'I hid under a beanbag,' Ellie said, proudly.

'And I found Sophie, didn't I Sophie? And she had the best hiding place, ever.'

'Did she, darling?' Catherine was avoiding Sophie's eyes, continuing to smile woodenly at her daughters. Sophie had a terrible sense of foreboding.

'Yes she did, she was in a cupboard! With all the brooms and buckets! And we couldn't find her for ages! And when we did, we found Dr Carver, too!'

The smile seemed to freeze on Catherine's face. Afterwards, Sophie seemed to remember Jo covering her face with her hands, while she herself felt like crying.

When Catherine spoke it was through clenched teeth. 'Could I have a word with you, Sophie?' Her lips hardly moved.

She'd make a great ventriloquist, Sophie thought, feeling light-headed, as she followed Catherine out of the room and down the hall. She wasn't afraid of anything Catherine would say, she just felt resigned to what she knew would be a good dressing-down, even though it was thoroughly undeserved. She had scant time to decide that she would not take it lying down, when Catherine turned on her heel and marched them both into the bedroom she had been sharing with James.

Sophie closed the door behind her and turned to face her employer.

'Well?' Catherine's face was white and furious. 'What have you got to say for yourself?'

'There's nothing to say.' Sophie crossed her arms

defiantly. 'It's not the first time he's bothered me. The very night I arrived at Prospect House he came on to me, and Mr McKinnerney sorted it out.'

'Did he?' Catherine's face was pinched and spiteful. 'And I don't suppose you did anything to encourage him, did you?'

'I didn't actually. I was trying to get away from him, if you must know.'

Catherine's eyes flashed, dangerously. 'You really expect me to believe that, do you? You can't leave any of them alone, can you? Callum. James. Alex.'

Sophie was furious. 'How dare you! Your husband only has eyes for you, in case you hadn't noticed. I have never encouraged Alex – it's not me who goes around chasing married men! And as for Callum, what I do in my spare time – '

'Are you implying something in that statement?' Catherine looked more menacing than Sophie had ever imagined possible.

'What, about Callum?'

'About married men. Because if you're saying what I think you're saying, you are making a very dangerous accusation.'

Sophie was exasperated. 'What exactly is the problem here? That Alex came on to me? That Gina noticed? I am not the one you should be angry with – Alex Carver is the villain of the piece. If you want to sack me, go ahead and do it – I just don't care any more.'

'Oh no. I don't think it will come to that.' Catherine's smile was evil as she turned to open the door. 'Anyway, you don't get out of it that easily. I've got plans for you.' And before Sophie could think what she meant by that ominous statement, she was standing in the hallway, the door firmly closed behind her.

She had one more port of call before she went to sort out the horses. Marching down the corridor, she rapped hard on the Carvers' door, hoping that he would be alone. She was in luck.

'Sophie! What a lovely surprise. Come in.'

'You must be joking. All I've come to say is that you nearly lost me my job this afternoon – '

'Sophie, I didn't – '

'I haven't finished yet. You almost lost me my job. Actually, I don't care very much about it at the moment, but what really riles me is that it's all a game to you. You seem to think that my feelings don't matter. That you can just take whatever you want. That when I say "no", I mean "maybe".'

'But – '

'Shut up and listen. If you come near me again you will be very, very sorry.'

'Threats, Sophie?' he laughed arrogantly. 'What are you going to do – tell your precious employer?'

'I've thought about that,' said Sophie, smiling sweetly.

'He won't do anything. He doesn't like unpleasantness.'

'I'm going to tell your wife all about you.'

There was a pause while he took this in, then he laughed again. 'She already knows all about me – that's why she wants a divorce.'

'No, you don't understand. What I meant was I'll tell her and everyone else about you. In court. At the divorce proceedings. Dish the dirt on her behalf, so to speak. Not nice for a doctor to be seen as a womaniser, really, is it?'

Alex was looking a little pale. 'You wouldn't!'

'Try me!' Sophie turned on her heel and was about to walk away, when she thought of something. Alex was still holding the door open with a shocked look on his face. 'By the way,' she told him, cheerfully, 'the reason I wouldn't bother to tell James is not because I don't think he would help – he would. The reason is that he has enough on his mind without worrying about stupid little problems like you.'

Alex regained his composure and sneered, nastily. 'You think he's so wonderful, don't you? Well, Sophie dear, things are not always what they seem. If he's half the man you think he is, why can't he keep a woman happy?'

He was still shouting down the hall after her when she slammed the door of her and Jo's room and began to pack her bags. It didn't take long, so, dreading another confrontation of any kind, she sneaked down the stairs and through the kitchen.

'Oh, there you are,' Mrs Clegg boomed, making Sophie feel weak with fright. 'There's a message for you. Mrs McKinnerney' – she said the words as if they were poison on her lips – 'has gone home in a taxi, with the children. She wants you to follow them later – her exact words were "when she can tear herself away" – with the horses and luggage.'

Sophie sighed. 'Thanks, Mrs Clegg.'

Mrs Clegg was watching her keenly. 'Now what's all that about, I wonder?' She was obviously hoping that Sophie would be able to enlighten her.

'Don't ask me, Mrs Clegg. I'm just the idiot that gets caught in the middle of it all.'

Mrs Clegg nodded, sympathetically; she understood that perfectly. 'Never mind, dear. You go and sort out all your jobs. I'll have us a nice pot of tea ready for when you've finished.'

Sophie felt weary. There was no point loading the horses into the box until the very last minute as they would only start to fret. She went to sort out the McKinnerney's luggage and was irritated to find that Catherine had only half-packed James's bag. Presumably because he had gone and left her and the children, she had decided not to bother.

Well, the buck stops here, thought Sophie. I suppose I'm the last one in this chain of responsibility. The dogs-body's dogsbody. Well aware that this wasn't her job –

and vowing to herself to start looking for another the very next day – Sophie began to wander listlessly round the room, half-heartedly throwing items into James's hold-all.

Even the thought of a pot of tea and – if she was lucky – some of Mrs Clegg's homemade scones didn't make the job any more appealing. Sophie emptied drawers and checked wardrobes with growing resentment. Catherine had packed all her own things carefully, leaving only James's.

Probably didn't like the thought of me going through her stuff, thought Sophie. Or couldn't trust me to do it properly; as if I didn't have enough to do.

Everything appeared to be in James's bag. Sophie struggled with the zip. Why was it that zips always became impossible to close on return journeys? she wondered. Even if the bag contained exactly the same items of clothing as on the outward trip, it would still be difficult to fasten.

. She struggled crossly for a while, then dragged out a sweater. That would have to go in with Catherine's, she thought, flopping down on the bed. She let herself relax for a moment, trying to shake the depression that seemed to be creeping gradually over her. Slowly, experimentally, she lifted the sweater to her face. It smelt of James. Not an unpleasant smell, but definitely of him. She buried her face in the material, trying to define the scent.

Sophie closed her eyes and inhaled, deeply. Brandy, a faint whiff of wood smoke, and the aftershave James wore, Sophie wasn't sure what it was. The smell was fresh, but not flowery or sweet; it brought the memory of the previous night's events flooding back to her. Sophie lay flat on her back on the bed and let the sweater fall over her face. Closing her eyes, breathing deeply, she wondered what it would be like to make love to James McKinnerney.

What had Alex said about James not being able to

satisfy his wife? Sophie found that hard to believe; in her imagination James was virility itself. Catherine had probably just told Alex that to arouse his sympathy. Sophie could imagine that, to a man like Alex, Catherine's supposed frustration would seem like a challenge and for Catherine, any opportunity to annoy her husband was a bonus.

Sophie felt exasperated. Why couldn't Catherine see what a nasty piece of work Alex Carver really was? Was it simply a case of the grass being always greener? She couldn't work it out. She herself thought James to be twice, three times the man that Alex was. Sophie let herself drift into daydreams. She imagined herself proving Alex wrong about James; she imagined herself arousing James more than he had ever been aroused before. Inflaming him to such a show of masculine passion that his powers to satisfy would never be doubted again.

What would it be like to feel James's weight on top of her, Sophie wondered. Would he still be reserved and proper in his lovemaking? Would he need much coaxing? Or would he throw his usual inhibitions to the four winds as Sophie slowly stripped before him? Would he have to be persuaded or would he fall on her eagerly, frustrated by months of reluctance from Catherine?

Face still pressed into the warm, fragrant sweater, Sophie breathed deeply, inhaling the lingering scent. She recalled his courteousness to her, his reluctance to talk about his problems, his loyalty. She rubbed the sweater over her face, imagining him in it, picturing his face above her. Sophie's skin felt warm and tingly in anticipation of James's imagined touch. Oblivious to her reasons, she began to unbutton her dress.

Holding the sweater in one hand, she caressed her face and neck with the pleasingly rough material, her other hand stealing furtively between her legs and into her panties. Sophie was carried away by her imagination; James was above her, trying hard to resist, but she was

140

urging him on. In her daydream, after many weeks of Catherine's unreasonable refusal to have him near her, James found the sight of Sophie's delectable body – ready and more than willing – too much.

Sophie pushed herself further on to the bed and slipped the sweater down her tingling body. Under her opened dress she wore only panties, and she imagined the sweater contained a highly excited James, as she let it slide, seductively, over her skin. The weave of the wool felt rough against her sensitive nipples; she teased them gently, until they felt swollen and ripe.

Would James like her breasts? she wondered. Would he want to run his tongue over them, suckle them until she moaned? The thought of James McKinnerney sucking eagerly at her full breasts excited her and she involuntarily slid the sweater further down over her belly and between her legs. She had, without realising it, discarded the panties, and the coarseness of the material felt like a particularly rough tongue as it stroked her already wet blonde bush.

Sophie pushed the bulk of the material between her legs and took hold of the arms, so that both her hands were full of the woolly material. Pulling first on one sleeve, then on the other, she lay back and let James McKinnerney's sweater cause quick shivers of excitement to run through her.

When she pulled the material back up to her face, she could smell her own scent mingling with his, which Sophie found almost unbelievably exciting. She felt she could come just thinking about him, but that wasn't what she wanted. She had to believe he wanted her, was lusting uncontrollably after her, would do anything for the chance to posses her. And so, with head flung back and imagination running wild, she plunged her fingers deep inside her hot wetness.

What would he feel like inside her? Sophie was weak with desire. Would he want to kiss her there first? Run

141

his tongue up the furrow of her womanhood, while she, impatient to feel him inside, wriggled and protested? The thought made her gasp and plunge her fingers inside herself once more. Would he make a noise? No, not James. He would be silent, just breathing, hard and heavy, above her.

Something seemed to cause Sophie's attention to slip at that point. She hung on tight to the thought of James inside her but a tiny, faraway alarm bell seemed to be ringing in her head. She had no time to explore this annoyance as she suddenly realised that she was sliding off the bed. Sophie tried to stop herself from falling but couldn't. She just had time to think that if James had been there, he would have heaved them both – still coupled – back up on to the bed, when she sat down hard on the floor. She came instantly, thinking of James lifting her bodily back on to the bed, her fingers still pressed far inside her.

Sophie was flushed and excited. She felt, for all the world, as though she had just enjoyed energetic sex with a demanding partner. Trying hard to catch her breath, she suddenly felt a moment of panic as she wondered what she should do with James's sweater, glistening, as it was, with the evidence of her arousal.

I'll put it in with my luggage, Sophie thought. Throw it straight in the wash when I get back to Prospect House and then leave it in the washroom. Everyone will assume it came back in James's bag.

She stood to button her dress and smooth her hair back into place. Catching sight of her pink face and shining eyes in the mirror, she decided not to go straight downstairs; Mrs Clegg would wonder what she had been up to.

And quite right, too, Sophie thought. What exactly had she been up to? Did this mean she fancied James? He was undeniably attractive but not really Sophie's type. He was too conservative – a bit stuffy, if she were honest. But, Sophie thought, a little private day-dreaming never hurt anyone and it had, at least, made her realise how much she was missing Callum.

She pottered around the room doing one last check under the bed and in the drawers. When she deemed the room inspected, and herself presentable, she dragged the bags into the hall. Mrs Clegg bustled by on her way to speak to Jo.

'Leave those there,' she called to Sophie. 'I'll get someone to take them down for you. You look worn out, dear! Oh and, by the way,' she called back over her shoulder, 'I think your dress is buttoned up wrong.'

Chapter Eight

'Hello, can I come in?' The voice appeared to come from a bunch of flowers held in front of a hidden face on Sophie's doorstep.

'I suppose so.' Sophie laughed, stepping back to allow the bouquet access.

'Thanks, it's freezing out there,' said the flowers in a voice strangely similar to Callum's. He lay the flowers on the table, where the cellophane and ribbons covered most of the surface.

'I came to say sorry.' Callum looked at Sophie, hesitantly. He rubbed his still gloved hands together as if he really didn't know what to do with them.

'Callum, you didn't have to bring me flowers.' The obvious pleasure on her face and soft tone of her voice told Callum that she was delighted that he had. He, in turn, seemed relieved that his peace offering had been so readily accepted.

'Oh, well then,' he said, airily, 'I'll take them back. The girl who sold them to me said that she wished men gave her flowers like these. She will be extremely grateful for them!'

'Don't you dare! But really, Callum, they're beautiful. Thank you.'

'My pleasure.'

They smiled happily at each other and Sophie was struck once again by the handsome openness of his face. He was like a breath of fresh air after a weekend of stale bad humour.

'Have you got time for a cup of tea?'

'I've got all the time in the world,' he told her. 'I've got the day off.'

'Oh great! Me too.'

'I know. That's why I asked for today. I thought I had some making up to do – if you'll let me, of course.'

'There's nothing I want more. Apart from,' she added, bitterly, 'to win the Lottery and get out of this place!'

He chuckled. 'Good weekend?'

'It was horrendous, Callum. Truly horrendous. I lost the will to live before we even got there – then it got worse!'

They laughed at the antics of their employers, comparing horror stories, Sophie filling Callum in on Catherine's latest outburst. Callum listened and sympathised until Sophie got to the bit about Alex Carver, then he frowned sullenly into his mug of tea.

'Is he who you were having trouble with?'

'I did, but it's all sorted out now.'

'If you need any help . . .'

She smiled and patted his hand. 'Thanks, Callum, but I really have got it under control.'

'Can I ask you a question?'

'It depends on the question.' She was guarded, not wanting to discuss Alex any further.

'Was it his glove?'

Sophie cast her mind back. She had almost forgotten the glove. Could it have been Alex Carver's? She hadn't thought of that. Callum mistook her confusion for hesitancy.

'I shouldn't have asked that. I'm sorry, Sophie. It doesn't matter.'

'No, no. I don't mind you asking . . .' Sophie's mind raced ahead. Should she tell Callum the whole story? She didn't really want to, not now that they were getting on so well together. Sophie had made up her mind – as she had driven the horsebox home the night before – that her mystery lover must now be consigned to the past. If she wanted any semblance of normality in her life, she had to make sure he never played his power games with her again.

This assumed end to their relationship – if it could be called that – left her feeling far from happy. It was, thought Sophie, unsatisfactory, to say the least, not knowing who the man was. But with a lot of determination, and a little help – which she was due to ask from Callum – Sophie was confident that she had seen the last of her mysterious seducer.

'Sophie, it's not important.'

She took a deep breath. 'I don't really want to go into details, Callum. I don't honestly know exactly what was going on myself. All I can say is that I'm not involved with anyone else, as of now. Also, I need to ask you for a favour.'

He was leaning towards her, eagerly. 'Anything.'

'Would you help me change the lock on that door? Also, I need locks for the biggest windows.'

He stared at her for a moment, then ran his fingers through his hair, obviously deciding not to question her further. Then he looked up and smiled. 'Sure. We can do it today, if you like.'

Sophie leant across the table to take his hand. 'Thanks, Callum.'

He didn't say a word but just pulled her out of her seat to his side of the table. Holding her close, his head against her breasts, he smiled up at her.

146

'I must tell you it's not normally in my nature to apologize.'

'Oh? Why did you then?'

'I missed you.' His voice was muffled as he mumbled into the soft material of her shirt.

'I missed you too,' she told him, meaning it. 'The funny thing is, I was going to apologize to you, too, but you beat me to it. So I didn't have to.'

'What?' Callum pretended fury. 'I said I was sorry when I didn't have to? Well you can just make amends and say it now!'

'No chance.'

'Come on!' He was undoing his jeans with a purposeful air. 'Your turn; apologise!'

'No way! It wasn't my fault, anyway.'

'It was, actually, but I was prepared to overlook that. Come on, Sophie,' his tone was cajoling. 'Say sorry.'

'Do I have to?' Sophie feigned annoyance.

'It'll make me feel better. It's a blow to my self-esteem if I have to admit I was wrong.'

'Oh, all right then. Sorry.'

'That was very grudging. Oh no, that won't do at all. Come on, properly.'

'Sorry, Callum, blah, blah, blah. How was that?'

'"Blah, blah, blah"? Oh no.' He undid his jeans and gestured for Sophie to take a look. 'See? My manhood could be permanently damaged by an incident like this. Only a proper apology will save it.'

They were both trying not to laugh, happy to be playing this game, delighted to be having fun together once more.

Sophie tried to look concerned. 'I'm most worried, Callum. How can I make amends and restore you to your – ahem – former glory?'

'That's more like it! Bended knees.'

'You must be joking.'

In answer, Callum freed his straining penis from the tangle of his trousers, and held it gently. 'Bended knees.'

But Sophie needed no prompting. It seemed ages since she and Callum had made love in the hay loft, and she wasn't going to miss an opportunity like this. Slowly she knelt on the carpeted floor, glad her tiny kitchen wasn't tiled. Resting her hands on Callum's knees, she stared solemnly up at him.

'Bended knees,' she told him.

Callum seemed incapable of speech. He was absent-mindedly stroking himself and smiling dreamily at her. Sophie kept her eyes fixed on his, and bent slightly to run the tip of her tongue up his penis. Callum's eyes widened, then a blissful look crossed his face.

'I was hoping you would do that.'

Sophie smiled and bent to do it again, stiffening her tongue to increase the pressure, making Callum shudder with delight.

'Oh Sophie! I've missed you. I've missed this,' he was whispering, almost to himself. Sophie smiled up at him again and watched his face as she took him full into her mouth. The effect was thrilling: Callum moaned and closed his eyes, his head rolling back in ecstasy. Sophie felt herself getting wet in response, and applied herself with renewed pleasure to Callum's marvellous prick.

She pulled his trousers aside so that she could ease one hand under him and was delighted afresh at the heavy handful of his balls. Gentle pressure made him groan more as Sophie slid him in and out of her mouth, his now-familiar smell and taste driving her desire.

'Sophie, wait!' When she looked up at him through her dishevelled hair, mouth wet and shiny, he tried anxiously to pull her upright.

'I wanted to make you come like that,' she told him. 'You know, give you a proper blow-job!'

'A proper one?' He was laughing, teasing her gently. 'How about an improper one?'

'Callum, you know what I mean!'

'I do, I do! But, my darling, I want to see you. I can't see you down there, and I've missed you.'

'Tell me what you've missed about me,' Sophie murmured into his hair, her arms around his neck.

'I've missed the sight of your gorgeous body,' he told her, sliding down her jeans and lacy knickers. 'I've missed kissing you here.' He opened her shirt and nuzzled her breasts, happily. 'And I've missed having you sat here.' He pulled her firmly into his lap towards his waiting penis.

Sophie groaned. She was wet enough to ease herself straight over him, but Callum was having none of it. He held her above him, his strong arms twitching as he took the weight of her. Sophie wriggled and squirmed, eager to feel her pussy-lips around him, to get the full length of him into her. But Callum was stronger. He eased her down so slowly that she hardly noticed how far into her he was until he moved, then she cried out in pleasure.

'Oh, Callum! I've missed you too.'

'Tell me, Sophie. Tell me how you've missed me.' He lifted her off him and held her there, the muscles on his arms and shoulders bulging.

Sophie couldn't reply. Not usually noisy during sex, she was gasping breathlessly; all she could think of was filling herself again with that wonderful prick. She was shaking, feeling hot and feverish as Callum plunged her down on to him again.

The effect was instantaneous. Sophie squealed with pleasure as his generous penis entered and claimed her. She was at his mercy and it felt wonderful. Callum hoisted her off him, teasing her clitoris with his straining bulk, and then down again, revelling in his exquisite power.

Sophie could feel her wetness spreading itself down Callum's prick, feel the heat inside her, and the light-headedness that precedes orgasm. Her cry of ecstasy as

149

she started to come surprised even Sophie; Callum felt the tightening around his penis and gave an involuntary moan.

Sophie was unaware of anything but for a sudden burst of colour exploding behind her closed eyelids. She rode out the crashing waves of her orgasm, her body rigid and her lips parted. Callum came moments later. Sophie felt the force of his coming gush into her like a fountain. For several seconds they were locked together in a rhapsody of pleasure, then they stayed locked together anyway, because it felt wonderful.

They spent the day together, Sophie being allowed to give Callum his 'proper' blow-job later, and then the pair of them took a long, hot shower. They had a heated debate about interrupting their day of pleasure to buy door and window locks – Sophie was tempted to postpone the trip but Callum thought it was urgent. Then Callum suggested he should prepare dinner.

Sophie was delighted. She had been worried that their trip to the locksmith would be an end to their day together. Watching Callum pile ingredients for their dinner into a bag, she realised that the best was yet to come; when he topped it all off with a bottle of wine Sophie was doubly happy – he couldn't be intending to drive home that night if he was drinking.

They drove back to the cottage in companionable silence. Callum secured the fixtures on the door and windows while Sophie scanned the Job Search sections of the papers, looking for alternative posts.

They had talked long and hard about their positions with the McKinnerneys and they both agreed that their jobs were far from safe.

'We could look for somewhere together,' Callum suggested, hesitantly. 'There are positions for couples.'

Sophie smiled. 'We're not exactly a couple, are we, Callum?'

'Well, no,' he laughed sheepishly, 'but we could be in time, couldn't we?'

'Maybe, but the last thing we need is to have to be a couple because we've taken a job which demands it.'

'I see your point. So . . . what?'

She kissed him. 'Let's just see what happens, shall we? If two jobs turn up fairly near each other, so be it.' He looked mortified.

'Callum, I don't want to lose you.' She struggled hard to find the right words, 'But I don't want us to get sick of the sight of each other before we've even begun.'

'You're right. But I want you to know, even if you find a job in the Outer Hebrides, I'll find one nearby.' They laughed and carried the papers into the kitchen so that she could read suitable ads out to him as he cooked.

Sophie watched covertly as he prepared the meal. He cooked as he made love, with a reckless, abandoned pleasure, unencumbered by the constraints of convention. He threw ingredients into pans, chatting and laughing, his face animated and open. Then he remembered the wine and pretended to be a waiter, tea cloth over his arm, anxiously awaiting her decision.

He really was good company. Sophie was touched by his good nature and delighted by his exuberant humour. Once the pans were bubbling and the kitchen was starting to fill with delicious smells, he brought his wine glass and came to sit opposite her.

'Shall we eat in here or in the other room?' he asked.

'There's something I wanted to say first.'

'Oh dear, that sounds ominous.' He was joking, but his face was serious. 'What's wrong?'

'I'm sorry. For not being entirely honest with you that night.'

He sighed. 'Sophie, that's your business, not mine. I was annoyed, yes. But I had no right to be.' He took a gulp of wine. 'Perhaps now is the time to tell you that I suppose I haven't been entirely honest with you, either.'

Sophie's heart twisted in her chest. What was he talking about? Suddenly she wasn't sure she wanted to carry on with this conversation. She thought briefly of asking him not to tell her, to leave her in blissful ignorance, but she knew it wouldn't work.

'What do you mean?'

He caught the strained tone of her voice and quickly reached over to hold her hand. 'It's not that bad, honestly.'

'Come on, out with it!' She pretended firmness, but her hand shook as she lifted her wine glass. 'No more secrets.'

'It's just that I think I know why Catherine has been such a bitch to you.'

'You do? Why?'

He took a deep breath. 'When I first came to work here – I hadn't been here more than two weeks – she came on to me while I was painting the paddock fence.'

'She can't have been married long, then, can she?'

'No, not long at all. Anyway, as you can imagine, I put her off. I wasn't rude, I just politely refused, telling her I didn't mess with what didn't belong to me.'

'Why didn't you tell me this before?'

'It never occurred to me. It was a two minute incident that we both obviously thought best forgotten. It was never mentioned again. I heaved a sigh of relief, put it down to married life not being quite what she expected, and didn't think about it again. Anyway, it was all a long time ago.'

Sophie wondered privately if this really was the reason that Catherine seemed to so dislike her; surely she couldn't still have her eye on Callum? As he had pointed out, it was all a long time ago. Still, Sophie thought, it confirmed what she herself had suspected for a while: Catherine had not been happy in her marriage for years. Had maybe never been happy. So why had she married James in the first place?

'I don't really think that that's why she's like that to me,' Sophie told Callum. 'I can't see even Catherine bearing a grudge that long.'

'I think she's jealous.'

'Of you and me?' Sophie laughed. 'I just can't see it.'

'Not just that. You're young. You're pretty. And most of all, you're unattached. No responsibilities. In Catherine's eyes there are many reasons to be jealous of you.' He went to attend to his pans and Sophie pretended to be looking at the paper; in fact her mind was elsewhere.

Put like that, it made sense in a warped kind of way. And it was a relief to be able to pin Catherine's animosity towards her down to something other than her own incompetence. Poor old Callum, Sophie thought, trying not to laugh. What a position to be in – having to make a decision whether to comply with Catherine's wishes and risk discovery, or to refuse and risk the sack!

They ate at the kitchen table. Callum was a good cook, and the food was delicious. All the more so, Sophie thought, because she hadn't had to cook it herself. They were just arguing amiably about whether to wash up there and then or to leave it indefinitely, when there was a knock at the door.

It was gone eight o'clock, rather late for one of Rosie's occasional visits. It could only be someone from Prospect House.

'Would you like me to keep out of the way?' Callum indicated the other room.

'No, stay, Callum. I've got every right to have friends here; there's nothing to hide.'

Catherine stood on the doorstep. Her smirk only faltered for a second when she saw Callum standing behind Sophie in the tiny kitchen.

'You'd better come up to the house,' she hissed at Sophie. 'Marcie Carver is here to see you.'

'To see me?'

'That's what I said. Hurry up!' She turned and marched back to the house, leaving Sophie with an ominous sinking feeling in the pit of her stomach.

'Shall I come with you?' Callum was reaching for his coat.

Obviously he can sense trouble, too, Sophie thought. 'No, really, I'll be fine. Wait here, I'll be back soon.' She kissed him briefly. 'And if you're bored you can always do the washing-up.'

She followed Catherine up the drive and around the house. It looked impressive at night, and Sophie had to take several deep breaths to stop herself feeling intimidated. She had a horrible idea that she already knew what all this was about. If she was right, she might be needing those job recruitment papers later.

Marcie Carver was waiting for her in the sitting room which had housed their very first meeting. She was looking out of the darkened window, her back to Sophie.

'She's here,' Catherine cried with impish glee, before shutting the door quickly behind Sophie. And, Sophie thought, no doubt listening at the keyhole.

Marcie turned, and Sophie couldn't tell if she had been crying or if her eyes were red from extreme tiredness.

'Sophie,' she said, for no apparent reason as she crossed the room to pour herself a drink. She didn't offer one to Sophie; it would have been refused, anyway. Sophie suddenly felt the need for a clear head.

'Catherine said you wanted to see me.'

'Yes.' Marcie stood still, swishing the amber liquid around in its glass, watching it catch the light. She seemed relaxed and graceful, rather like a beautiful and expensive cat seconds before it lashes out with razor-sharp claws.

'I suspect you know what this is about.'

'I'd like you to tell me.'

Marcie laughed and a shiver ran down Sophie's spine. This woman made Catherine look like an amateur.

154

'I bet you would, Sophie. But you see, I want to hear your version of events.'

'Which events are these?'

Marcie's eyes flashed. 'Don't play games with me, Sophie. It's not wise.'

'If I'm being accused of something – and it seems that I am – I want to know exactly what it is. I think that's only fair.'

'Fair? Suddenly you want things fair, do you? What's fair about you messing around with my husband? You tell me that!' She was spitting the words out venomously. Sophie could imagine Catherine's delighted reaction from behind the heavy door.

'I am not, and never have been, messing around with your husband. I know why you think that. I know who has encouraged you to think that. But I can assure you that you are wrong.'

'You're a brilliant liar, Sophie, I'll give you that. You could almost convince me. Unfortunately for you, you were seen. And by someone who doesn't know enough to lie yet. There is an old saying: "out of the mouths of babes . . ."'

'I don't believe this!' Sophie was outraged. 'She's even dragged the children in to do her dirty work, has she? If you're talking about when they saw me getting out of the cupboard, I was playing hide-and-seek, for Heaven's sake!'

'I imagine you were!'

'I don't have to take this! I'm not listening to any more of your stupid accusations.' Sophie was furious. 'You can't even see what's right in front of you, can you?'

'What do you mean?' Marcie was suddenly listening. Sophie poured herself a drink without being invited, protocol having long gone out of the window. Marcie seemed not to notice this lapse. The fire had disappeared from her and she was gazing stupidly at Sophie. 'I don't know what you mean,' she repeated.

Sophie sighed and flopped on to the sofa. What could she tell Marcie without hurting her too much? That her husband had been trying to get Sophie into bed from her first day there? That Catherine had thrown Sophie into the arena to deflect attention from her own indiscretions with Alex Carver? But Sophie had no proof of that. Catherine was a terrible flirt, true enough, but that didn't mean there was anything more going on.

'Mrs Carver, I'm not having an affair with your husband, I promise you. Have you talked to him about this?'

'Of course I have,' Marcie looked miserably into her glass, 'and he's denied it, naturally. But he's such a damned liar that I never believe him, on principle.'

'For once, he's telling the truth.' Sophie was trying to keep her voice down; she wanted to avoid giving any more voyeuristic fun to Catherine than was strictly necessary. 'At least, he's telling the truth about there being nothing between him and me, other than that – '

'It's just that Catherine said . . .'

Sophie held up a hand to silence her. 'I don't want to know what Catherine said. Honestly, I don't. All I can say is that I think I'm being used as a scapegoat in all this, and it's not the first time I've felt this way. I'm sorry about your husband's behaviour, but I'm not really the one you need to talk to.'

She was willing Marcie to pick up the clues and to point the finger of blame where it was deserved, but Marcie just continued to stare into her glass.

'Goodbye, Mrs Carver,' Sophie said and crossed the room swiftly to fling back the door. She was unsurprised to catch Catherine dithering in the hall, unable to vacate her vantage point quickly enough. Sophie ignored her and made for the front door, snatching up her coat on the way.

Back at the cottage, Callum was frantic. 'I was just about to come looking for you.'

'Don't bother – I'm here.'

'What is it, Sophie? What's happened?'

Sophie related the whole incident from beginning to end, finishing with Catherine's attempts to eavesdrop.

'They're all mad, aren't they?' Callum kept muttering. 'They're all bloody mad!'

Sophie's hand shook as she pulled paper and envelopes from a drawer in the kitchen before she hunted feverishly for a pen.

'Where's that one we had earlier?'

'Here. What are you doing now?'

She was writing urgently, furiously, pressing so hard that the pen tore at the paper. 'I'm writing my notice.'

'Are you?' Callum, not quite sure what was expected of him but eager to lend support, flopped himself down beside her. 'Excellent idea! But could I just ask where will you go?'

'Anywhere! I'll go home if I have to. Or I'll ask Rosie to put me up; she offered once before. Maybe I'll find another job really quickly, one with accommodation.' She looked doubtful. 'One thing's for sure, I'm not staying here.'

'You can stay with me, if you like.'

She smiled for the first time since she had returned from Prospect House. 'Thanks, Callum.'

'I've got a better idea! I'll hand my notice in too.'

'No, Callum, you mustn't. Listen, if you can't get something else fairly quickly, you may be glad of your job. Anyway, you've been here longer than me so you'll have to work notice, won't you? What will it be – a month?'

'Even more reason to write this letter now.'

Sophie sighed, she wasn't going to be able to dissuade him in this mood, she could tell. 'Your loyalty is touching,' she joked, 'but, seriously, Callum, don't do this for my sake. You've been happy here; you have to make your own decision.'

'I was happy here once but now it's really apathy that keeps me here. No, I'll be as glad as you to see the back of this place.'

'OK, OK. It's up to you. What are you going to put?'

Callum grinned. 'How about, "I can't work for you any more because you're all bloody mad!" Sound all right?' Their laughter was genuine and heartfelt.

Later, they walked through the dark lanes to the nearest pub. Although they hadn't discussed it, they both instinctively wanted to put some space between themselves and Prospect House. They stayed until closing time, making the most of having the roaring fire to themselves, and swapping tales of their earlier lives.

Sophie told Callum about her large family and her need to escape from the claustrophobic and humdrum existence that was life in her home village. Callum, in turn, explained his love of being outdoors as the reason he had become a gardener.

'That,' he said, cheerfully, 'and no qualifications owing to a misspent youth. I left school at sixteen, and was lucky enough to be taken on as a helper to the old guy who did the gardens here before me. When he packed it in – he had arthritis quite badly – I took over. Of course, when I first came to work here it was Mr McKinnerney's parents that had the place.'

'So; tell me more about this misspent youth. You're a dark horse, you are.'

'Oh no!' He looked quite prim. 'Don't get me wrong. I wasn't a real villain. No, I just couldn't be bothered to work at school. And in my ignorance it seemed like being a gardener was an easy option.'

Walking home in the biting cold, surrounded by all the smells and sounds of the countryside at night, Sophie was amazed at how unconcerned she was at her own plight. She linked her arm through Callum's. Tomorrow she would hand in her letter of resignation for a job which she had done for less than a month. She would be lucky to find another position quickly, especially one with accommodation. She would have little money to speak of and she didn't stand a chance of getting a decent reference.

For all this, Sophie felt as though she were walking on air. A weight had been lifted from her; she would not have to face Catherine McKinnerney for much longer. All she could think about at the moment was getting back in the warmth and spending the whole night with Callum. She shivered in pleasant anticipation.

They both struggled for ages with the catch on the door before common sense prevailed and they remembered that Callum had changed the locks. It seemed so long ago.

Once inside, light on, Callum bent to retrieve something from the doorstep. 'Hello,' he said, examining the package. 'What's this?'

Sophie turned from hanging up her coat and was overcome by a bad case of *déja vu*. This time it was a plastic bag containing a brightly-wrapped parcel, roughly the size of a small shoe box. She panicked.

'I don't want it!'

'You don't know what it is, so how can you say that?'

Sophie sat down heavily at the table. 'Oh Callum! It's all starting again! I can't stand it.'

He was patience itself. 'Look, Sophie, I don't know what's going on, remember? I can't help you if you don't tell me, can I?' She put her head in her hands, miserably, and he sighed. 'Let's start at the beginning. Now, do you know who has left this here?'

'No.'

'Do you know why someone is leaving things on your doorstep?'

'Not just on the doorstep,' she whispered. 'In my bedroom, too.'

He was shocked into silence for a moment and then he said, quietly, 'That's why you wanted the locks changed, right? Why didn't you tell me, Sophie? I could have – ' He stopped abruptly and ran his fingers through his hair. 'Why is this happening, Sophie?'

'I don't know.'

'Open the parcel.'

'But – '

'Open it, Sophie. Whatever it is can't hurt you, can it? I'm here with you. There are two of us in this together now. It's up to us not to let any of this get to us. Just remind yourself, we will be out of here soon.'

Relief washed over Sophie at the thought of leaving this place with Callum. He was right, just having him near made the whole mess easier to deal with. She couldn't let this incident spoil their day together. She picked up the bag. Callum reached for the kettle, feigning nonchalance, and began to make tea. Sophie turned the parcel over, her fingers trembling.

'Oh no!' cried Callum, slapping his forehead dramatically.

'What is it?' In her anxiety, Sophie dropped the parcel. 'What's wrong?'

'It's your birthday, isn't it, and you haven't told me.'

'You idiot! No, it's not my birthday. You frightened me half to death then.' She picked the parcel off the floor, smiling at his antics. 'But if it was my birthday, you needn't have worried; you've given me more than enough for one day.'

'Hey!' He affected a cowboy swagger, trying to make her laugh. 'I can give you more than that, baby. There's plenty more where that came from!'

'I meant the flowers,' Sophie said casually, then laughed at Callum's deflated demeanour. 'But the sex was good, too.' She ripped the paper from the package. Somehow the contents didn't seem so important now that Callum was here to witness them.

The tissue paper came away easily. Underneath was another gauzy piece of material – peach-coloured this time – wrapped around something heavier. Slowly, Sophie unwound the silky fabric and held it up. Callum whistled. It was a long negligée, the colour warm and enticing, with a panel of thick apricot lace set into the front. Sophie was speechless.

Callum wasn't. 'Bedtime, I think.'

'Callum!'

'Never look a gift horse in the mouth, I always say. I'll tell you what, though, there's no warmth in that thing. I know, I'll come to bed with you, just to make sure you don't get chilly.'

'It's not funny, Callum.' But even Sophie was laughing at his absolute refusal to think about the more sinister side of the gift.

He strode to the door of the cottage, flung it open to the freezing night air and leant outside. 'Thank you!' he bellowed into the darkness, before stepping back in. 'It's only polite,' he explained.

Sophie was trying to suppress school-girlish giggles. Her face was pink and she could hardly meet Callum's eye.

'That's not all he left,' she said embarrassed. She held up the object that the negligée had been concealing; it was a pink, plastic penis.

'Excellent,' crowed Callum. 'Got any batteries?'

He needn't have worried. Sophie felt quite unnerved to see that the vibrator already contained batteries, and she knew why. Her mystery lover had been intending to use it on her but had been denied access to the cottage because of the new locks. She didn't tell Callum this, and he didn't ask, but secretly, Sophie felt delighted that she had, for once, been one step ahead of her silent seducer. It would feel like an act of defiance to enjoy his gift with someone of her own choosing.

Callum was overcome at the thoughtfulness of their mystery benefactor.

'Look,' he proclaimed, 'there are batteries in it already. Isn't that kind?'

Sophie had to laugh; he was like a child with a new toy. He used it to stir his tea, before chasing her round the room with it on his head. 'It's Rhino-man!'

They were breathless with laughter when they finally collapsed on Sophie's bed and Callum urged her to go and put on her new nightdress. In the bathroom, trying it on, even she had to admit it looked exquisite. Sophie had never felt anything so soft against her skin. It seemed to float around her as she moved, caressing her body lovingly. The colour was perfect, lending a rosy warmth to Sophie's complexion, and the lacy panel gave tantalising half-glimpses of her full breasts and blonde bush.

When she stepped out of the bathroom, Callum was waiting for her on the bed, naked. She suddenly realised that she had never seen him like this before. In all their previous encounters it had been essential that at least some of their clothes stay on. She felt strangely shy. Then Callum held out his arms for her and her shyness evaporated.

They lay together, he half above her, kissing slowly and deeply. Sophie hadn't known she could be so excited by a kiss; before his hands even touched her she was breathlessly aroused. His eyes took in her voluptuous body encased in the alluring wrapping as his hands began to trace a gentle and appreciative pattern across the lace.

'You are very beautiful,' he told her, his pale blue eyes serious for once, as he gazed down at her. 'I don't know if I deserve you.'

Sophie thought of all the lies and deceit she had witnessed over the last few days. In all the unpleasantness, Callum's down-to-earth good humour had shone out like a lighthouse across a treacherous sea. She didn't speak, just pulled him down to meet her lips once more.

The weight of him against her, the hardness of his body and the clumsy care he took with her touched Sophie deeply. She could feel his prick nudging at her thighs and managed to wriggle one hand between them to stroke it. In answer, Callum lifted the layers of peachy material, exposing her flat stomach and long legs. Then, caressing her legs further apart, he manoeuvred himself on top of her.

It felt amazingly luxurious to be able to make love so unhurriedly and without the threat of discovery. Sophie relaxed more than she had ever been able to before, allowing Callum complete freedom to explore and appreciate her body. He took great delight in pleasuring every inch of her with fingers and mouth until she was begging to be properly satisfied. Then he rested on his elbows, smiling down into her eyes, watching their reaction as he entered and claimed her. He was careful, but firm, his penis caressing her inside as her eager womanhood returned the embrace.

Sophie rose to meet him, encasing and inflaming him, delighting in his sudden loss of control, his naked need of her. The expression on his face had changed. Sophie could see how much he wanted to claim her, possess her, wrap her in his desire; and she responded. He was plunging into her as if in a dream now. His eyes were glazed and he was gasping. Sophie could feel the hot, quick loosening in her stomach and hear her own breath catching in her throat.

She could hardly contain her disappointment when he came, quicker than expected, before her. His whole body stiffened in climax, before he finally shuddered and rolled to one side.

Sophie lay, confused and miserable, beside him, hot tears of frustration threatening to spill at any time. She felt bereft, let down, disorientated.

163

'Did you come?' he asked casually, hands behind his head. Sophie shook her head, fighting back tears, feeling that he should have known she hadn't come and that she had monstrously misjudged Callum's sensitivity.

'Well then,' he sighed, 'I'd better use this!' He produced the curving plastic penis which had been lying forgotten – by Sophie, at least – beside the bed.

Sophie squealed and thumped him. 'I thought . . .'

'You thought, what?' He laughed, teasing her with the proudly erect toy. 'You thought I'd let you down. Oh Sophie! Such lack of faith in me. I've never left a woman unsatisfied yet.' And with this rather boastful claim, he flicked a switch on the vibrator and set to work.

'If a job's worth doing,' he told her, easing the humming penis between her pussy lips, 'it's worth doing well!'

Sophie, deliciously wet already with Callum's sticky juices, felt the penis slide, cold and unrelenting, into her. As Callum angled it experimentally against her clitoris she jerked and shuddered, the buzzing seeming to pervade her whole body. The top of her head to the tips of her toes seemed to dance in time to the strange, primal music that was emanating from the very centre of her sex.

'Nice?' Callum was a master of understatement.

'Oh! Oh! Callum!'

'How does this feel?' He rotated the new toy expertly. 'What about this?' Sophie felt totally at his mercy and was delighted to be so; he was enjoying himself easily as much as she was. Just as she felt the waves of pleasure becoming more insistent, less controllable, readying themselves to rise and crash around her, Callum determinedly withdrew the source of pleasure. Before Sophie could object, he was running the still-humming penis over her body, tantalising and teasing, producing tiny electric shocks where she least expected them.

Her nipples rose in ecstasy at the vibrator's touch, her

tongue fizzed excitedly when Callum invited her to lick it, but best of all, they both decided, was what happened when he held it firmly between her buttocks. They jiggled and danced, delighting him, and sending shockwaves of excitement deep inside her.

Aroused and determined, Sophie took the vibrator out of Callum's grip and eased its curving firmness into her own eager womanhood. Callum, seeing her need, took over, lying her back so that he could give her as much pleasure as possible. Sophie came instantly. Not once, but over and over, a million tiny electric shocks of pleasure bursting inside her.

When they finally collapsed, exhausted and satisfied on the bed, Callum grinned impishly at her. 'It's going to cost a fortune in batteries,' he said, turning out the light.

Chapter Nine

*T*he clean, brilliant whiteness spread out before Sophie, transforming the familiar bridle path into something unexpected and enchanting. The grass, hedges and trees were all wreathed in a lacy frost, making them look sugar-coated and brittle. Under Firefly's hooves the ground crunched and, when they cantered up the long field, sparkling puffs of frost were thrown up behind.

It was a pleasure to be part of such a morning, Sophie thought, realising that it might be the last time that she took Firefly out on this, his favourite route. The large bay trod carefully, not sure of his footing on the icy ground, and snorted great clouds of breath, which seemed to linger in the stillness.

That was it, thought Sophie, the stillness. It was as if time itself were frozen. Everything was unusually quiet. No rabbits had darted across their path this morning to make Firefly start and skid. All the normal early morning sounds were muted somehow. Even the sound of the horse's hooves seemed muffled.

Anyway, Sophie mused, the peace and quiet had at least given her time to clear her head. She had left

Callum in bed – making him promise to be up when she got back – and had taken Firefly out, more to give herself time to think than out of necessity.

And now she had had time to think, Sophie felt sure she was doing the right thing. She had to leave this place, despite her loyalty to James and her growing affection for the horses in her care. Catherine was the real problem; her continuous hounding of Sophie really left no other option. Sophie reined in at the top of the hill and looked down on the fairytale landscape. Beneath her, Firefly pranced impatiently. He knew that if Sophie had a mind to allow it, she would let him gallop back to the woods. He skittered about on the spot while Sophie, lost in her own thoughts, held him expertly in check.

Sophie thought about Callum and her heart lurched. Were they doing the right thing? Was it really wise to think about leaving together when they hardly knew each other? But Sophie felt sure that they knew each other as well as they needed to – if nothing else, Prospect House had a way of making you realise who your friends were.

At last a frustrated snort from the large bay brought Sophie back to the present and she patted his neck. 'You want a good run, do you?'

He pawed the ground in answer. Sophie gave him a longer rein, letting him get the bit between his teeth, before she gently squeezed her legs to his shining flanks. It was all the encouragement he needed, taking off with all the power and conviction of an accurately aimed cannon. They thundered across the field, each hoof-fall sounding like a small explosion, Firefly's flared nostrils snorting steam like a train. Sophie didn't try to stop him; he would pull himself up when he reached the wood. For now, she hung on tight and enjoyed the feeling of so much horsepower underneath her.

At the entrance to the woods, Firefly did his usual swerving stop. It had nearly unseated Sophie the first couple of times she had ridden him but now she knew what to expect. She patted his heaving, sweaty neck, and tugged at his ears. The horse shuddered happily and shook his mane.

'Good boy,' she told him. 'I'll miss you.' She pointed his head towards home and he pricked his ears eagerly, no doubt anticipating his warm stable and fresh hay, Sophie thought.

She knew something was wrong when she saw the police car parked erratically outside the front door of Prospect House. Nobody ever parked there; or if they did, they risked Catherine's wrath. Glancing curiously at it, and trying to quell a mounting fear, Sophie rode around the side of the house – where everyone else parked – to the stables.

Unbuckling Firefly's bridle with trembling fingers, Sophie wondered what could have brought the police to the house. An accident? Her heart somersaulted, and she cursed her clumsiness as she dropped the bridle and tripped over the reins.

She did a makeshift round of the stables – only filling buckets which were completely empty – and then dashed up to the house. At the back door Callum was taking instructions from Jean; obviously he was on a mission of mercy.

'. . . they really won't eat those, Callum, so if there aren't any of the others, don't bother.'

Callum nodded, scratched his head, and looked up to see Sophie. 'Heard the news?'

Sophie shook her head, numb and frightened. 'What's happened?'

'Catherine's gone.'

'Gone? What do you mean, gone?' Sophie clutched the door for support.

'Gone. Disappeared. Vanished. Missing.'

'Oh, gone.' Relief washed over Sophie. She had

thought for a minute he meant that Catherine was ... it didn't bear thinking about. 'Where?'

'Sophie! Do pay attention, please. If they knew where she'd gone she wouldn't be missing, would she?'

'Come inside, dear.' Jean was alarmed at the colour of Sophie's face. 'Take no notice of him. Come and have some coffee. I'm staying here to man the telephone. Or should that be woman the telephone? Anyway, Callum is just running an errand in town for me, aren't you Callum?' She paused to glare pointedly at him.

'Oh, right. Clear off, Callum, is it? OK. See you later.' He kissed Sophie's cheek and pushed her into the kitchen.

Jean, seeing this, smiled wanly at Sophie. 'He's a nice young man,' she said.

'Whatever is going on, Jean?'

'Well, dear, your guess is as good as mine at the moment. Mrs McKinnerney must have left early this morning. She wasn't there when Mr McKinnerney got up, and you know how he likes to be up and about even before it gets light. Anyway, he assumed she'd gone to work exceptionally early –'

'She hasn't taken the children?'

'Oh no, dear. They are with their father at the minute. What made you think that? No, she left alone. As soon as he could phone her office, Mr McKinnerney tried; but with no luck. She never turned up there.'

'Oh, Jean! How awful.'

'He's now in the process of ringing round all her friends to see if anyone has seen her.'

'And the police?'

'Well, dear' – Jean looked less than impressed – 'to tell the truth I suspect they are only here at all because it's Mr McKinnerney's wife that's missing. They admit that they can't do anything unless there are suspicious circumstances. She's not even officially a missing person until she's been gone for twenty-four hours.'

169

'Suspicious circumstances?'

'Yes, you know, evidence that she might have been abducted. Or a reason to believe she may have done something silly. That sort of thing.'

'She has been acting strangely, though, hasn't she?'

'Well, yes, I suppose so. But you don't think she would . . .' The two women looked at each other. 'She'll turn up,' Jean decided. 'I expect she's just trying to shake him up a bit. Make him sweat. You know what she's like. Perhaps she just needed to clear her head.' But even Jean didn't sound convinced.

While Sophie was finishing her coffee, James arrived with the children. He looked old and tired, and, when he saw Sophie, very uncomfortable.

'Here they are, Jean. No school today, in the circumstances, we thought. Hello, Sophie.'

'Any news?' Jean asked with casual hopefulness.

'No, no,' James was trying to be cheerful. 'But I'll keep trying.' In the doorway he turned. 'By the way; the police have said that they may want to talk to everyone later, just to make sure there's nothing . . . well, anyway, you know.'

Jean and Sophie nodded.

'Also,' James hesitated, 'they need to know who was the last one to see her.' He shifted from one foot to the other.

The two women, who had both assumed that he would have been the last to see his wife at bedtime the previous night, were startled.

'Well . . . I mean, the last time I saw Mrs McKinnerney would have been when she helped me put the children in the bath.' Jean frowned as she tried to recall the exact time. 'It could have been six o'clock, maybe six-thirty. After that I went off duty.'

'Sophie?'

'About eight, eight-thirty, I suppose.'

James looked surprised. 'That late?'

170

Sophie nodded; she really didn't want to talk about this.

James cleared his throat. 'Do you mind me asking why? I mean,' he added quickly, 'you're not usually to be found up at the house at that time, are you?'

'Well, no.' There was no easy way of dealing with this. Sophie took a deep breath. 'Mrs McKinnerney came to the cottage to get me at roughly eight o'clock. She told me that Mrs Carver wanted to see me at the house so I came.'

'Marcie? Why . . .? OK, well, never mind that. So that was the last time you saw Catherine, was it?'

'No. When I came out from talking to Mrs Carver, Mrs McKinnerney was in the hall; but we didn't speak.'

'Ah, I see.' Poor James looked more confused than ever. 'Fine. So it's safe to assume that Marcie Carver saw Catherine after you did?'

'I would think so, yes.'

'Thank you, Sophie. I'll get on the phone to Marcie's place of work immediately. In the meantime, the police may still want to speak to you at some point, Sophie. I rather think,' he confided, 'that they are a little bored at the minute. I suspect that, under normal circumstances, an incident such as this wouldn't even warrant a visit.' He smiled half-heartedly, nodded to them both and departed; striding from the room as if he was single-handedly going to find his wife and bring her home.

'Where's Mummy?' demanded a tearful Ellie as soon as he had gone.

'We're not quite sure, dear,' Jean said gently.

'Disappeared!' Gina supplied, looking surprisingly cheerful.

'Like in hide-and-seek?' Ellie was doubtful; it certainly didn't sound like Mummy. On the other hand, she was willing to be convinced. 'Like at Jem's house?'

'Sort of.' Jean started laying out breakfast cereals

171

briskly. 'But because Mummy is a grown-up, she is allowed to go further.'

'Ah!' This was all starting to make sense to Ellie now.

'And that's why it takes people longer to find her,' Gina announced, wisely, pouring Co-Co Pops all over the table.

'I'd better go and finish sorting the horses out,' Sophie sighed. 'Give me a shout if there's anything I can do, won't you, Jean?'

'Can I come and clean tack later?' asked Gina.

'Now there's an offer I can't refuse.' Sophie ruffled the child's hair and smiled. 'I'll come and get you after lunch.' Peter slapped his spoon down into his Ready Brek, spraying the table top and floor.

'Business as usual,' Jean said grimly, reaching for a cloth.

Callum had no further news when he popped in to see her at lunch time. Their letters of notice still sat on Sophie's kitchen table, their presence fuelling her guilt.

'At least we didn't give those to her last night,' Sophie sighed. 'That would have made me feel even worse.'

'Even worse? What do you mean? It's not your fault that she's gone missing.'

'How do you know?'

'Now wait a minute, Sophie – '

'No, Callum, listen; even if I wasn't the last one to see her, even if Marcie did see her afterwards, she would still have been upset. And it would still have been my fault.'

'How do you work that out?'

'Marcie was as mad as Hell. She had come round last night to find out who was messing about with her husband; she suspected it was Catherine. So she comes over to tackle her about it once and for all, and Catherine – strangely enough – has another story to tell. One which the kids can back her up on; that I was seen getting out of a cupboard with Alex – even though it was part of an innocent game of hide-and-seek, as far as I was concerned. For all I know, Catherine may even have let Marcie talk to Ellie about what happened; nothing would surprise me. So Marcie is thrown off the trail, Catherine is off the hook, and I'm the villain of the piece.'

Callum looked perplexed. 'Anyone can see what Catherine's like around Alex Carver; you'd have to be blind not to. And he's no saint. I can't see why Marcie would fall for Catherine pinning the blame on you.'

'In the end, unfortunately, it comes down to what Marcie wants to believe. From her viewpoint it would be foolish to go around accusing one's neighbours of all sorts of unseemly behaviour. If Catherine gives her the handy cop-out of blaming the groom, I can imagine that Marcie would be only too happy to go along with it. These people aren't exactly big on telling the truth.'

'Still, that doesn't explain why Catherine's disappearance should be your fault.'

'I more or less told Marcie Carver that it was Catherine who was after her husband and not me.'

'Well, that's the truth, isn't it?'

'But Catherine was outside the door, listening.'

'So you think she's panicked and run off rather than face Marcie? Well, you're wrong. I know for a fact that Catherine left early this morning rather than last night.'

'How do you know that?'

Callum looked resigned. 'Don't say anything to anyone – James would be embarrassed. I heard him tell the police that her bed had been slept in.'

'Well then, he must have been the last to see her.'

'Apparently not. According to James they have taken to sleeping in separate bedrooms.'

'Oh, I see.' Somehow Sophie wasn't surprised, but the information didn't help her much.

'I think there's definitely more to this than meets the eye,' Callum said, getting to his feet. 'I don't think

Catherine would do anything if it didn't suit her. If she's gone off somewhere, she's got her reasons. Let's face it, if it had been any other family around here, the police wouldn't have raised a finger.'

'James said they may want to talk to me – us – later.'

'All you can do is tell them the truth about all this business with Catherine and Marcie. It might be important, but I doubt it.'

Sophie didn't have long to wait before she was summoned by the police. She and Gina were cleaning tack in companionable silence when a ludicrously young constable appeared suddenly in the doorway of the tackroom.

'Look out,' cried Gina, cheerfully. 'It's the fuzz!'

'Gina!' Sophie smiled apologetically at the policeman. 'I don't know where she gets it from.'

'It's not the worst thing I've ever been called,' he said, his rosy face turning even pinker.

'What's the worst thing?' Gina asked, sensing a chance to further her vocabulary.

'Er, I don't think I should . . .'

'Gina, go and find Jean. Tell her you can come and finish cleaning tack when I've talked to the policeman. Quickly! Go!'

Once the child had left – complaining that she never got a chance to join in any interesting things – Sophie caught the young man's eye and smiled. He blushed beetroot. Sophie was amused to see that even his ears had a delicate pink blush to them. He was going to be fun, she thought.

'Well,' she asked, wickedly, 'where do you want me?'

PC Day nearly fainted. He busied himself finding his notebook, dropped his pen – which rolled under a bench – and mumbled incoherently. Sophie retrieved the pen and he took it with shaky fingers. She moved further up the bench and patted the space beside her.

'Sit here. And feel free to ask me anything!'

The PC collapsed on to the bench, his legs suddenly having gone unaccountably weak. Despite there being no heating in the tack-room, Sophie couldn't help thinking that he looked rather warm. Trying hard to take command of the situation, PC Day fixed his gaze upon his notebook and flipped to a nice clean page.

'I just need . . .' His voice came out as a high-pitched squeak, letting him down terribly, and almost causing Sophie to laugh out loud. She checked herself just in time.

Leaning closer, she regarded him from under her eyelashes. 'What do you need?' she breathed.

PC Day seemed to be losing his nerve. Sophie knew she was being mean but she was enjoying herself too much to stop.

'I need to ask you a few questions,' he growled, overcompensating wildly for his earlier shriek.

'You're not going to arrest me, then?'

'Oh no!' He looked shocked, then laughed awkwardly. 'Not unless you've done anything, er . . .'

'Naughty?' she supplied.

He nearly dropped his pen again, then he laughed, nervously this time. 'No, no, I think naughty is all right. You're fairly safe with naughty.'

'Really?'

'Oh yes. Now . . .'

'Doesn't it depend on how naughty?'

PC Day began to suspect he was on unsafe ground. 'Well, yes,' he admitted, 'I suppose it does. Now, about . . .'

'Because,' Sophie slid imperceptibly closer to him on the wooden bench, 'I can be very naughty.'

'Can you?' PC Day was wondering how he had got into this situation.

'Amazingly, incredibly, outrageously naughty!'

The young constable swallowed hard and endeavoured to balance his notebook on his slowly blossoming erection. 'I'm sure you can, Miss, er . . .'

'Sophie.'

'Sophie. Yes. Quite. I'm sure you can be very, er . . .' He suddenly realised that his train of thought was completely shattered.

'Naughty.' Sophie said, helpfully.

PC Day's notebook wobbled dangerously, and he clutched at it with a desperate look in his eye; whatever else happened, that notebook must stay put. He tried to think where he had got to. 'Now, where were we?' he mumbled.

'You were about to arrest me, I think, for being naughty,' Sophie told him, holding out her slender wrists.

'No, no! I can't arrest you for that. What I mean is; I'm not here to arrest you.'

'That's a shame.' Sophie giggled. 'I've never been in handcuffs.' PC Day looked at her uncomprehendingly for a few moments, then quickly turned his attention back to his notebook.

His hair was very short, as if to make him look older than he really was. His skin still had the newness of youth. Sophie reckoned he was only about her age, although his attitude made him seem younger.

'We think you may have been the last person to have seen Mrs McKinnerney,' he gabbled, keeping his eyes fixed firmly on his blank notebook. 'We need to know how she seemed, what she said, if she gave you any idea of where she might have gone. It's just routine at the moment; we have no reason to believe there has been any . . .'

'. . . foul play?'

'Exactly! But we have to . . .'

Sophie had leant forward to pull her sweater over her head. 'Is it hot in here?' she asked, cruelly. 'Or is it me?'

The young man ran his finger round his shirt collar. 'I suppose it is, er . . .'

'What were you saying?' Sophie planted herself in front of him, her T-shirt straining as she leant forward. 'You have to, what?'

'We have to, er . . .' He frantically replayed the conversation in his mind. 'We have to do our breast!'

'Breast?'

'Best! Best!' He was puce-coloured and almost hysterical. Sophie relented.

'I saw Catherine McKinnerney at about eight-thirty last night. Only briefly, mind; I was heading back to my cottage.'

'Was anyone else with her?'

'No, but Mrs Carver was in the sitting room, and I assume she would have seen Catherine before she left.'

'Mrs Carver?'

'A family friend. Mr McKinnerney will have her address. Come to think of it, he may even have spoken to her by now.'

'So what time did you leave the house?'

'Roughly eight-thirty. Not much later.'

'Did Mrs McKinnerney give you any – '

'She hardly spoke to me. No clues. Nothing.'

'So you stayed in your cottage after that?'

'No, we went to the pub. The Bull's Head.'

'We?'

'Callum – the gardener – and I. We went out about nine-thirty and came back after the pub closed.'

'So you didn't see Mrs McKinnerney leave?'

'No, I didn't.'

'And you were back here by . . .?'

'Eleven-thirty.'

'Did you notice whether her car was still here?'

'No, I didn't.'

'And did you go out again?'

'No, I didn't,' Sophie smirked. 'I went to bed. With the

gardener. And,' she couldn't resist adding, 'we didn't get much sleep.'

PC Day swallowed hard, and decided to ignore her last remark. He hunched over his notebook. It was not only difficult to write when his book was balanced on such an impressive hard-on, it was damned uncomfortable too. 'Final question, Miss . . .'

'Sophie.'

'Thank you. Sophie. Final question: did you see or hear anything unusual last night , or at any time leading up to Mrs McKinnerney's disappearance?'

Sophie hesitated. She hadn't expected that question. PC Day, obviously surprised not to get a straightforward refusal, looked keenly at her. 'Sophie? Anything? Strange cars in the lane near the house? Unusual noises? Strangers lurking about?'

Sophie suddenly felt terribly cold. 'Well . . .'

'Yes?'

'It's probably something and nothing . . .'

'It usually is; but tell me anyway.'

'There has been a stranger . . .'

'A stranger? In the grounds? In the lane?'

'In the grounds.'

He leant forward, eagerly. 'Whereabouts in the grounds?'

'Well,' Sophie felt her face colouring up, 'around my cottage. Actually, in my cottage, one night.'

'A break-in?'

'Well, no. I suspect he had a key.'

'He?'

Sophie thought of the magnificent penis, ivory in the moonlight, on her second night in the cottage bedroom. 'He. Definitely.'

'Did you know this man?'

'No. Well, maybe.'

'Maybe?'

'He wore a mask.'

'How,' the PC asked, cleverly, 'can you be sure that it was a man? In the dark? If the person in question was wearing a mask?'

'Because,' Sophie felt her face going hot at what she knew she must tell him, 'because he had an erection – at least the size of the one you were trying to hide – which he insisted on showing me. Also,' she added, less sure of herself, 'I've seen him since.'

The young PC was staring, open-mouthed, at her. They gazed in mutual embarrassment at each other for several seconds and then PC Day stood, importantly, and with some difficulty, in front of her.

'I think you should come up to the house whilst we sort this out,' he said.

All Sophie could think afterwards was that she was glad that Callum wasn't there. Once the young constable had established that Sophie had seen a prowler in the vicinity of the house, things started to move fairly quickly. It had suddenly become obvious to her that to tell half the story to the flustered PC was just going to look very suspicious, and Sophie realised, with dreadful certainty, that a full explanation of her dealings with the stranger was probably going to be called for.

James McKinnerney had looked confused, and then aghast, when questioned about the likelihood of any strangers being on the estate legitimately.

'No, I've hired no extra groundsmen, not at this time of the year. Callum is more than able to cope in the winter months. What is all this about?'

'A stranger, sir. Hanging around the grounds.'

'A stranger?'

'Miss Ward has reported seeing someone.' Sophie had rapidly become Miss Ward in an attempt not to appear too familiar when CID arrived – as it now seemed inevitable that they must.

'On the estate?'

'And in town,' Sophie said, miserably. She was already regretting the decision to come clean. But, she thought, what if the prowler had had something to do with Catherine's disappearance? She couldn't risk keeping quiet.

'In town as well?' PC Day was relieved to be on familiar ground. 'A stalker, maybe? How many times have you actually seen this man?'

'I don't know.'

'Can you describe him, Sophie?' The anguish in James's voice was palpable.

'No, he . . .'

'Height?' PC Day was finding his feet again.

'Tall. Six feet, maybe.'

'Hair colour?'

'I don't know . . .'

'You don't know?' James looked at her anxiously, his tone sharper than Sophie had heard before. 'Why don't you know?'

'I told PC Day; the prowler was wearing a mask. And another time it was dark.' James was staring at her in horror. Very slowly he lowered himself into a chair and put his head in his hands.

Sophie suddenly remembered the notes and the presents which she had been given. Specifically she remembered the curving pink vibrator, now sat in her bedroom; she blushed. 'Could we talk about this some-where private?' she asked PC Day quietly.

The young constable was beginning to feel out of his depth. 'I think that might be a good idea,' he told her, faintly. 'But I think we should wait until CID get here before we take the questioning any further.'

James wordlessly showed them to his study. His face was ashen as he closed the door; his eyes unable to meet Sophie's. She hunched herself into a huge padded leather chair, an enormous cloud of desolation settling around her. Why hadn't she told someone about the prowler earlier? Whatever were the police going to think? PC Day had rung the police station – panic in his voice – to ask for advice on what to do next. The words 'prowler' and 'mask' seemed to have had an ominous prominence in the conversation, with the result that two CID officers were on their way. Sophie felt wretched. PC Day, anxious to wash his hands of the whole embarrassing mess, refrained from even speaking to Sophie as they waited. Occasionally, as he glanced around the room, he caught her eye, but he looked away quickly every time.

It was a relief for both of them when he had an idea. 'Did you say that you had kept the notes and, er, gifts that you had been given? Perhaps it might be useful if you could go and get them; it'll save time when CID arrive. They may just help us to identify your prowler.'

'He's not my prowler,' Sophie snapped, but rose to collect the things anyway, glad of an excuse to escape the oppressive atmosphere.

In the cottage she flung several items into a bag: the negligee, the silk scarf, the note which had been left in her bedroom – the one from the saddlery shop was long gone – and, with a grim smile, the vibrator. She suddenly felt very angry at having to show these things to total strangers. What sort of clues were they going to get from a pink plastic penis, for Heaven's sake? She imagined the vibrator being passed round a courtroom. 'And here is Exhibit A, Your Honour.' She laughed out loud. No way, she thought, was she going to let some jumped-up teenager make her feel guilty about her sex life.

With renewed vitality she strode to the kitchen door, marched across the yard, and went into battle.

Unfortunately for Sophie, the two CID officers could hardly be classified as 'jumped-up teenagers'. Although neither of them was an awful lot older than the hapless PC Day, they were of a different breed, as Sophie realised immediately.

181

One was large and sweaty, with bow-legs – presumably, thought Sophie, from the strain of having to carry the considerable weight of his body. His harsh crew-cut emphasised a bullet-shaped head which seemed to disappear into his shirt collar, without making any concessions for a neck. Despite his alarming appearance and blundering clumsiness, he seemed anxious to please, leaping up when Sophie arrived, offering her a seat, and smiling broadly, as if meeting her were the highlight of his week.

His presence made the large room seem suddenly smaller, as he lumbered around trying to find a chair big enough to accommodate himself comfortably. It was not until he made some banal and inappropriate comment about the weather – earning him a contemptuous snort from his colleague – that Sophie noticed the other man in the room.

This officer, obviously higher ranking, was as compact and careful in his movements as the first was large and bullish. He watched his partner with cold, bored eyes, clearly irritated by what he seemed to see as too much fuss. He was short and flashy; his suit, his haircut, and his briefcase were all openly expensive and chosen to impress.

While the first man reminded Sophie of a labrador – a little brainless, but good-natured enough – this one was more like a terrier – snappy and awkward. Sophie didn't like the way he looked at her with a mixture of annoyance and lasciviousness. She had met his type before; their lack of stature turned them into bullies.

Just let him try, she thought; she was in no mood to be pushed around.

'Hello, Miss Ward,' the large bouncy one beamed. 'I'm DC Ashwell, and this is DS Bettridge. We would like to ask you a few questions about this stranger, if that's okay.'

'Of course.'

Ashwell grinned at her. 'So, Miss Ward, let's talk about this man. How many times have you seen him, to date?'

'I don't know. As I told PC Day, I've never seen his face, so I may have met him countless times and not realised it.'

Bettridge, who appeared to be bored with the conversation already, looked up quickly. 'All right, how about you tell us from the beginning all the times you have had any contact with him,' he said nastily.

Sophie gave him a hard stare. Right, she thought, you've asked for this. She took a deep breath, and began. She told them of the time the mystery man appeared in her bedroom, of his entering without breaking in, and her suspicion that he had a key.

She played down what had actually happened then; moving rapidly on to the gift in her bedroom, the note, and their next rendezvous in the saddlery shop.

Sophie told it all in a dispassionate voice, leaving nothing out, and not allowing herself the luxury of a glance at the faces of the two policemen until she had brought them up to date with the last incident – the package on the doorstep.

What she did see when she looked up was very satisfactory. Ashwell was struck dumb. His eyes were as round as saucers, his mouth gaped slackly, and he scratched his head several times – looking like a parody of himself – as he tried to collect his wits. Sophie wondered briefly how long that would take, before she noticed DS Bettridge. He was sitting far forward on his chair. The bored expression on his face had been replaced by a beady-eyed, eager look. With a jolt, Sophie realised it was not her story that had aroused his interest; his eyes were not searching her face, but roaming her body – it took him several seconds to realise that she had stopped talking.

When he finally snapped to attention, Sophie was glaring at him. 'Did you write all that down?'

'Well, no.' He looked a bit put out but regained his composure quickly. He nodded at his colleague. 'That's his job.'

Sophie looked at the still gaping Ashwell who suddenly realised that something was expected of him and looked around nervously. 'What?'

'Shouldn't you have written that down?' Sophie enquired.

'Well, not really,' he stammered. 'We're still trying to establish whether this, er, prowler could have anything to do with Mrs McKinnerney's disappearance, aren't we?'

'Course we are, Ron.' Bettridge smiled, almost fondly, at him. Ashwell looked relieved.

'What I don't understand,' the large man mused, obviously encouraged by his superior's support, 'is why you didn't tell anyone about these, er, meetings, Miss Ward?'

'Yes,' sneered Bettridge, 'I don't understand that either.'

'I expect,' snarled back Sophie, defensively, 'there are a lot of things which you don't understand' – she emphasised the 'you' – 'but let me enlighten you; I didn't think it was anyone else's business.'

'Well,' Ashwell smiled kindly, trying to diffuse the situation, 'it might be, or it might not be. We don't know. We need you to tell us what went on. We need to try to find out as much as we can about this man.'

'What exactly do you want to know? I told PC Day that the man wore a mask when he came to my room.'

'Quite so.' Ashwell nodded wisely, as if he routinely entertained masked men in his own room. 'But we really need to elaborate on this description if we can.'

'The only thing I can tell you for sure is that he was roughly six feet tall.'

'What was he wearing?'

'Dark clothes. A ski mask. Gloves.' Sophie remembered the feel of the soft leather gloves, and resolved to play that down.

'Hair colour?'

'No idea; it was too dark.'

'Eyes?'

'Yes; two, I think.' Bettridge's head shot up and he regarded her, coolly.

Ashwell laughed, uneasily. 'Oh yes. Two. I see. Very good. No, seriously, though, did you see the colour?'

Sophie glared at him. 'It was dark,' she intoned, slowly and clearly. 'As I told you.'

'What about his voice?' Bettridge asked, ignoring her irritation. 'Did you notice anything about his voice? What did he say to you? Did you notice an accent? What sort of language did he use?'

'He didn't speak.'

'He what?' Even Bettridge was taken by surprise.

'He didn't speak,' Ashwell clarified for his colleague, helpfully.

'I heard,' snapped Bettridge, looking as if he could happily have slapped Ashwell.

'Oh, I thought you said . . . well, never mind,' Ashwell said hastily as Bettridge rounded on him. Sophie was enjoying the entertainment. For some reason Laurel and Hardy kept springing to mind.

'So,' Ashwell continued, 'if this man was masked and he didn't speak, weren't you frightened?' He sounded quite awe-struck.

'I didn't have time to be,' Sophie said, casually. 'He'd tied me to the bed before I even had time to think.' She thought Ashwell's eyes were going to pop out of his head.

'Tied you . . .'

'. . . to the bed, yes.' Suddenly Sophie thought of

185

something that could prove useful. 'I could give you a very detailed description of the man's penis.'

Ashwell's face went purple and he began to splutter. Bettridge glanced at him in irritation, rather than concern, and finally leapt up to clap him on the back. He used, Sophie thought, rather more force than seemed strictly necessary.

'Get a grip, Ron,' he hissed eventually, and Ashwell, eyes watering and face still red, tried mutely to reassure his superior that he was fully recovered.

'Did you say . . .?'

'Yes?'

'His . . .?'

'Yes?'

'. . . penis?' Ashwell whispered the word, cringing as he did so.

'Yes,' Sophie said, loudly. 'His penis. I got a good look at it. It was – '

'I don't think that will be necessary,' Bettridge interrupted quickly; much to Ashwell's relief. 'It's not as if we can feasibly use the information. I think we would be more interested to know how you came to see this man's, er, member.'

'Member? Oh, yes, I see. Well he got it out, didn't he?' Sophie informed them.

'And what,' Ashwell asked, nervously, 'did he do with it?'

'Well, not much, really,' Sophie had to admit. 'Although afterwards he came and sat on the bed and he touched me.'

'In what way?' Ashwell asked, before he had had time to think the question through.

'Let's put it this way,' Sophie said, leaning forward confidentially, 'there's not much point looking for fingerprints.'

Bettridge exploded in a fit of temper. 'Are you trying to tell us that a total stranger, with a mask on, got into

186

your bedroom in the middle of the night, and touched you intimately, and you never said a word to anyone?'

Sophie thought hard. 'That's about it.'

Ashwell was only now recovering from the shock of it all. 'You said that he, er, you know, touched you. Well, that's assault.'

'Only if' – Sophie leant forward again, as if to make herself clearer – 'I didn't want him to do it. And I did. Very much.'

Ashwell was blushing fit to burst, while Bettridge was looking as if he couldn't believe his ears.

'That's fair enough,' stuttered poor Ashwell. 'That's your choice. Nobody can judge you for that.'

Sophie smiled. 'What a relief.'

'And the next time, in the saddlery shop,' Ashwell struggled gamely on, a light sweat becoming visible on his forehead, 'when he . . .'

'. . . when we had sex,' Sophie prompted.

'Sex?'

'Sex, yes. It's when two people – '

'I know what sex is!' Ashwell shouted. Then, remembering his manners, added, 'What I meant was – '

'What he bloody well meant was how did you manage to have sex without seeing his face? I'd quite like to know that, too,' intejected Bettridge.

'It was very dark.'

'Again? You seem to live in a world of perpetual darkness, Miss Ward. How dark could it be in a public place?'

'Oh, very dark,' she assured him. 'Especially once he had turned off the light and I had the scarf over my face.'

'Scarf?'

'The scarf he gave me. This.' Sophie took it out of the bag, and they both stared at it, as if, by doing so, everything would suddenly become clearer.

'How,' Bettridge asked, making an obvious attempt to

curb his temper, 'did he get a scarf over your face without you being able to identify him?'

'I put it on myself,' Sophie said, as if to a very dim child. 'He asked me to.'

'And you did it?' Ashwell asked, faintly.

'Do you do everything you're asked to do by total strangers?' Bettridge enquired, sneeringly, but with a glimmer of hope in his eyes.

'Oh no!' Sophie pretended to be shocked. 'What do you think I am?' The two men exchanged glances.

'Perhaps we had better see the things he left,' Ashwell decided, sure he was on safer ground. The two men studied the note. No clues on that or the scarf they both agreed, although Ashwell politely requested that they be allowed to take the note. Sophie shrugged; she had no problem with that. As they put it carefully into a plastic bag, she had a sudden vision of them doing the same with the vibrator, and giggled.

Bettridge looked up quickly, his eyes glittering. 'Anything wrong, Miss Ward?'

'No,' she sniggered, 'not at all.' They eyed her suspiciously, then sat back to wait for the next possible clue. At that moment there was a knock at the door, and Jean entered with a tray of coffee cups. She patted Sophie's arm on the way out and smiled encouragingly.

If only she knew, thought Sophie, watching Ashwell fumble dangerously with the delicate china. At last, cups perched on chair arms, they were all ready to resume. Sophie pulled the negligée out of the bag with a flourish and held it up for maximum effect. She wasn't disappointed. Bettridge whistled. Ashwell gave an involuntary twitch that made his coffee cup rattle alarmingly on its saucer.

'And that's not all.' Sophie smirked, producing the shiny pink object out of the bag. 'This was left with it on my doorstep.'

Bettridge spluttered his bourbon biscuit across the

room, while Ashwell gazed in innocent mystification at the object.

'It had batteries, too,' Sophie said, switching it on. 'But they are a bit run down now – I had a night of passion with the gardener,' she confided. All suddenly became horribly clear to Ashwell. He let out a cry of recognition, clapped his hands over his mouth, and sent his coffee cup spinning, spectacularly, across the room.

'For Christ's sake, Ashwell!' Bettridge was rapidly losing his temper. 'Pull yourself together! Go and get a cloth. I don't know why I always end up working with you; you're a bloody liability!'

Ashwell lumbered thankfully from the room, crushing the remains of the bourbon biscuit underfoot. Bettridge watched him go and then turned an oily and unconvincing smile on Sophie.

'Now then, Miss Ward. Sophie.'

'Miss Ward,' she corrected him, irritated.

'I'm Alan,' he said, forcing a smile.

'I'm still Miss Ward.'

'Fine, fine.' He took a deep breath, then started again. 'Now, Miss Ward, what we really need to know is; does this, er, prowler have any significance to Mrs McKinnerney's disappearance?'

'You don't think I'd have told you all this if I was sure he hadn't, do you?'

He leant back. 'Well, you might.'

'And why would I do that?'

'Perhaps you like the attention of police officers.' He was smiling his grossly unpleasant smile again.

'Well I don't,' Sophie said firmly. 'So there goes that theory.'

He looked as though he'd been slapped, but recovered quickly. 'So you think he may have played a part in your employer's unexpected departure, do you?'

'No, I don't. Well, he might ... Look, you're the detective; you work it out. I don't know, I'm only the groom.' Her voice was rising, out of control. She fought to bring it to its proper level.

Bettridge pulled his chair closer. 'Don't get upset, Miss Ward, I'm not here to distress you. We just want to find Mrs McKinnerney. Now, tell me again about this saddlery shop.' Sophie ran through the story again doggedly, Bettridge nodding and taking notes.

'So, you can't remember anything else about him? What he was wearing?'

'A cotton shirt!' Sophie suddenly remembered.

'Excellent! And he kept this on?'

'Yes, I told you; he obviously wanted to get away quickly afterwards.'

'And you couldn't chase after him because . . .?'

'He had stripped me naked; probably on purpose.'

Bettridge nodded, encouragingly. 'And . . .?'

'And because I was wearing stockings and suspenders, which had got all twisted,' Sophie confided. 'They are so difficult to rearrange in a hurry.'

'Also, he had you . . . how?'

'Over the stool,' she told him. 'He had me over the stool, my back to him, while he held on to me.'

'You were kneeling, I take it? And he was . . .?'

'He knelt down, too. He just sort of hoisted me up . . .' She suddenly became aware of the glazed expression on Bettridge's face, and the straining of the material at the crotch of his expensive suit.

'Go on, Sophie; then what?'

Sophie leapt to her feet. 'Why? So that you can get your kicks out of my story? No way! You pervert. You're supposed to be finding Catherine, not giving yourself a hard-on. I've had enough of this; I'm off.' She snatched up her bag, shoving the scarf, negligée, and vibrator into it.

In the doorway, she nearly knocked over Ashwell, dithering around with a bucket of water. 'And you're as

190

bad!' she shouted at him, to his surprise and mortification.

'Wait, Sophie! Miss Ward! Come back!' Bettridge came after her down the corridor, his erection making running difficult; but Sophie wasn't stopping. She turned in the hallway, so that they came face to face.

'No more questions,' she snarled. 'Don't bother me again.'

'But . . .'

'Is there a problem here?' James McKinnerney strode into the middle of the melée, obviously on his way out somewhere, and looked angrily at Bettridge. Sophie had only a moment to feel gratitude before she was overcome with a sense of unreality. She had forgotten to mention finding the glove to Bettridge and Ashwell; a genuine mistake, but prophetic. For there, on James McKinnerney's right hand, was the other one of the pair.

Sophie threw the stable rubber back into the box of grooming kit and patted Firefly's gleaming flank. He grunted and jerked at his head collar, rolling his eyes round to look at her. She led him into his stable, making Jasmine, in the next box, kick out at the dividing wall skittishly.

Sophie sighed. All the horses were nervous and excitable, and had been since she had returned from the house. They seemed to be picking up on her own jumpiness; even Jigsaw had suddenly become so highly-strung that she had had problems getting him into his loose-box. It was no great surprise. Since Sophie's outrage at DS Bettridge's questions, and her utter shock at seeing James wearing the intruder's other glove, things had only got worse.

Dominic had arrived to accuse James of cruelty to Catherine. He had rounded this performance off by berating the police for their failure to find his sister. Telephone calls to friends of the family had made it clear that Catherine had not just gone visiting; only the phone call to Marcie Carver had thrown up anything new.

'There was no one at home,' James had said, 'and when I phoned Marcie's work number, she wasn't there either, which is most unlike her.'

Marcie's secretary had informed James that Mrs Carver had taken a sudden, but necessary, few days off. It had taken all of his charm to persuade the woman of his urgent need to speak to her boss, before the young woman would give him a telephone number. It was the number of a Health and Fitness centre nearby.

Eventually, Marcie was reached and confirmed that she and Catherine had spoken to each other after Sophie had left the previous night.

Had it really only been last night? Sophie thought, wearily; it seemed so much longer ago.

'We argued,' Marcie had sobbed over the phone to James, 'and I called her some horrible names. I'd had enough! She even tried to blame it all on your groom; she said she and Alex were having an affair. When I got home I gave Alex an ultimatum and then I came straight here; I didn't want to be there when he made his decision. Oh, James, I'm so sorry; it's all my fault.'

James had relayed all this to the staff, his face betraying nothing. Sophie only heard half of it. She was still in shock at the thought of James being her secret lover. On the one hand, she would rather it had been him than a total stranger but, she thought, what about all this talk of loyalty he had spouted? And how could he stand there, looking so concerned for his missing wife, when only the night before he had paid a visit to Sophie's cottage with, she was certain, less than honourable intentions? She just couldn't be sure what she felt when she looked at James any more, so she had kept her eyes on the ground.

'We still can't track down Alex Carver,' he had said, carefully, 'but it's not impossible that he may have spoken to, or seen, Catherine last.' Or – the implication had hung, unspoken, in the air – he may be with her at this very minute.

Sophie slipped the padlock on to Buzz's door – her last job every night before she locked up. Stacking water buckets in the furthest corner of the stable, she only dimly registered the outer stable door being swung shut. It occurred to her that she hadn't secured it properly, and it had caught the wind.

It was only when Firefly began to kick and snort that she looked up in surprise and saw the masked man standing between her and the outside door. The ripple of fear and excitement that shuddered through her was overtaken rapidly by a furious anger.

How dare he, she thought, bitterly. How dare he think it's all right to come to me; today of all days. After what she had been through; all the questions, the insinuations, the disgusted looks – disguised as concern – and the smirking faces of the police. Sophie stood, feet slightly apart, fists clenched. She searched her emotions for the trickle of fear she had first felt – and found it had gone. This man had an identity; he was James McKinnerney – she knew that now.

But, she realised, relishing the thought, he doesn't know that I know. She felt a thrill of exhilaration; for once she was ahead of him in the game. Now she was the one that held the knowledge, the position of power. She knew the face behind the mask. The hands which had roamed her body so greedily had an owner. Sophie held this information about his identity to her like a concealed weapon, to be brought out if, and when, she needed it.

'What do you want?' she asked, and was gratified to hear her voice ring out loud and clear, without a hint of nervousness. The man made a move towards her.

'Stay there!' she snapped. He hesitated. Behind him one of the horses – Sophie couldn't see which – was pawing at the door of the stable, rattling the heavy wood on its hinges.

'How dare you?' Sophie's voice was dangerously low, but perfectly controlled. 'Do you know what I've been through today, because of you? Have you any idea how it felt, trying to explain to those two imbeciles why I had let a total stranger do those things to me – something I find hard to explain even to myself?' She was furious now. 'They wanted to know everything. Times. Places. Positions. Even' – her voice broke slightly – 'what I was wearing.' The figure came towards her again, arms outstretched, and Sophie backed quickly away.

'Stay away from me!' she yelled. 'I know you! I know who you are!'

The man froze. Sophie could see him more clearly than ever before. He was tall, taller than Alex Carver, she could see now. He was too heavily built to be compared to Callum, with his tight, lithe body. The clothes were dark, anonymous. The mask was the same ski-type one he had worn the first time he had appeared at Sophie's bedside.

Sophie remembered the meetings. She recalled the excitement and the arousal – such as she had never felt before – the urge for more which she always felt after-wards. The anger had gone. In its place Sophie felt a sort of grudging gratitude towards the man who had awakened such potential for enjoyment inside her.

'James,' she said, softly. 'I know you're James.' The figure hadn't moved. 'It's got to stop,' she told him. 'I didn't tell the police it was you. Nobody knows; I won't tell. But it's got to stop.'

The man was still frozen. Then he reached out to clutch the nearest stable door for support. 'How . . .?' It was the only word he had ever spoken. Sophie felt suddenly, irrationally, that she didn't want to hear him speak.

'No more,' she told him. 'Just go.'

194

He turned and almost seemed to stagger to the door. Sophie watched dispassionately as he struggled with the latch on the door and let himself out in to the darkening night. When she locked up five minutes later, the mystery man had slipped from her life as if he had never been.

Chapter Ten

'You can try,' Jean told Sophie, doubtfully. 'But I warn you; he's in no fit state to be sensible.'

'Daddy's drunk,' Gina informed Sophie, cheerfully. 'He had a party all on his own, and now he's pickled.'

'Hurry up and eat that breakfast!' Jean ordered. 'It's school today for you; my nerves won't take another day of you winding your brother and sister up.'

'Good,' said Gina. 'I can't wait to tell Fiona that Mummy ran away and Daddy got drunk after the police had gone.'

'You'll do no such thing!' Jean shrieked, then, turning to Sophie, she rolled her eyes. 'Perhaps she should have another day off school.'

'Is it true about Mr McKinnerney?'

'Drunk as a lord,' Jean confirmed under her breath. 'Can't get any sense out of him. It's all very well, but that phone hasn't stopped ringing. I've had to deal with his parents, her boss, and any number of concerned friends . . .' Jean seemed uncharacteristically flustered.

'Is there anything I can do to help?'

'Probably not, dear, but thanks for the offer. I tell you; it's a good job that I don't take to the bottle at the first sign of trouble. It seems to be the natural reaction to every problem around here.' She beckoned Sophie away from the children and said, under her breath, 'That's not the best of it. I nearly had to break up a fight last night!'

'Jean! No! Who?'

'Mr McKinnerney and Mr Hamilton.'

'James and Dominic? Why?'

'Don't ask me, I couldn't make any sense of it. Mind you, Mr Hamilton has been very unpleasant about his sister's disappearance – blames James for it, you know.'

'Poor James.'

'Exactly my feelings. As if he hasn't got enough to put up with. Anyway, with any luck we shouldn't have to see the other one for the next few days.'

'Which one? Dominic?'

Jean nodded. 'He's got some sort of audition somewhere so that should keep him out of the way.'

'He's not too distraught at Catherine's disappearance to pass up the chance of a part then?' They laughed, then Jean spotted the letters in Sophie's hand.

'Oh dear. Don't tell me, let me guess – letters of resignation?'

Sophie held them up ruefully. 'I'm afraid so.'

'Oh, I can't say I blame you dear. I suspected you wouldn't want to stay for long from the minute you arrived. Well, who would?' She sat down wearily. 'And Callum, too? Oh dear. I don't know what's happening to this household, I really don't.'

'It's going to the dogs,' Gina explained.

'Gina! Eat that breakfast – now.'

'So,' Gina began slyly, digging in to her Co-Co Pops, 'am I having a day off, or do I get to tell Fiona all about this?'

'You evil little toad,' Sophie said, ruffling her hair. 'Be nice to Jean; she has a lot to put up with.'

'Haven't we all in this house?' murmured Jean as Sophie went to find her employer.

James was slumped in his chair in the study, staring morosely in to a glass of whiskey.

'Mr McKinnerney? Could I speak to you?'

'Come in, Sophie.' Although he had obviously been drinking, he did not seem particularly drunk, and he didn't seem embarrassed to see her, as she had imagined he would. 'I won't offer you a drink,' he said, without moving, 'as I'm sure you've got more sense.'

Sophie didn't say anything. She moved closer, holding the letters tightly. She knew that now was not a good time to deliver them but, in the circumstances, James McKinnerney was hardly in a position to object.

'Sit down.' He waved vaguely at another chair, and Sophie, who had had no intention of staying, sat. She was curious: was he going to mention his role as her mystery lover, or not? Would he apologise, and, if so, what would his excuse be? Would he beg her forgiveness, or at least her confidence? Or would he brazen it out, and try to pretend it was all a bad dream? That it never happened? The latter seemed most likely, judging by his lack of embarrassment and preoccupied demeanour. He seemed almost to have forgotten about it completely; perhaps he had had more to drink than Sophie had first thought.

He appeared to have forgotten she was there. She took the opportunity to study his face covertly. He looked older than his years again today – that was surely only to be expected – but in that weathered, comfortable way that truly handsome men have.

Sophie felt the familiar pang of loyalty to him and then berated herself; she must try to remember that any loyalty she felt for this man was totally misplaced. It was easier to remember if she recalled what she had been through, all because of him. Still, she thought, if he wanted to pretend their love-making had never happened, so be it – that suited her right down to the ground.

Staring at the large hands holding the crystal glass, Sophie knew that the memory of being caressed by those hands would never leave her. It felt strange knowing that his lips had been the ones which had descended so hungrily on hers in the darkness of the saddlery shop. Those fingers, Sophie thought weakly, have explored and aroused even my most intimate places.

And now, she realised sadly, that all that was over. He seemed not to have even noticed that she was still here.

'Mr McKinnerney?'

He started, then focused slowly on her, giving her a confused smile. 'I'm sorry, Sophie. I'm in a bit of a daze.'

She wanted to hand the letters to him and leave but, instead, blurted out, 'Are you all right? Can I do anything to help?'

'I wish you could but, no, I suspect not.' He frowned. 'Would you say that it was my fault that my wife has gone missing?'

Sophie stared at him. 'I don't know,' she said carefully. 'Was it?'

He looked up quickly. 'I haven't done anything to her, Sophie. She just went. I didn't even see her go. What I mean is, did I drive her away, do you think?'

Sophie wanted to say 'no' but how could she? If there was one thing she was sure of, it was that she didn't know James McKinnerney as well as she had originally supposed.

'I don't know. No one really knows . . .'

'No one really knows? Good God, Sophie! I thought you would be on my side. You saw what she was like! You took the brunt of her bad temper too.'

'What I was trying to say, was that no one knows what goes on in anyone else's marriage,' Sophie said, her temper rising. 'I only know what you've told me.' Implicit in her statement was her new-found distrust of anything he had told her in the past.

199

'And what you've seen! Despite her tantrums and her always goading me, I could never do enough for her. I could never harm her. Never! And now she's gone, anyway, despite my patience, my giving way all the time. And everyone – you included, it seems – believes it to be my fault.' His face was an angry red, and he slumped back sulkily in his chair.

Sophie fought hard to contain her mounting fury. Was he really so selfish that he had forgotten what had gone on between them? If he loved his wife so much why had he felt the need to search out her, Sophie?

'I suggest,' she said carefully, 'that you think very hard about what you are saying. Catherine probably thought that she had very reasonable grounds to leave you.' She wanted him to acknowledge their affair – if it could be called that – but still Sophie found it hard to speak about it directly.

'What do you mean? What grounds?'

Sophie was angry now. 'You know very well what I mean. It's no use you playing the wronged husband, not after what you've been up to, and especially not with me! It just doesn't wash.'

'Sophie, what are you talking about?' His face was ashen and he looked at her genuinely aghast.

'You know.' Sophie looked down, feeling herself blushing, despite the anger she felt at James for putting her through this. 'With me. It's no wonder she was so unpleasant to me. Did she know?'

'Did who know what?'

'Oh come on! It's too late to play stupid games.'

'Sophie, forgive me, but I really don't know what you're talking about.'

'You. And me. The cottage. The saddlery shop.' Her face was burning hot and she was finding it hard to raise her face to his. Why should I be ashamed? she thought furiously, willing herself to meet his eye.

'You? And me? I'm sorry . . . I don't . . .'

Sophie saw the confusion and bewilderment on his face and, with a sudden flood of panic, realised she had made a terrible mistake.

'It wasn't you, was it?' She felt pinned to the chair, devastated. Back to square one, she thought, suddenly uncertain of everything and everyone around her. But worse than that, James McKinnerney was leaning towards her, regarding her with curiosity and concern. 'Perhaps I will have that drink,' she whispered.

James seemed suddenly to be completely sober, as if the cold shower of Sophie's false accusation had been powerful enough to combat hours of heavy drinking. He poured her a large whiskey, and passed it to her shaking hands.

'I think you'd better tell me what all this is about.'

'I thought it was you.' Sophie felt wretched; drained. Another, just as worrying, thought was creeping in to her mind: if it wasn't James, who was it?

'You thought what was me, Sophie?' His voice was kind, but Sophie couldn't meet his eye.

How could she have made such a terrible mistake? She couldn't even bring herself to answer. Tears burned hot behind her eyes and her head was pounding. Suddenly the horrible truth hit James.

'Oh, Sophie! Not that intruder that the police were talking about? Is that it? Why would you think that was me? Talk to me, please. I do so want to get this sorted out, for my own peace of mind, as well as yours.'

Sophie would have laughed out loud if she hadn't been so miserable. Ask James for help? He couldn't even sort out his own life. 'It doesn't matter,' she croaked.

'It does matter – it matters very much. First of all, I want to know why you thought that that prowler was me.'

'Your glove,' she told him. 'Someone had been in my cottage and dropped a glove. Yesterday I realised it was yours.'

201

'Sophie, I couldn't honestly tell you when I lost that other glove,' he assured her. 'I haven't worn those gloves for months; I haven't needed to, it hasn't been cold enough. I may have lost the other one last year, for all I know. Now, how did this glove get into your cottage?'

'Someone left it there. Well, not in the cottage itself, but someone had been in the cottage.'

'How did they manage that?'

'They had a key.'

'A key? I have the only other key apart from yours.' He was thinking hard.

Sophie explained that the spare key was kept in the hall, and what Catherine's response had been to Sophie's request that it be kept somewhere safer.

'She really does have it in for you, doesn't she?' James marvelled. 'Now, Sophie, if you really don't want to, you don't have to tell me, but I would very much appreciate knowing what happened between you and this man.'

Sophie swallowed hard. 'Well, I suppose, everything.'

'Everything? What do you mean?'

'I could hardly call it a relationship – if I'm honest, it was just sex.'

'Ah, I see.' But it was obvious he didn't. He was trying not to look too taken aback. Sophie already knew what his next question would be and she was dreading it. 'Were you, er, shall we say, consenting?'

'Yes,' she whispered.

'Why, Sophie?'

'Because' – she forced herself to look him in the eye – 'because, secretly, I always hoped it was you. And because,' she added, refusing to be ashamed, 'I enjoyed it.'

It took several seconds before James even registered surprise, then he was out of his chair and pacing wildly behind his desk. 'Is this true? Do you think I could do those things? What must you have thought of me? We must get to the bottom of this. Is there anything you can tell me about this man that will help us find him?'

'He wore a mask.'

James was aghast. 'A mask? Good God! There must be something . . . did he speak?'

Sophie shook her head. 'He was always completely silent.'

James flopped back down in his chair. 'I just don't understand. What must you have thought of me,' he repeated, 'if you believed it was me doing those things to you?'

'I enjoyed "those things",' Sophie said, refusing to let him see her embarrassment. 'I just hoped you enjoyed it as much as me; and I flattered myself that you did.'

'Oh Sophie!' He put his head in his hands, wearily. 'I would never, ever do anything like that.' He raised his head to look at her earnestly. 'But please don't think it's because I don't find you attractive. I . . . I'm very much in love with my wife, still. Even after everything.' He was mumbling now, almost to himself. 'But in actual fact, I do. Find you attractive, that is. Very much so. Too much so, maybe.'

'You don't have to say that to make me feel better,' Sophie snapped, trying to cover her discomfort. 'I don't want or need your sympathy.'

James looked at her hard, without a trace of pity, and then sighed. 'I wish I was just saying it for that reason,' he told her. 'But the truth of the matter is that you bring a freshness and an honesty to this house that I find very appealing. If I'm truthful, Sophie, I have to tell you that I have had – how can I put this – feelings for you. When we talked on the balcony at the Newton-Smith's party, it was purely my own lack of courage, not loyalty to Catherine – I wasn't feeling much loyalty, that night – which stopped me doing what I wanted to do.' He laughed ruefully. 'That and the fact that I wouldn't have demeaned you by acting like the lecherous old "Lord of the Manor!"' They both laughed self-consciously.

'I'm sorry,' Sophie said quietly, 'for suspecting you. I should have known better.'

'And I'm sorry,' he said gallantly, 'that you should come to my home and be treated this way. All I can do is apologize. Of course, none of this helps us to find out who the prowler is.'

'Was. I saw him off last night.'

'How?'

Sophie related the incident in detail and James listened carefully. 'There was one thing,' she said eventually, loath to get back on the subject but knowing she had no choice. 'I accused the man of being you and from his reaction I had no reason to doubt that I was right.'

'What do you mean?'

'Well,' she said, thinking hard, 'whoever it was, they were quite happy for me to think it was you behind that mask.' James regarded her keenly, then leapt to his feet.

'Do you know, that actually makes sense, now I think about it. Look, Sophie, do you mind if I check a few things out? I'm not trying to get rid of you but I've got a feeling that between us we may get to the bottom of this yet.'

'No, it's fine by me.' Sophie got to her feet stiffly. 'I must go and get some work done anyway – the horses will think they've been abandoned otherwise. Just one thing; do you think this prowler has any relevance to Catherine's disappearance?'

'I don't know, Sophie. But I'm as determined to find out as you are. I feel as though I too have been wronged in all this. If someone is trying to make it appear that it is me doing these things, then I want to know why.' He sighed. 'Don't imagine that I will rest until I know what's going on; I don't like being set up like this.'

He had his hand on the door, ready to open it for her. 'By the way, Sophie, I meant what I said. That night at the

Newton-Smith's – remember? When we put Catherine to bed? I wanted you that night.' He was stumbling over the words, determined to say what had been on his mind, and so make her feel better about the misunderstanding. 'I dreamt about you that night; that's why I left early the next morning.' He laughed self-consciously, 'I couldn't face you after what we had done together in my imagination the previous night.'

Sophie laughed too. How could she have judged James so wrongly? 'Now that's what I call a guilt complex!' she told him.

He was serious again almost immediately. He put his hand on her arm. 'We will get to the bottom of this, Sophie, I promise.' She smiled at him and left, oblivious to the fact that she was still clutching the two letters.

'Oh, Sophie!' Callum was exasperated when he saw the envelopes still sitting on her mantelpiece. 'What am I going to do with you?' He handed her the coffee cups and went back into the tiny kitchen to fetch milk and sugar.

'Do I really have to tell you?' she called after him provocatively, stretching out in front of the fire. She was feeling quite pleased with herself; the meal she had just cooked for Callum had actually been rather good. This was unusual for her. Growing up in a large family had meant that everyone had taken turns with each and every job. This enforced helping in the kitchen had been the bane of her life. Although, Sophie had to admit, cooking for two – one of them Callum – felt very different. Perhaps, she thought, she would eventually really get to enjoy domesticity but somehow she doubted it very much.

'How did you manage to forget to give them to him?'

Sophie had to think hard to remember what they had been talking about, then she shrugged. 'Oh, the letters.'

There had been no point telling Callum about how she

had wrongly accused James of being the mystery man. In fact, so much had happened in the last couple of days that it seemed strange that Callum didn't know the whole story. On reflection, Sophie thought, it was good that he didn't; it was a relief not to have to answer any more questions about it. So many people seemed to have had to be told her most intimate secrets that Sophie felt utterly unsettled.

'I just couldn't do it,' she confessed. 'He's in such a state about Catherine. Jean told me that he and Dominic have almost come to blows over all this. If I had handed him the letters it would have felt like I was kicking him while he was down.' Sophie didn't add that they had had more pressing matters to discuss than her and Callum's resignations.

'You're too soft.'

'That's why you like me.'

'No,' he said, bringing in a tray containing the milk jug and sugar bowl. 'I like you for many reasons, but that isn't one of them.'

'Tell me.'

'Tell you what?'

'Some of the reasons.'

'No, you'll get big-headed.'

'Do you like me because you've just found out that, as well as all my other talents, I am an excellent cook?'

'No.'

'No?'

'Well, in all honesty, I couldn't care less about that. Anyway, you're not an excellent cook.'

'What!'

'You forgot something.'

Sophie racked her brains. 'Forgot something? What do you mean?'

'Pudding,' Callum affected a thick Yorkshire accent. '"A meal's not a meal without pudding," my Dad used to say.'

'And what did your Mum say at that point?'

'Usually told him to stop moaning and get on with the washing-up.'

'Well, you can stop moaning, too. You're very honoured that I cooked for you at all. After all those years of having to do it at home it comes second only to ironing as the job I least enjoy.'

'Well, as it happens, it's not a problem.'

'Oh good.'

'I took the liberty of bringing something for us.' He grinned wickedly at her, and Sophie felt a thrill of anticipation run through her. She had a strange feeling that whatever it was, it would not be a normal end to the meal. She smiled to herself. If there was one thing she could say for Callum, it was that he was never predictable.

'What is it?' She could smell a rich, sweet aroma drifting in from the kitchen.

'Wait and see.' he leered.

'You are thoughtful,' she sighed, wrapping her arms around his neck. 'Is there anything I can do?'

'Yes.' Callum sniffed the air. 'It's nearly ready. Get undressed.' Sophie thought she had misheard him.

'Sorry?'

'Get undressed; it's about ready, I reckon.'

'Aren't we going to eat first?'

'Sort of.' He grinned his lop-sided grin. 'Trust me, I'm a gardener.' And so saying, he disappeared back in to the kitchen. Sophie did as she was told, trying hard to place the delicious smell drifting enticingly into the living room.

What was he up to now? she wondered, undressing and lying in front of the fire. At length, Callum came back in. He stopped to admire her voluptuous body, then turned out the two small lamps, leaving the flickering firelight to throw shadows over her curves. When he returned from the kitchen the next time, he was holding something behind his back. The smell hung so thick in the air now that Sophie could almost taste it. It was rich, luxurious; it smelt wonderful.

'Chocolate?' asked Sophie. 'My favourite! Chocolate pudding? Chocolate mousse? What is it, Callum?'

He produced a small china jar with a handle, rather like a paint pot, and a thick, soft brush. 'Chocolate Sophie!' he announced, to her confusion. 'Lie down.'

She lay back, realising with growing delight what he intended to do, and watched as he stirred the smooth brown mixture with his finger. Then, drawing a line down her belly, he invited her to lick the rest off. Sophie did so, with great relish; it was just as delicious as the smell had promised. She tried to dip her own finger into the sweet thickness, but he pushed her back on to the rug.

'No. That's not the dessert. You are!'

'But I want some.'

'Then, I'm very much afraid,' he said, starting to unbutton his shirt, 'that you will have to eat it off me. It's the rules.' He stripped in the warm firelight as Sophie stole stray drips of chocolate from around the top of the pot and watched him. She never got over the wonder of Callum's body; it was the body of an athlete, of someone who lifted and carried and dug the ground. This was no half-hearted physique, like those of the men Sophie saw in town; men who sat behind desks all day, and stumbled to the gym twice a week. Callum had the hard, honed muscles and tanned complexion of a man thoroughly out of place in an office. His hips were slim and, when he joined her, naked, in front of the fire, his skin had a warm tightness that made Sophie shiver.

Beside the golden brown of his body, Sophie's skin looked ivory pale, the soft light from the fire lending it an appealing pinkness, not lost to Callum's appreciative gaze.

'Lie back,' he instructed her, holding the pot in one

hand and the brush in the other. Sophie giggled, and did as he said, squirming as perfectly round drops of chocolate appeared on her belly like warm pennies.

Callum was delighted. 'Spots!' he cried. 'The dreaded chocolate plague! Only I can save you now.' And he bent to scoop up the thick sweetness with his eager tongue. Sophie squealed as he dived to catch one wayward drop as it tried to escape round her waist, but Callum held her still as he licked it up, then raised his head to grin at her. She had to laugh: the wicked, lop-sided smile, and the chocolate ringing his mouth combined to give him the air of an overgrown child run amok in a sweet factory.

'Hungry?' he asked, 'I am!' He was over her with the pot again, this time turning her navel into a tiny chocolate well and urging her not to move. Sophie tried hard to keep still as he drank the liquid chocolate from her belly but his probing tongue, and the feel of his hair brushing her sides, made her squirm again – and the well overflowed.

'Oh no! Look out. Quick!' He swooped down again catching dribbles and trickles here and there. When he eventually stopped to catch his breath, Sophie laughed to see that he even had chocolate in his hair.

In mock fury, he grabbed the brush and daubed bold designs on both her breasts then, before she could retaliate, he was upon her, devouring her, it seemed to Sophie, as his mouth licked and sucked the chocolate from her body.

Reaching over his shoulder, determined to have her revenge, Sophie grabbed the brush and slapped it wetly across his chest. Callum gave a hoot and grabbed the brush off her.

'You'll pay for that,' he promised. 'Right, now you can lick it off. Come on!' And Sophie set to work with a vengeance on the sticky trail across Callum's taut chest. When she raised her head he was watching her and smiling, the smudgy mark around his mouth giving him the appearance of a renegade clown.

'Stand up,' he urged and, kneeling before her, he dipped the paintbrush into the pot once more. He painted circles spiralling out from her nipples, the brush gliding across them like a feather. Down her belly he painted a line, pausing only to coat the inside of her navel again, making a neat chocolate cup. Then, replenishing his brush, he slid it, dripping, between her legs, shiny drops sticking in the bush of blonde hair like dew on a spider's web.

Sophie steadied herself against Callum's shoulders as he gently parted her pussy lips and began to coat her womanhood. She stood very still so as not to break his concentration, for Callum was engrossed in daubing the thick sweetness over, and into, her.

'Chocolate-coated Sophie,' he murmured at last, rocking back on his heels to survey his handiwork.

Sophie's body had taken on a startling appearance – like the enormous faces that adorned the wings of exotic butterflies to deter predators. Or maybe, Sophie mused, it was the war-paint of a warrior woman belonging to an undiscovered tribe. Whatever it was, it made Sophie feel primitive and reckless.

'My turn!' she said, grasping the brush and pulling Callum to his feet. As she moved, she felt the sliding looseness of the unfamiliar substance inside her. It felt strange and exciting.

She used the brush to define Callum's muscles, looping strokes across his chest, and a criss-cross of marks for the washboard tautness of his belly. She giggled as she gave his prick a jaunty chocolate hat then, licking that off, she proceeded to paint it properly, until it stood – smooth and shiny brown – in front of her.

Before she had a chance to savour the enticing chocolate-coated penis, Callum lay down on the rug and pulled Sophie down to straddle his face. Without further ado,

210

he plunged his mouth into her glistening sticky-sweet womanhood and began to gorge himself. Sophie leant over him, slipping sensuously as their chocolate-slick bellies met, and took him in her mouth. They lay, a head at either end, filling their noses and mouths with the rich sweetness of each other.

Callum's tongue was deep inside Sophie, lapping eagerly to reach every last drop of the chocolate; and then, when that was gone, carrying on for the sheer pleasure of being inside her.

Sophie, for her part, smelt, touched, and tasted chocolate – until she couldn't remember what the usual smells and tastes of sex were at all. The sticky dribbles ran down Callum's penis and dropped on to his balls, making him wriggle as Sophie strained to reach them with her tongue. When the chocolate was gone – just the drying designs on their bellies gluing them together – Sophie was relieved; she enjoyed the feel and taste of Callum just as much without embellishment.

His rigid, smooth-headed penis and the rough, heavy balls were both exhilaratingly strange and dearly familiar to her by now, and she applied herself to them with the firmness that she knew he enjoyed. This was not easy as his tongue was causing her all manner of distractions and she groaned as he flicked playfully at her clitoris. She tried hard to concentrate. Callum's penis was hard and tight, his gasps indicating that he was not far away from coming.

Sophie herself was melting, opening to him, her own juices mingling with the residue of chocolate on his lips. Her knees felt weak as his tongue once more caressed her, entered her and claimed her. She felt him deep inside her and was overcome with a desire for it never to be over; for it to go on and on, the two of them locked together forever.

Callum's mouth was coupled with her pussy lips, and she felt – rather than heard – his moans of pleasure reverberating through her body. It felt that the vibrations reached every corner of her body, her very being responding to his special music.

He was coming now – unearthly gasps escaping from him – his groans triggering Sophie's responses, and she soon joined him, shuddering and panting; they were so locked together in embrace that they resembled some strange two-headed creature.

Eventually they took themselves off to the bathroom, their shrill delight echoing through the cottage as they discovered chocolate in places about their bodies that they had hitherto been unaware it could hide.

Their daily routine seemed to have gone out of the window, Sophie couldn't help thinking, as she watched Callum teaching Gina how to juggle. It couldn't be good for the children: Gina was missing school again today, Ellie hadn't gone to playgroup, and Jean – usually so efficient and organised – was reduced to tending the ever-ringing phone.

James appeared to be lying low after yesterday's indulgence, and Sophie felt edgy and uncertain; everything seemed to be in limbo. It was the third day Catherine had been missing, although it seemed much longer. Sophie wondered if anything would ever be the same here again. Even the horses seemed to be waiting for her return. Firefly was skittish and snappy, and Jasmine was just not eating properly. The only creature who seemed unaffected by the heavy atmosphere was Buzz, who was just as awful as ever.

It was funny, Sophie thought, how Catherine could still affect their moods so drastically, even when she wasn't there. She sighed, and went back to the mucking out. In the yard, Gina was trying – unsuccessfully – to persuade Callum to take her to the cinema.

'You'll like it, Callum, honestly.'

'What's it called, this film?'

212

'101 Dalmatians.'

Callum winked at Sophie. 'What's all that about then, I wonder?'

'Lots of dogs,' Gina told him.

'Oh! Dalmatians! I thought you said "Damnations!" I thought it was about someone who swore a lot.'

Gina squealed in fury and thumped him.

'I'll miss her,' Callum confided to Sophie when Jean had called the child in for lunch. 'She's a good kid, considering what she has to put up with.'

'Forget that,' Sophie told him, sternly. 'You've got a job to do; remember?'

Callum's face fell. 'Why do I have to do it?'

'We agreed.'

'You agreed!'

'We both agreed, Callum.'

'Oh, all right. All right!'

'Have you changed your mind? About leaving?'

'No, of course not. Have you?'

'No. Look,' she relented, 'if you really don't want to give the letters to James . . .'

'It's OK, I'll do it.' Callum took them off her and hung his head. 'A man's gotta do what a man's gotta do and all that. Wish me luck.'

'Oh good grief, Callum! You're only going to hand in our letters of notice, you're not going to the gallows or anything!'

'''Tis a far, far better thing, that I do now . . .'

'Right! That's it! Give them here. Better still, I'll come with you – make sure you get there. I know you: you'll decide to drain and sweep the swimming pool on the way and never get round to it!'

'What a good idea.'

Sophie sent Callum to find James while she popped into the kitchen, where Jean was dishing up the children's lunch. If possible, it was even more fraught than

213

usual. The two younger children were fretting over their mother's absence while Gina merely took advantage.

'I don't like fish fingers,' Gina was announcing as Sophie entered. 'I liked them yesterday but I don't like them today.'

'Oh yes you do.' Jean's face was determined. She pulled a face at Sophie then turned back to the child. 'It's that or go hungry.'

Gina pushed her plate away. 'I'll go hungry, thanks.'

'Fine.' Jean scooped up the plate, and put it near the dishwasher. 'No pudding for you then.'

'What's for pudding?'

'Nothing if you don't eat your fish fingers.'

'I'm eating mine,' Ellie said reproachfully.

Gina shot her a dirty look. 'Well I hope you like frog-spawn,' she whispered, 'because that's what's for pudding.'

Ellie went white. 'Jean,' she asked carefully, 'Do I like frog-spawn?' Sophie's heart went out to poor Jean. She recalled the last time they had chatted.

'I'm getting too old for this,' the nanny had confided. 'My sister's just bought a lovely little retirement cottage in Sussex. I was thinking . . .'

'Oh no, Jean,' Sophie had said, laughing. 'You've got years in you yet. Anyway, we can't all leave at once! I'm sorry, but you'll have to stay for a while. You don't escape that easily.'

They had joked about it, but Sophie knew full well that the past few weeks had been an enormous strain on all of them. Jean had been there for the children all their lives – arriving in the house on the first day that Catherine brought Gina home from hospital – and would not make the decision to move on lightly.

Still, as she had told Sophie, she wasn't a young woman any more, and Peter would not be a baby for long. 'They will need one of these new nannies with bags of energy and footballing skills.'

Sophie had laughed, but she could see Jean's point. Sophie watched her now, persuading Gina to try the fish fingers once more.

'Callum likes fish fingers,' Sophie mentioned casually, ensuring that they at once became Gina's favourite food. Jean gave her a look of pure gratitude while simultaneously pouring juice, mopping Peter's chin and trying to decide – at Ellie's earnest request – whether she preferred Snow White or Sleeping Beauty.

Once they were safely through the main course, Jean produced sponge pudding and custard – much to Ellie's relief – and then began the clearing up, gratefully allowing Sophie to make coffee for them both.

'They'll have a hard time replacing you,' Sophie told her in admiration, 'when you decide to go.'

'I couldn't leave at the moment,' Jean said. 'Not until everything is settled. I wouldn't dream of upsetting the children further; certainly not before the right person is found to replace me.'

The children – out of earshot in the hall – were trying, shrieking and laughing, to climb on to Brin's back for a ride. So it was only by chance that the two women heard the familiar sound of tyres on gravel. With Catherine's disappearance still heavy on their minds every car on the drive, every door slamming, every key in the lock – for the front door was now kept locked – had taken on a new significance.

Jean and Sophie, adept at feigning nonchalance in front of the children, glanced quickly at each other. Then Gina's clear voice rang through the house.

'Look, everybody – Mummy's home!'

Sure enough, when Sophie peered through the hall window behind Gina, she saw that the child was right. Climbing out of a car, which Sophie didn't recognise, was Catherine. She looked different, Sophie thought. Smaller. Paler. A confused and less vibrant version of herself.

As Sophie watched, the driver's door opened, and Alex Carver leapt out, quickly opening the boot and depositing what could only be Catherine's bags on the gravel drive. He did this as though they were hot, or as if he feared that any contact with them meant he ran the risk of catching some terrible disease.

Catherine watched him, her eyes huge with bewilderment, as he threw them before him, the exasperation etched on his face.

All Sophie could think of was that they were not exactly a good advertisement for adultery. Catherine looked as though she would burst into tears at any time, while Alex resembled the 'before' picture in a promotion for indigestion relief. In the hall, Jean and Sophie gave each other another cryptic glance, as Ellie bounced from door to stairs, shouting for her father and generally working Peter up into a frenzy of excitement. Gina, Sophie couldn't help noticing, looked decidedly unenthusiastic.

'I suppose this means school tomorrow?' she asked, miserably. Jean ignored her and rushed to open the door, but was stopped in her tracks. James had appeared at the top of the stairs. Callum trailed behind him, still holding the letters.

'Is it her?' James asked, as if he couldn't bear the disappointment which might result from opening the door to find out for himself. Jean nodded in confirmation.

Everyone stood back as he descended the stairs. Even Ellie stopped yelling and skipped over to hold her father's hand. James looked down at her and smiled briefly, then handed her to Jean.

'Jean, would you be kind enough to take the children to the playroom?' he asked, prompting Gina to cheer up instantly.

'I want to watch if there's going to be trouble,' she whispered to Sophie. Jean hastily bundled the children upstairs, Gina protesting about the unfairness of it all.

216

Callum and Sophie gave each other a meaningful look as James opened the front door. 'I haven't managed to give him these yet,' hissed Callum.

'Never mind that, just stick around in case there's any hassle,' Sophie whispered back.

She needn't have worried; James was a gentleman to the last. He descended the front steps slowly, almost languidly, nodding at Alex Carver as if he were merely a taxi-driver who had brought Catherine home from a party. She stood with her back to Alex, watching James, her eyes brimming and her bottom lip trembling.

'Catherine.' James said her name as if he were pleasantly surprised to have her drop in on him unexpectedly.

'He doesn't want me,' she wailed shockingly, the floodgates opening as she flung herself into her husband's arms. Alex Carver was looking alternately embarrassed and defiant, as if he wasn't sure whether to expect sympathy or violence.

James calmed his wife quietly and then turned to Sophie. 'Would you mind taking Mrs McKinnerney upstairs, Sophie? Thank you.' Sophie, cursing that she was going to miss the drama, put a perfunctory arm around Catherine's shoulders and led her upstairs.

'He didn't want me!' Catherine kept exclaiming, as if she could just not see why that should be. She looked at Sophie from mascara-smudged eyes. 'He said I should be in a mental hospital!' She began wailing again, and Sophie patted her back, trying to find an iota of sympathy for this woman who had caused so much trouble.

'Then he asked me to take the bags in,' Callum moaned, when they met up to compare stories later.

'Oh no! So you didn't hear what he said to Alex either?'

'Aha! That's where you're wrong. I took the bags up the steps, but I stayed by the front door – just in case.'

'Oh well done, Callum! So, what did James say?'

'He was brilliant!' Callum's eyes shone at the memory of it. 'Alex Carver was really squirming and James just stood there for ages, letting him stew. In the end Alex tried to tell him that nothing had happened between him and Catherine; and how he had persuaded Catherine to come home. James didn't say anything. Then Alex tried to say that he thought Catherine needed professional help and James said, "Ah, I see. Like a doctor, you mean?" And Alex went bright red.

'Then James said, "Well, I'm sure we all respect your professional opinion." And Alex got all stroppy. He said he didn't have to bring Catherine home, that he wanted no part in her schemes – '

'He what?'

'Wanted no part in her schemes. That's what he said.'

'I wonder what he meant by that?'

'Who knows? They're all as barmy as each other. Anyway, James didn't question him about it so it must have made sense to him. So then James just said, "No, it wouldn't look too good, would it?" and turned to come indoors.'

'Was that it?'

'No, wait! That's more or less what Alex said; "Is that it?" As if he expected a fight. And James turned to him and said, "Where are my manners? Thank you for bringing my wife home!"'

Callum and Sophie both laughed at this.

'Yes,' Sophie said, 'that sounds like James.'

Callum pretended to cringe, as if expecting a blow. 'But I still didn't manage to hand the letters to him.'

'Oh Callum!'

'Well, how could I? It didn't seem right, somehow.'

'You're right, I know. It's just that sometimes I think the time will never be right, and we'll be here for ever.'

'Well with any luck, things should start to settle down a bit from now on.'

Sophie remembered these words later in the day as

she, Callum, and Jean waited nervously in the sitting room of Prospect House. Their work was done for the day and the children had had an early night in preparation for Gina's being back at school the following day.

'I think,' Jean had confided to Sophie, 'that this could do Catherine a lot of good. I know it's been a shock for her, Alex turning her down. It's dented her ego, she's used to getting what she wants.'

It had seemed less like he had turned her down, Sophie thought, and more as though he had turned her in. Catherine had more of the attitude of a returned prison escapee than of a homecoming wife and mother. Sophie had also found out, after a chance remark from Catherine, that Alex Carver had given her some kind of injection. 'A tranquiliser, of some sort,' she had reported to James later. He had been furious.

'That explains why he didn't just put her in a car and send her home. Tranquilisers! Bloody quack doctor! I'll have him for professional misconduct for this.'

He had calmed down eventually and asked that all the staff come to the house that evening, although he didn't specify why. Sophie was amazed at his ability to still care so passionately about how his wife was treated when she had so callously disregarded his feelings.

'Love.' Callum told her. 'It makes idiots of the best of us.'

'Speak for yourself!' Jean laughed.

At that moment James entered, shutting the door quietly behind him. They all fell silent and he stood, nervously, as if he didn't remember why he had called them there himself. At length he realised that they were all watching him expectantly, and he launched into what he wanted to say.

'Thanks for coming, all of you. I am well aware of how much extra time you have had to put in on my behalf over the last few days. You have done it without complaint, and for that alone I am extremely grateful.

Having said that, I don't want to take up too much more of your time again this evening, but I would like to say a few words.

'It has been an awful time for us – all of us – and I have been very touched at the way you have all carried on, being cheerful and conscientious, despite everything. I would like to be able to tell you that you will not have to put up with this sort of upheaval and unpleasantness again.' He rubbed his eyes wearily. 'But I'm afraid I just can't promise. Between us four – and I don't really want this to go any further – Catherine needs help. I'm not talking hospitals,' he added quickly, 'but maybe something gentler, less intrusive.'

Sophie marvelled at his tolerance. Heaven help the psychotherapist who got Catherine, she thought.

'Anyway,' James continued, 'the important thing is that she is home now and, hopefully, will soon be well. I want to thank you all once again for your tremendous support. I'm glad that all of this hasn't driven any of you away.' Sophie and Callum exchanged guilty glances.

'Now,' James told them, 'comes the clearing up after the event. Jean, perhaps you would be good enough to help me contact all the people who have been ringing about Catherine, tomorrow? Just to let them know that she's alive and well. The Marshalls. The Fields. I expect that Marcie Carver is getting her own version of events at this very moment.' He laughed without humour. 'We won't worry about her. I made certain I phoned Dominic the first opportunity that I got. He said he would be round to visit Catherine tomorrow on his way to London.'

'That's all we need,' muttered Jean. At that moment the doorbell rang and she went off to answer it.

'Sophie,' James said quietly, 'I would appreciate a little chat with you afterwards. Something you definitely should know.' He didn't have time to elaborate before

Jean entered, closely followed by DC Ashwell and DS Bettridge.

Ashwell was grinning fit to burst. 'Lovely!' he kept saying, to no one in particular and for no apparent reason. Bettridge, as usual, looked disinterested and sullen, as if he could think of at least a thousand more important things to be doing than this.

Jean introduced them – more for Callum's benefit, than anyone else's – and then Ashwell, who was so excited he could barely stand still, blurted out, 'We've found her car!' Everyone gazed at him, mystified, until James realised what it was that he was talking about.

'Ah! Catherine's car?'

'Mrs McKinnerney's car.' Ashwell took out his notebook importantly, and read off a number plate. 'But,' he continued, 'I'm afraid your wife wasn't in the car.'

'But that's a good sign, we think,' Bettridge quickly interjected.

'It means she's not been in an accident,' Ashwell explained, rather weakly.

'Yes, I see,' James said. Sophie could see he was trying to think of a kind way of telling them that Catherine was home. Callum beat him to it.

'She'll be pleased,' he said.

'Sorry?' The smile was frozen on Ashwell's face.

'Mrs McKinnerney,' Callum said, slowly and clearly, 'will be pleased that you've found her car.'

'And you are . . .?' Bettridge's eyes were fixed firmly on Callum.

'Callum. Mr McKinnerney's gardener.'

'Ah!' Bettridge glanced at Sophie, obviously trying to remember the context in which he had heard mention of the gardener before.

'Oh!' cried Ashwell, in horror, remembering first. Callum looked from one to the other, before clearly deciding that they were completely mad.

'Actually,' James said, not at all sure what was going

on, 'I have some important news for you regarding my wife.'

'Lovely!' said Ashwell, poised over his notebook.

'She's upstairs.'

'Upstairs? Lovely! Excellent!'

'It's not "lovely" or "excellent",' snapped Bettridge. 'Why weren't we told?'

'He's telling you now,' Callum said, exasperated. 'What's up with you people? I don't know!' He turned to Sophie. 'Shall I meet you later in the pub?'

'Sure,' she said, trying not to laugh at the comical faces of Bettridge and Ashwell. 'I'll see you down there.' Callum departed, muttering to himself.

James, like Sophie, appeared to be trying to keep a straight face, but he had more control. 'It just remains for me to thank you, gentlemen,' he said politely, 'for all the concern you have shown for my wife's disappearance.'

Ashwell looked crestfallen. 'Right you are, then, Mr McKinnerney. And, Miss Ward, if you ever want to talk to us about that other thing . . .'

'I won't.'

'Right you are, then. Lovely.' Jean showed them out.

James closed the door behind all of them and then came to sit opposite Sophie on the matching sofas.

'Well,' he began nervously, 'I've been talking to Catherine and, with a little persuasion, she confirmed something that I was just beginning to suspect. You should brace yourself, Sophie – it is rather disturbing news, I'm afraid.'

Chapter Eleven

'Dominic?' Sophie's anguished cry rang through the room, and she quickly clapped her hand over her mouth as if deciding, too late, that the information should be kept secret.

Catherine – who had decreed that all her own behaviour over the last few days could be accredited to illness – had taken to her bed, delighted to have such a good excuse to do so.

As with everything else, Sophie thought, bitterly, she had not done it by halves. Jean was up and down the stairs like a thing possessed, whilst Catherine sat, in glamorous splendour, giving orders.

'Well he's not that bad,' Catherine responded testily. Sophie could have hit her. James hovered at the side of Catherine's bed, looking alternately embarrassed and angry.

'I think,' he said, carefully, 'that the least Sophie deserves is a full explanation for all this. I also think,' he added, looking hard at Catherine, 'that you should try your very best to handle this with tact and humility.' Catherine, for once, appeared to be listening.

James turned in the doorway. 'Try to remember,' he

said ominously to Catherine, 'that the outcome of all this rather depends on Sophie's good nature. Sophie, I shall be downstairs if you need me.' The two women watched the door close.

Sophie sat down heavily on a pink wicker chair, her mind in a whirl. 'Dominic?' she said again. 'Why? And how do you know?'

Catherine had the decency to shoot her a sympathetic glance. Whether it was down to her own compassion or James's thinly-veiled threats, Sophie couldn't tell.

'I am sorry, Sophie. I know this must be an awful shock for you. Your mystery man, prowler – whatever you want to call him – really was Dominic. We planned it together.'

A feeling of unreality was rapidly overtaking Sophie. She looked round the room at the lacy white curtains, the vast bed with its hand-embroidered bedspread, the cuddly toys lined up on the window seat. It's like a child's room, thought Sophie, only we're not children any more. We are adults, and the games we have been playing are adult games.

Still her eyes roamed around the room, taking in the pastel coloured cushions and the silver hairbrush on the dresser – anything rather than come to rest on Catherine's face. 'Why?' she asked, eventually. 'Why would you want to do that to me?'

'It wasn't you. We weren't trying to do anything to you,' Catherine said, laughing as if it was all some silly misunderstanding. 'It was James who should have been the real victim.'

'James?'

'Yes, James, my husband.' Catherine spoke as if to an imbecile and then, suddenly remembering James's words, checked herself. She sighed. 'It was for the money really.'

'For the money?' Sophie was incredulous.

'It's a lot of money,' Catherine said, defensively. 'Well,

it could have been a lot of money.' She sighed again at what might have been.

Sophie was having no problems looking her in the eye now. 'So that was what it was all about, was it – money?'

Catherine nodded. 'I would have needed some of my own – if I'd left James,' she explained, as if this would make it all seem suddenly reasonable.

'And where,' Sophie asked through clenched teeth, 'do I come into all this? Just out of interest?'

Catherine was starting to look nervous. 'Well, we thought – Dominic and I – that if we made it look as though James was having an affair with you, I could legitimately leave him and take him to court for half his money.'

Sophie was holding on tight to the arms of the wicker chair. Her knuckles were white and her whole jaw ached where her teeth seemed to be locked together. 'And it didn't occur to you,' she hissed, 'that someone could get very badly hurt in all this?'

Catherine shrugged. 'It was a risk we had to take, really.' She seemed quite carried away with her own cleverness. 'We planned it down to the last detail.'

'And that's supposed to make me feel better, is it?'

Catherine ignored her. 'Of course we thought about trying to get you and James together without involving Dominic, but we knew that was a long shot. You know what James is like, a real old stick-in-the-mud. So no chance of that. But actually,' she said thoughtfully, 'when we saw you we did wonder whether your charms might be enough to break the habits of a lifetime.'

Sophie listened, aghast. She could hardly believe, even knowing Catherine as she did, how little she cared for other people. She was, thought Sophie with grudging admiration, the most spectacularly selfish person that she had ever had the misfortune to come across.

'Anyway,' Catherine continued, anxious for Sophie to

appreciate the full extent of her cleverness, 'we thought it would be good practice for Dominic.'

'For Dominic?'

'You know, to test his acting skills.' She giggled. 'He tried so hard to imitate James's voice, but in the end he just couldn't do it. That's when we hit on the idea of a silent seduction.' She sounded quite excited.

Sophie stood slowly and wandered across the room to look out of the window. 'Do you have any idea what you've put me through?' she asked eventually. 'Can you possibly imagine what it's like to keep looking at total strangers and wondering if it's them? To not know whether you see the person every day, without realising?'

Catherine looked quite taken aback, as if this had never occurred to her. Sophie wasn't surprised; Catherine never saw anything from any point of view but her own, it was clear.

'I've said I'm sorry,' Catherine said petulantly.

'You're only sorry because you got caught out,' Sophie said. It was all becoming clear. 'You're only sorry because you told Alex Carver your little scheme and he wanted no part of it. It wouldn't have occurred to you to be sorry if everything had worked out the way you planned.'

Catherine looked down at her hands. When she lifted her head again, Sophie was astounded to see tears in her eyes. 'He didn't want me,' she gulped.

'He did want you,' Sophie reassured her, 'but he didn't want all the trappings. Unfortunately for you, he wanted a good time with no strings attached. When he found out you were planning to leave James, he panicked; that wasn't what he had had in mind at all. You see, he's basically happy with Marcie. She understands him. And she puts up with all his womanising, which most women wouldn't – '

'She's horrible to him!'

'As horrible as you are to James, would you say?'

Catherine looked down at her hands again. 'Anyway,' she mumbled, 'I don't understand why you got the police involved.'

Sophie turned on her vehemently. 'I didn't get the police involved – you did! By disappearing! It was only when you went missing that they turned up, so don't blame me for that. What's more, you're very lucky that the police weren't involved after the first time that Dominic played his little trick. How did you know that I wouldn't call them there and then?'

Catherine shrugged. 'We didn't, really. But once we knew you weren't going to call them in after the first incident, we guessed we had you. Anyway, if you had called them in, what could you have told them? Not much. There weren't many clues around, but the ones that were there all pointed to James.'

'So you were quite prepared to drop James in at the deep end with the police as well, were you? You really are unbelievable! All I can say is, what a good job that you went off when you did. Heaven knows where it would all have ended otherwise.'

Catherine looked quite tearful again. 'I've blown it, haven't I? What an idiot! I can't believe I've messed things up so badly.'

At last, Sophie thought, remorse! 'You may not have completely blown it,' she said, looking down at the weeping woman. 'James has obviously convinced himself that all this stems from some sort of illness – temporary insanity, or something. He's so glad to have you back he's obviously not going to make a big thing of it. He must really love you,' she added, 'because in his position, most men would have come close to murdering you by now.'

'I meant,' snapped Catherine, 'that I've blown it with Alex!'

Sophie turned on her heel and exited the room before

227

the temptation to slap Catherine became too great. Out in the hallway, she leant her head back against the wall and tried to think. So she now knew the identity of her masked seducer. She knew who he was. She knew why – as much as she was ever going to, anyway. What she didn't know was what she was going to do about it.

Dominic! She shook her head. What a truly amoral pair he and his sister were! And they had come very close to getting away with it all. If Sophie had remembered that glove in her interview with the police, she would have dropped James right in it, without ever meaning to. She re-ran her secret meetings with Dominic in her head. All she could really think about was how she would ever face him again. Her cheeks burned in humiliation and she walked woodenly towards the stairs.

Perhaps, she thought desperately, I won't have to face him. Perhaps I can avoid him, at least until I can get away from here permanently. But even as she allowed herself the luxury of this fantasy, she remembered James telling them last night that Dominic would visit his sister today on the way to his audition.

Well, thought Sophie, clutching the wide banisters for support, at least he should be good at the audition; he'd had enough practice at deception over the last few weeks.

She imagined him reporting his antics with Sophie back to his sister – the two of them amusing themselves at her expense – and a blind fury gripped her. Why should they get away with this, she thought. Just because James indulged Catherine like a spoilt child – ignoring her many faults, closing his eyes to her nastiness – it didn't mean Sophie had to do the same. As for Dominic, Sophie was determined not to let it end here. But what could she do? It was too late to go to the police now; and she had to admit she had been a willing accomplice.

Somehow, she thought, I don't know how, but somehow, I'll face him. As she passed the sitting room door it opened, and James poked his head out.

'Sophie,' he called after her. She turned to face him. 'I just wanted to say – '

'I don't really want to hear it,' she told him.

He hung his head. 'I'm sorry, Sophie.'

'Everybody's sorry. You're sorry. Catherine's sorry. I'm sorry – I'm sorry I ever came here!'

He moved towards her. 'I feel that I've let you down.'

She felt furious with him. He had let her down, as surely as if it really had been him behind the ski-mask. If he hadn't been always so willing to accept and forgive Catherine's behaviour . . .

'You must wonder why I put up with her,' James said, as if he was reading her mind, 'but I do love her, Sophie. Sometimes – a lot of the time, actually – I wish I didn't. But I do.'

Sophie suddenly felt utterly tired of them all. 'You won't be surprised to hear that I'm leaving,' she told him. 'But you might be surprised to hear that Callum is coming with me.'

He looked for a moment as though he might object, then thought better of it. 'I'm not at all surprised,' he admitted. 'I will, of course, give you both excellent references. And you're welcome to stay at the cottage until you've found somewhere else.' She nodded. 'And Sophie?'

She looked at him, defiantly.

'I am sorry, truly. Catherine admitted it all when I talked to her yesterday. I think she assumed that Alex Carver had spilled the beans about her plan. I didn't know what to do. If I'm honest, I have to say that I was tempted to ignore the whole thing. It doesn't endear her to me, knowing what she and Dominic had planned. I had to speak out, if only so that you could know the man's identity. I hope I did right.'

Sophie didn't know what to say so she just nodded

and turned to go. In the doorway she stopped. 'What time is Dominic due here today?' she asked.

'About two o'clock, I think. But, Sophie, I don't think it's a very good idea for you to – '

The door slammed and she had gone.

The wind sung a wild song in Sophie's ears. She narrowed her eyes against the rush of air, her cheeks stinging where Firefly's whipping mane caught them as they pounded up the long field. The only sounds were of her own blood pumping fiercely through her heart, and Firefly's heaving snorts. She could feel the thumping of his great, heavy feet falling, but the actual sound was muted by the wet clay soil.

He was reaching the top of the hill now, Sophie being flung backwards and forwards as he laboured up the steepest part – rather like riding a huge rocking horse. His feet must feel awfully heavy to him, she thought, what with all the sodden earth pulling him down. But still she pushed him and still he responded.

That, she thought, was the kind of horse that Firefly was: he had a huge heart and was always eager to please. As they reached the top of the hill, Firefly swerved to a stop in his usual place.

'Not today,' Sophie told him. 'Today we're going the long way round.'

She turned his head left and squeezed him into a canter around the outside of the woods. Firefly was happy to oblige. Great clods of brown clay were left whirling in the air behind them as he got his haunches under him and found his stride.

They galloped across the field, Firefly's black mane and Sophie's blonde hair streaming out behind them as they thundered along the path. Turning the corner, Sophie could see someone up ahead, making repairs to the fence that bounded the McKinnerney estate. It was

Callum. Firefly saw him too; his brown furry ears flicked forwards, then back again, to await Sophie's instructions.

'Whoa, boy,' she told him. Firefly made a huge show of going too fast to stop, putting on the brakes in a skidding, swerving pantomime that still managed to shower Callum with mud.

'Cheers, Firefly,' he said sarcastically, when the huge bay eventually stood, snorting dramatically, beside him. He leant across to pat the horse's great neck and, taking hold of the reins, smiled up at Sophie.

'Are you feeling better now?' he asked. She had phoned the pub the previous night to tell him she wouldn't be meeting him. She had excused herself with a headache, the real reason being the shock of James's news about Dominic. Despite, or maybe because of, her insistence, James would not let her speak to Catherine that evening. Sophie had had to spend a restless and unpleasant night waiting until she could get the full story in the morning.

She had not seen Callum since the meeting which James had called in the sitting room the day before. It took her a few moments to remember this, and so realise what Callum was talking about.

'You still look a bit pale,' he said with concern. 'Should you be out, do you think?'

'I'm OK,' she told him. 'I just had a bit of a shock, that's all. Nothing to worry about,' she added quickly, not really wanting to give a full explanation. 'But I have got a confession to make. I told James we were leaving. He was very good about it – says I can stay in the cottage until I find something else,' she gabbled. 'Anyway, at least he knows.'

Callum was watching her closely. 'Well, that's all right then. Look, Sophie, are you sure you're feeling OK? Has something upset you?'

She couldn't look at him. She made a big show of letting out Firefly's girth a notch or two; in actual fact,

231

she was trying not to cry. She was all right, she thought, until she was shown some sympathy, then all her defences came down at once and the floodgates opened.

Callum stepped forward and caught her as she dismounted unsteadily. Supporting her, and still holding Firefly's reins, he secured the horse to a fence post and held her to him.

'Tell me, Sophie, please.'

'I can't!' Her sobs were muffled, grudging. She didn't want to cry over Dominic – he wasn't worth her tears, she kept telling herself.

'Hey,' Callum told her, gently, 'don't think that I'm going to lend you a hanky again; I didn't get the last one back!'

Sophie gave a giggle – half-hiccup, half-laugh – and burst into tears. Callum said nothing. He just held her against him tightly, stroking her back and murmuring into her hair. 'It'll be all right,' he told her. 'Whatever it is, it will be all right. We'll be out of this place soon. Hush, Sophie. Don't cry.'

She was angry with herself. 'I'm sorry, Callum. I'm being stupid. I'm really sorry . . .'

'It doesn't matter. Hush. I might have some good news for you anyway. A new job – for both of us. How's that, eh? Once we get out of here we'll both feel better, won't we?'

She blew her nose and wiped her eyes, hope suddenly surging through her. 'Another job? Where? Together?'

'A long way from here,' he said vehemently. 'That fact alone makes it all the more appealing as far as I'm concerned.'

Sophie laughed; his enthusiasm was infectious. 'So tell me about it.'

'Two jobs, for a couple – groom and gardener, same as here. But with occasional chauffeuring duties thrown in for me, and some light housework for you. The money is about the same as we are getting now, I think, but with

232

self-contained accommodation, so I wouldn't be paying rent – which means we would be better off in the long run.'

Sophie was so excited, she had to stop herself from leaping up and down. She felt as though a weight was slowly, but surely, being lifted off her. 'Oh, Callum! Let's go for it!'

'I've already phoned for details and we've got to send references as soon as possible; but it sounded quite promising. So, how does that grab you?'

She flung her arms around his neck. 'It grabs me! It grabs me!' They were dancing round together, eyes shining happily at the prospect of leaving the McKinnerneys' employ.

'Yeah,' yelled Callum. 'Escape from Alcatraz!'

'If we can get past the searchlights,' laughed Sophie. 'I can just imagine Catherine in a gun turret!'

'Oh don't!' Callum gave a mock shiver of fear. 'Of course we haven't got the jobs yet – they might like me, but be a bit dubious about you! No, seriously, try not to get too excited; so much depends on the references.'

'Don't worry about that,' Sophie said with a grim smile. 'If there's one thing we can be sure of, it's that we will both get the best references that they've ever seen.'

Callum looked at her questioningly. 'You sound very sure.'

'I am. Let's just say, the least they owe me is good references for both of us.'

'How intriguing. Are you going to tell me what it's all about?'

'No.'

'Well then, Miss Ward, I shall just have to get the information out of you the only way I know how!' He backed her, giggling, against a tree and placed a hand either side of her so she couldn't escape. 'Now I have you!' he crowed, in the worst German accent she had ever heard. 'You will talk!'

'Never!'

'Then I will make you talk!'

'You fiend!'

Firefly regarded them both with a serious expression, then bent his head to crop the grass, ignoring their antics.

'You leave me no option. Prepare yourself for the ultimate torture!'

'Oh no!' she squealed. 'Not the ultimate torture! What is the ultimate torture?'

'The ultimate torture,' he said, obviously trying to think of one quickly, 'is, well, it's . . . actually I haven't thought of it yet. But,' he leered at her comically, 'it will be torturous. And it will be, er, ultimate!'

Sophie was laughing so hard at his expression that she couldn't reply.

'What!' he cried, stepping back. 'You dare to laugh at me?'

She leant against the tree, doubled up. 'Oh Callum! You should see yourself. You look so funny!'

He looked at her sternly, fighting the laughter. 'You are insolent,' he informed her, 'and you will pay.'

Striding across to Firefly, he unclipped the head-collar rope which Sophie had left on underneath the bridle. Callum fumbled with it, his back to her before he turned. He had looped and knotted one end of the soft yellow rope. Firefly watched, briefly interested, and then turned his attention back to the grass.

'You will be very sorry,' Callum told her, in his dreadful accent, 'that you saw fit to mock me!' Quick as a flash, he had looped the rope around her wrist, and pulled it so that it held her snugly.

She laughed. 'Have you thought of the ultimate torture yet, or are you just tying me up indefinitely? I only ask because I've got to get back and get some work done at some time today.'

Callum regarded her coolly. 'This is not the time for

234

humour, young lady.' So saying, he caught her other wrist and tied them both deftly together behind the tree.

'Callum!'

'I am not Callum.'

'Untie me, now! What do you think you are doing?'

'Aha! Now you decide to take me seriously. Well, it is too late; you must face the ultimate torture!'

'Callum!' She tried to undo the knots behind her, laughing at his mock-serious face. He was really getting into the part, striding backwards and forwards in front of her, regarding her through narrowed eyes. Pausing opposite her, Callum looked her slowly up and down. Sophie stopped struggling and gazed defiantly back. A thrill of excitement ran through her.

Callum's eyes lingered over her body, then flicked back up to her face. 'I have thought of the ultimate torture.'

'I thought you might have,' she breathed.

He approached, close enough to touch her. 'You will not cry out,' he told her. 'Otherwise I will, er . . .' He looked around desperately. '. . . Otherwise I will do something horrible,' he finished, lamely.

Sophie sniggered.

'Was that a snigger? I think it was. I do not like sniggers!' They were both having to try very hard to keep straight faces. 'You will pay!'

He pushed himself up against her and placed a kiss on her lips. Before she could get her breath he was kissing her neck, her ears, her throat. Sophie gasped, and pushed herself hard into him. She could feel the coarse bark of the tree behind her and the comforting solidity of Callum in front of her.

His lips were rough, insistent; she responded with her own eagerness, feeling the swell of his penis against her, and his hands loosening her clothing. He pulled her jacket over her shoulders and left it to hang from her arms, which were still secured around the tree. He unbuttoned her blouse, watching her face as he did so, and then popped open the front of her lacy bra. Her breasts seemed to fall eagerly into his large, warm hands. Sophie moaned happily as he took their weight and bent to plunge his unshaven face between them.

Over Callum's shoulder she could see Firefly observing them curiously, and she laughed, then shivered with pleasure as Callum's mouth claimed one of her nipples.

'Callum! Callum!' He lifted his head to her. 'Untie me, now. Anyone could see us out here!'

'You have not been listening to me,' he said, bending his head to give his attention to the other large, pink nipple. 'And anyway,' he mumbled, 'who is this Callum you keep talking of?'

'A joke's a joke,' she told him, 'but I don't want to get caught tied to a tree!'

He ignored her, and she felt his fingers expertly unhooking the top of her jodhpurs and sliding the zip down over her underwear.

She caught her breath. 'Callum!'

But still he ignored her, the blond head working its way down her body, whilst his rough hands pulled at her jodhpurs.

'Callum!'

He grinned up at her, and then deliberately pulled her jodhpurs to her ankles. Then, watching her reaction intently, he reached up both hands and hooked his thumbs into the sides of her panties.

'Don't you dare!' she growled at him, fighting outraged laughter at his nerve. 'Callum!' But her laughter had confirmed her pleasure to him, and he whisked the panties down to join the jodhpurs.

'If you don't untie me now, Callum, you'll be sorry!'

But he stepped back and snapped, 'Stand upright!' And, despite herself, she did. 'Now,' he told her, 'you are ready for the ultimate torture.' His eyes roved the pleasing, heavy roundness of her breasts, the pale flatness of her stomach, and the golden triangle of soft hair.

'Do you have anything to say?' he asked.

'I want you, Callum,' she whispered. Every inch of her body was quivering with anticipation. She felt exposed and wanton; she didn't care now whether anyone saw them or not. She merely cared about her own satisfaction. She wanted his work-roughened hands all over her body, and she wanted it now. She watched his lopsided grin spread across his face and she burned to have his mouth on hers.

'Please, Callum,' she urged. 'Now!' The game was over, forgotten in favour of something much more pressing, more urgent. He leant over, planting his lips on hers. Sophie could feel his penis strained tight inside his trousers. She wanted to free it for him but her hands were still behind the tree with no hope of releasing them.

'Undo your trousers,' she told him. He stepped back and complied, his penis springing joyfully from its dark prison. He watched her watching him, as he proudly handled his prick. Then he was on her again, pushing her back against the tree, the hardness at his groin insinuating itself into her soft wetness.

Sophie could feel the unrelenting bark against her back but, no matter how she wriggled, she couldn't open her legs wide enough to allow Callum entry. Her ankles were still held together by the tight jodhpurs.

'I want you,' she told him again. 'Please, Callum, I need you inside me.'

His breath was catching in his throat as he slid his hand between her legs and plunged his fingers into her warmth. Sophie was moaning and squirming, trying to make room for the blunt hardness which she could feel pressing insistently against her thigh.

'Please, please,' she begged, her womanhood enflamed with its own desire.

He pulled her down the tree a little way and suddenly

she could bend her knees. It was all the leeway he needed. With an animal urgency which Sophie shared, he guided his quivering penis into her, and Sophie felt her body close around the welcome intrusion.

There was no time or inclination to make slow, unhurried love today. Their naked desire was mutual, Sophie arching her back against the tree as Callum's erection thrust into her again and again. Their hips met in furious harmony, drawing back only to renew the pleasure within seconds, Sophie delighting in the sublime friction that had turned her clitoris into a mass of explosive nerve-endings.

When she felt her muscles clench and the orgasm begin to clutch her body, she braced herself against the tree and let Callum have his final pleasure with her. He was gasping, saying her name over and over; holding her shoulders as he made his last swooping plunge into her before his climax claimed him and he leant, shuddering, against her.

Sophie could feel their combined wetness on and in her; she shivered. At once Callum pushed himself off her and pulled the blouse and jacket round to protect her from the cold breeze. Tucking his now-sated penis back into his trousers, he hopped quickly round the tree and untied the halter rope.

'You didn't mind?' he asked quietly, as she sorted out her dishevelled clothing.

She stood up straight, her legs shaking a little from their former unfamiliar position. 'I didn't mind at all,' she whispered, kissing him. 'In fact, I'm going to do the same thing to you when you least expect it.' She kissed his cheek, and they laughed happily.

'So,' he said, as he gave her a boost back into Firefly's saddle, 'do you want to meet me at lunch time?'

Sophie pretended to think about it. 'Well . . .'

'Go on! You know you want to. Come to my shed,' he

urged, sidling up to hand her the reins. 'I've got cream of mushroom soup in my flask today.'

'My, my!' Sophie shook her head in wonderment. 'You know how to live, Callum, don't you.' She looked down haughtily at him from the saddle. 'I'll think about it.' And with a laugh, she wheeled Firefly round towards home. The horse took the bit and set off like a rocket, glad to be on the move once more.

'And don't bring the horse this time!' Callum shouted after her, brushing mud off himself for the second time that day.

'Aha!' Callum said, opening the door of the shed to Sophie that lunch time. 'I knew I'd got you with that promise of mushroom soup. Works every time. Women just cannot resist my mushroom soup.'

She laughed, a touch distractedly. She had just seen Dominic's old car parked behind the house and, despite her promise to herself not to let him upset her further, she was feeling a little shaky.

'What I don't understand,' she said, 'is why we're meeting in your old shed when I have got a perfectly nice, centrally-heated cottage only a stone's throw away.'

'Because my shed has style and, er, spiders,' he informed her, 'while your cottage merely has warmth, comfort, cooking facilities ... yes, I suppose you have a point!' They laughed.

'Oh well,' Sophie said, 'I'm here now, so you might as well show me that job advertisement.' Callum pointed it out, and they sipped at the hot soup as she read it. 'Sounds good, doesn't it?'

He nodded. 'That's what I thought. Did you ask James for the references?'

'I forgot,' she lied. In fact she had been on her way to Prospect House when she had spotted Dominic's car and had veered off towards the stables. She was not ready to face him yet.

'We'll have to get them today,' Callum assured her. 'I said I would send them straight off. I can get them if you like.'

'Whatever.'

'Are you all right, Sophie?'

She smiled. 'I'm sorry, I didn't mean to be off-hand with you. I've just got something on my mind.'

There was silence for a while and then he said, 'It's about that glove, isn't it?'

She sighed. 'I suppose so.'

'Do you know who left it?'

'Yes.'

'Do you want to tell me?'

'No.'

It was his turn to sigh. He leant over to stroke her cheek. 'The sooner we get out of this place, the better.' She smiled.

They chatted for a while until Callum rose, and packed the flask and sandwich box away. 'Right then, I've got a lovely job lined up for this afternoon. I've got to clear the swimming pool and get it all covered for the winter. What about you?'

'I need to borrow a hammer and nails – I want to mend those broken jumps up in the paddock. I can't help wondering if Gina's been sabotaging them to postpone the jumping lessons.'

'Don't worry about those; I can sort those out, if you like.'

Sophie shook her head. 'No, I'll do it today. Besides, it won't take me long.' In actual fact the jumps had been broken for some time and their repair wasn't urgent. But, Sophie thought, it would keep her out of the way of anyone visiting or leaving the house – notably Dominic. Callum obligingly sorted out the necessary tools for her and asked if she wanted any help.

'I don't think so, thanks. What are we going to do

about those references? Did we decide?' She stepped out of the shed and Callum pulled the door to behind them.

'I could go and ask now,' he said. 'If James gets his act together, I could have them ready to send off tomorrow.'

Sophie stopped dead. Dominic's car was still sat there. She turned confused eyes on Callum. 'Tomorrow?'

'The references. Send them off tomorrow ... Oh look, never mind. I'll go and ask now. Are you sure you feel all right?'

'Yes! No! You mustn't! Don't go up there now.'

'What? Why? Don't be silly, Sophie. The sooner we send them off, the sooner we know about the job, don't we?'

'Don't go up there yet.'

'Why not? What's wrong?'

'Dominic's there.'

'Dominic, eh? Well, seeing as he's more often here than not, anyway, I can't say that I'm surprised. What have you got against Dominic all of a sudden?' He was looking at her, curiously.

'Well, he's just ...'

'Well, he's just Dominic. Not the Prince of Darkness, just Dominic.' He took hold of her shoulders gently. 'Why don't you go back to the cottage, Sophie? I'll tell James that you're not feeling too well. I can go and mend those broken jumps – '

'No!' she cried stubbornly. The last thing she wanted was Callum telling James that she was ill. Catherine and Dominic would really have something to laugh about then. 'No, I can mend them. I'm feeling fine.'

'If you're sure.'

'I'm sure.'

They made their way round the back of the house, Sophie keeping her head down. Callum glanced at her occasionally, then up at the house, as if there were clues to be found to Sophie's strange behaviour in its ivy-covered facade.

241

Sophie, despite having had all morning to think about it, still had no idea how she would cope if she had to see Dominic. Her legs felt heavy and weak. The expanse of gravel at the back of the house had never seemed so wide as it did now that she wanted to get across it quickly. All the time she was here, she could be seen from the house. She imagined Catherine pointing at her from a high window and Dominic being called to his sister's side to share her amusement at Sophie's humiliation.

Sophie's legs felt leaden, as if she were wading through water. Only another few strides, she thought, and then I'll be into the gardens and they won't be able to see me.

At that moment her plans for escape were thwarted as, with a crunching stride, two figures came briskly round the side of the house: James and Dominic. Sophie's legs seemed to buckle under her. She could not take her eyes off Dominic. Her face felt hot and prickly, as if she were starting a fever.

Callum was looking at her with alarm. 'Sophie, what's wrong?' But she couldn't speak.

Dominic looked different today. He had forgone the baggy sweaters and casual trousers for a stripy shirt and a long leather coat. He exuded, even more than usual, an air of pampered confidence.

'Sophie,' he said unctuously, making her shiver. 'And how are you?'

'Just get in your car, Dominic,' snapped James. Callum was looking incredulously from Sophie to Dominic and back again.

'I just wanted to speak to Sophie,' Dominic said, planting himself before her. 'How are you, Sophie? Are you going to wish me luck? For my audition?'

She couldn't lift her head up. She didn't want to see him, or hear him, or even, she thought, feeling suddenly sick, smell him.

Dominic bent down to peer into her face. 'Shy, Sophie?' He laughed nastily. 'Surely not?'

Her cheeks were burning as she lifted her face to him. It cost her an effort, but her eyes blazed. 'You bastard,' she said quietly.

Dominic laughed again. 'Now that's the old Sophie that I know and love,' he said, stepping back a pace, despite himself. He pulled himself up to his full height. 'Well, Sophie, what do you think? Will I get the part?' He leant forward, his eyes twinkling playfully at her. 'The question is, am I a good enough actor? What do you say, Sophie?'

'Get into your car!' barked James. 'Don't you think you've done enough? Get in, go away, and don't come back!'

Dominic ignored him, addressing himself to Sophie once more. 'Do you know, Sophie, that was the easiest job I ever did. I hardly had to act at all.' He leant towards her, conspiratorially. 'In fact, sometimes I even forgot I was acting.'

Several things happened at once. James stepped forward to grab Dominic's arm, presumably to propel him towards his car. Catherine flung open a bedroom window, looking suitably melodramatic and shouting something unintelligible. And Callum, who had been standing, as tense as a tightly-coiled spring, exploded across the gravel in Dominic's general direction. Sophie watched, as if in a dream, as Callum's huge, solid fist landed squarely on Dominic's freshly-shaven jaw. There was a noise – not unlike the sound a boot would make crushing a shell – and Dominic's face was suddenly, shockingly, awash with blood. He staggered backwards, looking surprised rather than pained, and sat down heavily on the gravel.

Sophie, Callum and James all stood looking at him in fascinated horror as he clutched his mouth and moaned. Catherine's voice carried across the courtyard.

243

'What's going on? What are they doing to you, Dominic?'

Dominic tried to reply and couldn't. He seemed to be preoccupied with something he was holding between his thumb and forefinger. 'My tooth!' He looked genuinely aggrieved. 'You've knocked my tooth out!'

Callum nodded. 'Looks that way.'

'I've got a very important audition today,' he whined.

Callum raised his eyebrows. 'Is that right?'

Sophie was trying to keep a straight face. Even James was looking on with smug amusement.

'It's my front tooth!' Dominic wailed.

'Well, I hit you at the front of the mouth,' Callum explained. 'So it would be.'

Dominic struggled to his feet, made a move towards Callum, then thought better of it. 'I can't even talk properly,' he lisped incredulously. 'How am I going to do an audition like this?'

James took him by the arm and steered him towards his car. 'I suggest,' he told his brother-in-law earnestly, 'that you keep your mouth shut. Who knows, you may not be required to speak.' He opened the car door, inserted the still-protesting Dominic, and leant down with an uncharacteristic sneer.

'I hear you're rather good at silent parts,' he said quietly, as he slammed the car door and stepped back.

Dominic fumbled around, trying to fit the key in the ignition with shaky fingers. He wound the window down to say something, forgot what it was that he wanted to say, wound the window up again, and screeched off erratically down the drive. They watched him go, each locked in their own private thoughts. Then James turned to Callum.

'Rather nice that, Callum. Thoroughly enjoyed it.' He shook Callum's hand warmly, making him wince.

'I was on my way to see you,' Callum said, flexing

bruised fingers. 'It was about references. I thought I might have blown it.'

'Blown it? Certainly not! Worth a good reference, that was. Come up to the house with me now, and you can tell me what you need. Excellent!'

Sophie watched them walk up to the house in amazement; they were both so elated at the manner of Dominic's departure that they seemed to have forgotten she was there.

Halfway across the courtyard, Callum turned and smiled sheepishly at her. 'Are you coming, or shall I see you later?'

She shook her head, a bemused smile playing across her lips. 'I think I'll go and do those jumps,' she said dazedly. He nodded and blew her a kiss.

She continued her interrupted journey across the courtyard, through the gate, and into the paddock. The hammer and nails chinked together in her pocket as she strode along, every so often overcome with the uncontrollable urge to laugh out loud.

Chapter Twelve

*T*he car wound its way along the coastal path, pausing only so that its occupants could ask directions from a decidedly windswept postman. At the top of the hill it turned off the main road, leaving the breathtaking cliffs and distant, booming sea behind, and began to pick its way down a smaller road into a sheltered valley.

One by one, various cottages came into view, looking strangely deserted, their occupants having sensibly shut out the biting wind and ensconced themselves in front of fires and television sets. Occasionally the twinkle of Christmas tree lights could be seen behind the curtains, one householder having been brave enough to string coloured bulbs around the low eaves of his, or her, bungalow. The bulbs shivered perilously in the high wind, tinkling dangerously against the brickwork every time there was a lull in the strong gusts.

At length, the houses gave way to several small shops: a post office, a baker's, a grocer's and, inexplicably for such a tiny village, an estate agent. The car drove past all these, and stopped beside a white cottage, surrounded by a low stone wall. Inside the house, a woman appeared excitedly at the window, waving wildly, while the front door was flung open by another, slightly younger, woman.

Sophie leapt out of the car and rushed down the path to the cottage. 'We got the jobs!' she cried.

Jean pulled her into the house. 'Come and tell us all about it.'

Callum hung back to lock the car, much to the amusement of Jean's sister, watching from the window. 'Now who's going to come all the way down here to steal your car?' she asked when he came in, her eyes bright with mirth. 'Especially an old banger like that.'

Callum feigned outrage. 'How dare you say that about Miranda? I was led to believe that you were such a nice lady too. Has Jean been telling fibs about you?'

The older woman took his arm, chuckling. 'She has if she's told you I'm a nice lady, I'm afraid!'

In the kitchen, Jean and Sophie were chatting animatedly. Jean paused when she saw the other two. 'Hello, Callum, dear. And congratulations on getting the job. I see you've met Norma, my sister.'

'Oh we're old friends by now,' said Norma, waving away the formalities. 'And this is Sophie, is it? Nice to meet you, dear. Good of you to find a replacement for Jean, too. I thought I'd never prise her away from those McKinnerney's.'

'It wasn't as easy as that, you know,' Jean told her. 'I could hardly leave the children before they had someone else, could I?'

'I don't know,' Norma sighed. 'In my day it was common practice for mothers to look after their own children. You should have just left her to it. She'd have soon learnt to cope.'

'But she didn't want to; that's the whole point. Poor little mites – they've had enough upheaval without throwing them on their mother's mercy. Honestly, Norma, you have no idea what that place was like.'

Callum agreed. 'It was, and still is, a madhouse,' he assured Norma.

'But your sister,' Sophie told her, 'was still wily enough to get out before we did.'

Jean laughed. 'Now I want to hear all about your new job,' she said, pouring tea from a large, spotty teapot. 'And then you can tell me how the new nanny is faring.'

Norma produced a vast fruit cake and loaded slices on to plates for them. 'Made it myself,' she told Callum, proudly. 'There are still some things an older woman can do best,' she said, winking at him.

'I'm sure,' Callum agreed, winking back.

'They make a right pair,' Jean laughed, as they all made their way into the sitting room. 'Watch her, Sophie! She doesn't get the chance to monopolize a young man as often as she'd like to.'

Jean seemed different, more relaxed and jovial than Sophie was used to seeing her. Sophie thought about how much pressure they had all been under and was glad that Jean's departure had come when it did, for her friend's sake as much as anything. She told Jean what their new jobs would entail, Callum adding his comments as and when he saw fit.

'The place we're going to is really run down,' Sophie told the sisters. 'A real mess. It doesn't look as though it's had any maintenance done on it for years. It seems the whole estate is owned by this elderly chap – I'd guess he's in his seventies – who just let it go into decline when his wife left him.'

Jean shook her head. 'It's not going to be too much for you two, is it?'

'Oh no.' Sophie sipped her tea and explained. 'We've got as much time as we need, really. She looked at Callum and they laughed. 'It turns out that this old chap has a new love in his life and she wants the place restored to its former glory.'

'He's got builders renovating what will be our accommodation first, the idea being that we can move in fairly quickly and I can get started on the gardens,' Callum said. 'I don't think it will be long before it's ready. It's one of the newest buildings on the estate, so it's not as bad as the rest of the place.'

'The living quarters are nice,' Sophie told Jean. 'Quite separate from the main building, and bigger than my cottage at Prospect House.'

Callum agreed. 'There was one problem,' he said, glancing at Sophie with a smile on his face. 'Have you told Jean?'

'No, not yet,' Sophie laughed, turning to her friend. 'When we saw the job advertised it specified that the employer wanted a couple so, naturally, we wondered whether they would expect us to be married. Some of them can be quite strict about things like that. Anyway, we had decided that we wouldn't mention it until after we had the interview. That way, if they really liked us, it maybe wouldn't matter as much.'

'Oh, isn't it silly,' cried Norma. 'In this day and age, too!'

'Anyway,' Callum continued, 'he was obviously impressed with the references – James gave us excellent ones, so he could hardly fail to be, really – and the interview went well.'

'We were offered the job on the spot,' Sophie supplied. 'So then we had to tell him,' she finished with a giggle.

'And he wasn't at all phased.' Callum was trying not to laugh now, too. 'He introduced us to his lady friend. We had such a shock – she was only about Sophie's age! And he told us that she was his sixth "wife." How did he put it, Sophie?'

'Apparently, they aren't actually married themselves. He said, "Do you honestly think, at my age – and faced with a willing twenty-year-old – that the first thing I thought about was asking her to marry me?"'

Norma gave an outraged shriek. 'Oh, the naughty old devil! Sounds like a man after my own heart.'

'And I thought,' Callum laughed, 'that at least working for an older man things would be a bit less frenetic and there wouldn't be all the bed-hopping and affairs that went on at Prospect House. It just shows how wrong you can be!'

'This girl that he's fallen for was his former housekeeper,' Sophie interjected. 'Which I suppose explains why the house is such a mess!'

They laughed again, and then Jean leant forward and tapped Sophie's knee. 'You know, you'll have to be careful if she was his previous housekeeper.'

'In what way?'

'They're always the worst, sticklers for it being done exactly how they would have done it themselves.'

'I don't think she had time to do much housekeeping,' Sophie said, winking at Norma. 'Anyway, it sounds as though I will be needed elsewhere most of the time. The new lady of the manor has this dream of starting up her own riding stables and I'm to manage it once it's up and running. She seems to have a good business head. She wants to open the house, once all the renovations are complete, as a specialist riding holiday centre. You know, for families.'

They all thought about this for a few minutes, and then Jean leant forward again, eagerly. 'So, tell me about the children. How are they? Are they missing me, or have they settled?'

'They're fine,' Sophie assured her. 'Of course, they're missing you, but not in a bad way. They talk about you a lot, it's only natural. And Gina plays up all the time, so no changes there!'

'And what about Jo? Is she enjoying it? Is she happy?' Jean asked anxiously. 'Does she love them?'

Sophie smiled. 'She adores them,' she said quietly. 'She's very good with them. After having sole charge of

Jem and Tara Newton-Smith for all those years, even Gina's bad days are a breeze for Jo. Gina tried her usual trick, the other day – you know the one, "I don't like shepherd's pie today; I liked it yesterday, but not today!" Jo never batted an eyelid. She just said, "Don't you worry, Gina, I've got a lovely beetle crumble in the oven you can have some of that instead!"'

They all laughed. 'I've never seen Gina clean her plate so quickly,' Sophie said.

'It just seems a shame to me, still,' said Jean, shaking her head. 'Jo's only young herself; she should really be with people her own age. Making a few new friends.'

'Don't worry too much about that,' Sophie said conspiratorially. 'I saw the applicants who came to be interviewed for Callum's old job at Prospect House and I thought there was a lot of potential there! In fact, I was beginning to wish I was sticking around.'

'Oh, were you?' Callum narrowed his eyes at her in mock suspicion. 'I didn't know anything about that! Jo seems to be doing fine,' he agreed, chasing cake crumbs around his plate and prompting Norma to trot off to fetch him some more. 'She's got this clause in her contract that lets her have weekends off. She and Rosie go gallivanting up to the University. I don't honestly know what they find to do there.'

Sophie kept her head down. She had only had to look at Jo's face – with its enigmatic smile – to know exactly what she and Rosie found to do at weekends. 'Yes,' she said, casually, 'Rosie has been introducing her to lots of new people. You mustn't worry about Jo – she's much more capable than the Newton-Smiths ever let her believe herself to be.'

'Oh, I never doubted her capabilities for a moment,' Jean said. 'It's just that Gina can be so difficult sometimes – it's easy to forget why she plays up. And Ellie has always needed such a lot of reassurance. And Peter, he's still only a baby – '

251

'Jean! They're fine! I promise! If you don't believe me, go and visit them the first chance you get. But I swear to you, they really are happy. It was a godsend, the Newton-Smiths deciding to send their two away to school when they did. For Jo as well as for you and the children. Look, Gina's sent you a letter – sort of – and there's a drawing from Ellie.'

Jean took the note and picture into the kitchen where they could hear her sniffing quietly to herself for several minutes.

'She knows she's done the right thing,' Norma assured them. 'But it's bound to be difficult for her for a little while. She brought them up, practically. Still,' she whispered, 'I know what she needs; a friend of mine is going to give me one of her dog's puppies when they're old enough. It will be my Christmas present for Jean.'

Sophie was about to say that it would hardly make up for what Jean saw as the loss of three children, when she stopped. She cast her mind back many years, to her childhood; and specifically to the birthday when she had been presented with a puppy of her own. She remembered the sleepless nights, the constant cleaning up of unspeakable substances, and the endless patient persuasion necessary to get the creature house-trained.

'I think,' she said, smiling at Norma, 'it could be just what she needs.'

BLACK LACE NEW BOOKS

Published in August

A VOLCANIC AFFAIR
Xanthia Rhodes

Pompeii. AD79. Marcella and her rampantly virile lover Gaius begin a passionate affair as Vesuvius is about to erupt. In the ensuing chaos, they are separated and Marcella is forced to continue her quest for sybaritic pleasures elsewhere. Thrown into the orgiastic decadence of Rome, she is soon taking part in some very bizarre sport. But circumstances are due to take a dramatic turn and she is embroiled in a plot of blackmail and revenge.

ISBN 0 352 33184 4

DANGEROUS CONSEQUENCES
Pamela Rochford

After an erotically-charged conflict with an influential man at the university, Rachel is under threat of redundancy. To cheer her up, her friend Luke takes her to a house in the country where she discovers new sensual possibilities. Upon her return to London, however, she finds that Luke has gone and she has been accused of theft. As she tries to clear her name, she discovers that her actions have dangerous – and very erotic – consequences.

ISBN 0 352 33185 2

THE NAME OF AN ANGEL
Laura Thornton

Clarissa Cornwall is a respectable university lecturer who has little time for romance until she meets the insolently young and sexy Nicholas St. James. Soon, her position and the age gap between them no longer seems to matter as she finds herself taking more and more risks in expanding her erotic horizons with the charismatic student. This is the 100th book in the Black Lace series, and is published in a larger format.

ISBN 0 352 33205 0

To be published in September

SILENT SEDUCTION
Tanya Bishop

Sophie is expected to marry her long-term boyfriend and become a wife and mother. Instead, she takes a job as a nanny and riding instructor for the wealthy but dysfunctional McKinnerney family. Soon, a mystery lover comes to visit her in the night. Is it the rugged young gardener or Mr McKinnerney himself? In an atmosphere of suspicion and secrecy, Sophie is determined to discover his identity.

ISBN 0 352 33193 3

BONDED
Fleur Reynolds

When the dynamic investment banker Sapphire Western goes on holiday and takes photographs of polo players at a game in the heart of Texas, she does not realise they can be used as a means of revenge upon her friend's cousin, Jeanine. In a world where being rich is everything and being decadent is commonplace, Jeanine and her associates still manage to shock. Dishonesty and double-dealing ensue. Can Sapphire remain aloof from her friends' depraved antics or will she give in to her libidinous desires and the desires of the dynamic men around her?

ISBN 0 352 33192 5

Published in October

FRENCH MANNERS
Olivia Christie

Gilles de la Trave persuades Colette, a young and beautiful peasant girl to become his mistress and live the life of a Parisian courtesan. However, it is her son Victor that she loves and expects to marry. In a moment of passion and curiosity Colette confesses her sins to the local priest but she is unaware that the curé has his own agenda: one which involves herself and Victor.

ISBN 0 352 33214 X

ARTISTIC LICENCE
Vivienne LaFay

Renaissance Italy. Carla Buonomi is determined to find a new life where she can put her artistic talents to good use. Dressed as a boy, she travels to Florence and finds work as a young apprentice to a master craftsman. All goes well until Carla is expected to perform licentious favours for her employer. One person has discovered her true identity however and he and Carla enjoy a secret affair. How long before Carla's true gender will be revealed?

ISBN 0 352 33210 7

If you would like a complete list of plot summaries of Black Lace titles, please fill out the questionnaire overleaf or send a stamped addressed envelope to:-

Black Lace, 332 Ladbroke Grove, London W10 5AH

BLACK LACE BACKLIST

All books are priced £4.99 unless another price is given.

---------✂----------------

Please send me the books I have ticked above.

Name   ....

Address   ....

           ....

           ....

     .... Post Code   ....

Send to: **Cash Sales, Black Lace Books, 332 Ladbroke Grove, London W10 5AH.**

Please enclose a cheque or postal order, made payable to **Virgin Publishing Ltd**, to the value of the books you have ordered plus postage and packing costs as follows:
    UK and BFPO – £1.00 for the first book, 50p for each subsequent book.
    Overseas (including Republic of Ireland) – £2.00 for the first book, £1.00 each subsequent book.

If you would prefer to pay by VISA or ACCESS/MASTERCARD, please write your card number and expiry date here:

....

Please allow up to 28 days for delivery.

Signature   ....

---------✂----------------

BLACK
lace

WE NEED YOUR HELP . . .
to plan the future of women's erotic fiction –

– and no stamp required!

Yours are the only opinions that matter.

Black Lace is the first series of books devoted to erotic fiction by women for women.

We intend to keep providing the best-written, sexiest books you can buy. And we'd appreciate your help and valued opinion of the books so far. Tell us what you want to read.

THE BLACK LACE QUESTIONNAIRE

SECTION ONE: ABOUT YOU

1.1 Sex (*we presume you are female, but so as not to discriminate*)
   Are you?

   Male ☐
   Female ☐

1.2 Age

   under 21 ☐   21–30 ☐
   31–40 ☐   41–50 ☐
   51–60 ☐   over 60 ☐

1.3 At what age did you leave full-time education?

   still in education ☐   16 or younger ☐
   17–19 ☐   20 or older ☐

1.4 Occupation _____

1.5 Annual household income

    under £10,000   ☐   £10–£20,000   ☐
    £20–£30,000   ☐   £30–£40,000   ☐
    over £40,000   ☐

1.6 We are perfectly happy for you to remain anonymous; but if you would like to receive information on other publications available, please insert your name and address

_____

_____

_____

_____

SECTION TWO: ABOUT BUYING BLACK LACE BOOKS

2.1 How did you acquire this copy of *Silent Seduction*?

    I bought it myself   ☐   My partner bought it   ☐
    I borrowed / found it   ☐

2.2 How did you find out about Black Lace books?

    I saw them in a shop   ☐
    I saw them advertised in a magazine   ☐
    I saw the London Underground posters   ☐
    I read about them in _____
    Other _____

2.3 Please tick the following statements you agree with:

    I would be less embarrassed about buying Black
    Lace books if the cover pictures were less explicit   ☐
    I think that in general the pictures on Black
    Lace books are about right   ☐
    I think Black Lace cover pictures should be as
    explicit as possible   ☐

2.4 Would you read a Black Lace book in a public place – on a train for instance?

    Yes   ☐   No   ☐

SECTION THREE: ABOUT THIS BLACK LACE BOOK

3.1 Do you think the sex content in this book is:
      Too much   □   About right   □
      Not enough   □

3.2 Do you think the writing style in this book is:
      Too unreal/escapist   □   About right   □
      Too down to earth   □

3.3 Do you think the story in this book is:
      Too complicated   □   About right   □
      Too boring/simple   □

3.4 Do you think the cover of this book is:
      Too explicit   □   About right   □
      Not explicit enough   □

Here's a space for any other comments:

SECTION FOUR: ABOUT OTHER BLACK LACE BOOKS

4.1 How many Black Lace books have you read?   □

4.2 If more than one, which one did you prefer?

4.3 Why?

SECTION FIVE: ABOUT YOUR IDEAL EROTIC NOVEL

We want to publish the books you want to read – so this is
your chance to tell us exactly what your ideal erotic novel
would be like.

5.1 Using a scale of 1 to 5 (1 = no interest at all, 5 = your
     ideal), please rate the following possible settings for an
     erotic novel:

     Medieval/barbarian/sword 'n' sorcery   ☐
     Renaissance/Elizabethan/Restoration   ☐
     Victorian/Edwardian   ☐
     1920s & 1930s – the Jazz Age   ☐
     Present day   ☐
     Future/Science Fiction   ☐

5.2 Using the same scale of 1 to 5, please rate the following
     themes you may find in an erotic novel:

     Submissive male/dominant female   ☐
     Submissive female/dominant male   ☐
     Lesbianism   ☐
     Bondage/fetishism   ☐
     Romantic love   ☐
     Experimental sex e.g. anal/watersports/sex toys   ☐
     Gay male sex   ☐
     Group sex   ☐

     Using the same scale of 1 to 5, please rate the following
     styles in which an erotic novel could be written:

     Realistic, down to earth, set in real life   ☐
     Escapist fantasy, but just about believable   ☐
     Completely unreal, impressionistic, dreamlike   ☐

5.3 Would you prefer your ideal erotic novel to be written
     from the viewpoint of the main male characters or the
     main female characters?

     Male   ☐   Female   ☐
     Both   ☐

5.4 What would your ideal Black Lace heroine be like? Tick as many as you like:

Dominant	☐	Glamorous	☐
Extroverted	☐	Contemporary	☐
Independent	☐	Bisexual	☐
Adventurous	☐	Naïve	☐
Intellectual	☐	Introverted	☐
Professional	☐	Kinky	☐
Submissive	☐	Anything else?	☐
Ordinary	☐	_____	

5.5 What would your ideal male lead character be like? Again, tick as many as you like:

Rugged	☐		
Athletic	☐	Caring	☐
Sophisticated	☐	Cruel	☐
Retiring	☐	Debonair	☐
Outdoor-type	☐	Naïve	☐
Executive-type	☐	Intellectual	☐
Ordinary	☐	Professional	☐
Kinky	☐	Romantic	☐
Hunky	☐		
Sexually dominant	☐	Anything else?	☐
Sexually submissive	☐	_____	

5.6 Is there one particular setting or subject matter that your ideal erotic novel would contain?

_____

SECTION SIX: LAST WORDS

6.1 What do you like best about Black Lace books?

_____

6.2 What do you most dislike about Black Lace books?

_____

6.3 In what way, if any, would you like to change Black Lace covers?

_____

6.4   Here's a space for any other comments:

_____

_____

_____

_____

_____

Thank you for completing this questionnaire. Now tear it out of the book – carefully! – put it in an envelope and send it to:

Black Lace
FREEPOST
London
W10 5BR

No stamp is required if you are resident in the U.K.